THE BIG LOST

A NOVEL

‡

RR CARROLL

PUBLISHED BY

4T2 BRAND, LLC

NEOSHO, MISSOURI

The Sawtooth Pack also known as the *Wolves of the Nez Perce*, have been at the heart of the wolf recovery movement in the West for over fifteen years. Countless letters of support for the pack have come to the *Wolf Education & Research Center's* mailbox over these years. Many of these have expressed gratitude for the Center's work in educational outreach and for helping to further develop the sound science that promotes wolf re-introduction in the wild lands of the West.

Many of the original pack have moved over to the other side but one Sawtooth Pack member remains. The one the Nez Perce Tribe called Piyip, or "Little Brother," continues to provide a living reminder of the importance of the wolf in a complete and healthy ecosystem for the many visitors that come to see him each year near Winchester, Idaho.

Piyip, as a descendant of the "Elder Eight" wolves, offers a living symbol of the importance of all creatures, great and small, in our natural environment. While his original pack awaits his departure from the earthly side of his wilderness, Piyip dutifully fulfills his role as an ambassador for his wild cousins and is a joy to all that have been privileged to know him.

This story is dedicated to

Piyip.
Wolves of the Nez Perce

PUBLISHED BY 4T2 BRAND, LLC

Copyright © 2011 by

Ronald R. 'Tex' Carroll, Ph.D. and 4T2 Brand, LLC.

This is a 4T2 Brand, LLC book, published in the

United States

www.4t2brand.com

Cover & interior design by the art department of

4T2 Brand, LLC

Editors

Cheryl Carroll

Sandra Sargus

ISBN: 978-0-9833568-0-6

ALSO BY RR CARROLL

‡

Almost Guatemala, novel
The Old Cowboy's Box, short stories

Chopo My Pony, children's book
Mustang Ghost, children's book

Rounder, The Tales of Rounder M. A. Dilla,
narrated compact disc.

The Big Lost

Prologue
THE GATHERING

FROM THE SHADOW OF THE TIMBER, the first wolves moved out of the darkness. The pack had remained hidden among the trees during the early morning hours and waited for the first light. As the pair crossed into the new sun on the pristine powder, the low angle of the light extended their shadows. A large female moved into the lead. She cleared a path through the fresh snow for the rest to follow. Her color was clean, as white as the surrounding scene. It made her just about invisible except for a small grey star just under her neck.

The Chilly Buttes pack needed a kill. They had hunted all night without success and they were hungry. There was a particular nervousness and urgency about their movements. The largest male fell in behind the female quickly and took a position to her right flank. In his wake, the other pack members dutifully fell into line. The array of predators had their target in view and flowed like water steadily downhill. They were intent on the herd of elk methodically grazing at the river's edge.

At first, the big animals appeared undisturbed by the sudden nearness of the intruders. A few noticed but most continued grazing on the sweet fall grass. Several of the wolves playfully dipped their noses and bit into the stream as they crossed the water to the other side of the river, masking their intent. The wolves were quickly on both sides of the shallow river and moving steadily around the isolated members to the rear of the herd. Still there was no sign of nervousness among the browsing elk. The leaders intently took stock of the prey as they passed the herd at a steady lope. With the hunters now moving among them, the herd began at last to nervously separate into bunches of three or four. The small groups began to move away from the threat.

Without warning, the white female suddenly came forward and lowered her head as she extended her tail and broke into a determined run. With an equal reaction, a large elk cow instantly matched the wolf's pursuing speed with a burst of her own. Another wolf took up the chase and the three, the hunted and the hunter, joined in a primordial race. As the cow crossed over the streambed to the other side, the pack's largest male and two others joined the pursuit. The frantic elk, her head held defiantly up, moved deliberately amongst several others of the herd in an attempt to dislodge her pursuers, but the predators ignored the ruse. The water around her body seemed to explode as the elk cow violently crossed the stream once again. Relentlessly, the others of the Chilly Buttes pack on the other side greeted her and gave her no relief.

The speed of the closest pursuer brought the hunter alongside the tiring prey. Without breaking stride, the wolf made a heroic leap and grabbed, with a determined grip, the lower neck of the cow just above the large shoulder muscle. The practiced jaws and teeth deeply penetrated the hide and brought red gushing to the surface. With it came a call of panic that eerily echoed across the valley. The wounded animal shook mightily and shed her assailant along with a spray of water stained crimson. Panicked, she kicked at the female who had taken a bite of the hamstring and was holding on fiercely. Yet again, the cow broke free and plowed through the icy water to the bank on the other side. The water's resistance took its toll and the weary fleeing elk struggled up the slippery water's edge. She slipped back awkwardly before desperately struggling onto the bank.

As she fought to regain her balance the pack's largest male mercilessly met her head on. The elk, in defense, dipped her head to ward off the new threat, but the wolf used his heft to ferociously grab and lock its jaws onto her neck. This time her frantic shaking and twists failed to free her from the bite. She clumsily stumbled and went down on her front knees. Again she called. But this time the effort was weaker than before. Two of the hungry wolves moved decisively onto the downed cow's rear and violently pulled one leg away from the body. The fated animal slumped to the ground and exhaled deeply. The breeched vein pumped out her spirit rapidly as the weaker, slower members of the Chilly Buttes pack gathered nervously around the hard won victory. The feast would soon follow.

‡

Crows, magpies and eagles surrounded the carcass remnants as the satiated wolves rested in the late afternoon sun. The birds now had their turn to feed, and were quickly and noisily making the most of the opportunity, before the winners of the prize might choose to return. Several wolves were at the river's edge for a drink, and only the pack's best female protected the gory banquet.

A singular male coyote approached from the opposite side, away from the sentry, and cautiously moved toward the half-eaten kill. A third the size of his larger cousin, the coyote wisely hesitated as he well understood the consequences if he misjudged the situation. Hunger for a meal drove him, however, to make his decision. He trotted quickly to the carcass and pulled at a tendon at the rear. His meal was far from leisurely, and he made frequent glances back over his shoulder toward the female guardian. She continued to sun herself paying the interloper little mind so the coyote moved deeper into the hollows of the carcass. He nervously retrieved a large chunk of the prize and struggled to swallow it whole. The warm flesh satisfied. In the sweetness of satiated hunger, he had let himself forget whose kill it was. It was a fatal error. The female wolf grabbed the scavenger by the back of the neck and with a powerful jerk broke his spine. The snap of structural bone echoed another call of death across the valley. The remainder of the pack joined in quickly and took delight in paying the lowly coyote a bitter final lesson. After the savage encounter was done the birds again moved quickly back onto the feast, unconcerned by the fate of the coyote.

Custer County sheriff's report & incident log
8:40 a.m.
A caller reported a lost wallet near the park.

ONE   THE BIG LOST

THE COLD PENETRATED GERALD CAHALAN'S FLESH and the aggravating chill worked its way determinedly into his skeleton. His extremities ached, and he wanted to stand up and exercise the warm blood back into his hands and feet. The hunter suspected that his toes and fingers were turning blue from the cold, but the discomfort would have to wait. He had labored too long in the dark of the predawn to prepare the camouflage and pack the snow all around his hideaway. He wouldn't give that away now just because he was cold.

From the vantage point of the hunter's blind, Jerry's view was ideal, and he had a clear sight overlooking the meandering Big Lost River below. He was about a half mile off Trail Creek Road where it intersected with Highway 93, near the two remnant mountains known as Chilly Buttes. Jerry had built his hideout up the trail of the dry creek known as Elkhorn. While he had worked in the predawn darkness, the first winter snow had slipped in as a surprise. The storm had moved quickly eastward out of the Sawtooth Mountains and over the Challis National Forest making its way toward the Yellowstone. In its path, it had painted the scene white which now made the blue steel barrel of Jerry's .270 rifle stand out in contrast.

As the eastern morning glow grew brighter behind the mountains at Jerry's back, he cradled his hunting rifle in his arms and waited in silence. Jerry strained his eyes to see movement in front of him. He slowly moved his rifle into position and pointed the barrel downward in the direction where he hoped to catch sight of his prey—if he had the hunter's luck.

Custer County sheriff's report & incident log
2:42 a.m.
Deputy spoke to revelers who were
disturbing the peace in Challis.

Two   THREE POSITION SAFETY

IN THE SLOW MOVEMENT FROM DARKNESS TO LIGHT, Jerry recalled the day his permit arrived from the Fish & Game Department in Boise, and the thrill and anticipation it invoked. He remembered saying aloud, "I'm going to hunt the gray wolf," and doing a quick dance step on the hardwood floor just inside the front door.

He recalled, too, the conversation he had had with the gunsmith in Colorado that afternoon.

"What kind of game are you after Doc?" Spencer Abrams had spoken loudly into the speakerphone as he stared at his neatly organized workbenches and the shiny shop floor. "I'm assuming you'll be after elk or is it bear?"

"No sir, I'm after gray wolf up near Mackay, Idaho. A place called Chilly Buttes. You know it?"

"I do—been there several times. So, you're going to be one of the first timers this year? It's been over forty years since anyone could hunt wolves in that country."

"I want a special gun Spencer. Can you help me out?"

"Depends. What kind are you looking for?"

"From what I read in the trades, you build a fine .270, and that's what I want. I want one that's all business, lean and handsome and to the point—no frills."

"I guess you've read reviews on my customs. I can build you one, but we are running a bit late on time. I don't rush the rifles I build. Usually a custom takes me four or five months to put together. I'm assuming you are going to want to be out the first of the season, right?...that won't give me my normal time window."

Jerry broke in, "I'll pay extra for your undivided attention Spencer. This hunt is a once in a lifetime for me. Tell you what—I'll put a five-hundred dollar bonus on the end of the order on delivery day. How's that sound?" Jerry smiled, expecting the bonus to seal the deal.

"You make a tempting offer Doc." Spencer paused for a second, "I suspect we can do business on those terms. I'd like to run through the specs though; I need to make sure this is what you want."

"That'll work. Go ahead."

"Okay, for starters, I use a black synthetic stock. No spit. No polish. It's a no-nonsense stock for all weather and all conditions. I then mount a 24-inch barrel with a narrow fore end and grip. The barrel ends at the muzzle with a slender taper of .610 inch exactly. We put it together on a stainless Remington Model 700 action. It has a fluted bolt shank which will slide smoothly along the raceways and the fluting is in a spiral pattern. I don't know if you are aware, but by fluting the bolt shank there will be less friction between the shank and the receiver housing—makes for a quick reload. You know, in case you miss the first shot."

"There is one unique feature I put on my customs Doc. I use a three-way safety. It's the old Mauser style safety. It locks the firing pin adding a bit of extra assurance that the rifle fires only when you're ready. Finally, to put the crowning touch to this beauty, I will mount a 3-9X Nikon Monarch UCC scope. And for all of that, when your piece is finished it will weigh a tad over seven pounds.

Oh, and I'll include special hand loaded ammunition. How does that sound to you?"

"Do you prefer a cashier's check or money order?"

"A personal check is good enough. Fifty percent up front and fifty percent upon delivery would be fine. And, of course, the bonus if I get it done."

"I'll Fed-Ex the check tonight and, can you engrave my initials on the barrel?

"Certainly, you want GC, right?"

"No I would like GBC and the year, if that is not too much to ask."

"No sir, it's not. Oh, and one other thing, I would like to come and pick the rifle up from you personally."

"That's preferred Doc. We'd love to have you come to Colorado. Then we can give the little beauty a proper try out on the range to make sure you are satisfied. I will look forward to seeing you and I'll call you as soon as your rifle is ready." Spencer Abrams smiled. He liked these kinds of orders for these kinds of clients. And he looked forward to seeing pictures of his work lying across a trophy wolf in the wild lands of central Idaho.

Custer County sheriff's report & incident log
9:50 a.m.
Deputy Quick helped fire volunteers deal
with two small fires near Willow Creek Summit.

THREE   WOLVES EAT SNOW

IN HIS HIDEAWAY, concealed from everything but God, Jerry knew all he had to do was to wait, to endure, to suffer the cold. Lying motionless, he thought about trying to call to the pack but then thought better of it. Sooner or later the predators would come to him if he would just be patient. The hunter would become the hunted then. Jerry enjoyed that irony as he peered again through the scope.

Then, without warning, a brace of elk appeared in the virgin light about two hundred yards below Jerry's hide-away. The big animals filled the lens of his riflescope. The pair was moving rapidly up the slope and prancing nervously. The fresh snow was flying behind them as they cut a new trail.

They appeared to be moving away from something, a threat of some kind. An outstanding bull with a full rack was in the lead. His companion cow pranced closely on his right flank, staying close to the regal male. Jerry could see a cloud of mist erupting from the animals' nostrils as they moved quickly closer to where he hunkered down.

At that moment, just as suddenly as the elk had come into view, what was making them nervous presented itself to the hunter. Two large wolves were the first to appear, breaking free from the shadows of the tree line and bobbing up and down in the new powder. The two were then joined by two more, and then three others followed in an ordered line behind the leaders. Within less than a minute, the panorama from Jerry's snow blind took in a pair of edgy elk, and what he figured was the Chilly Buttes wolf pack.

Jerry nervously checked his rifle to make sure he was ready. He placed the three-position safety to the red but then looked at it again to make sure he had done it right. He was anxious. Suddenly all the prep came to this moment; to this opportunity.

The canines arrayed on the field were intent on making the kill and thus showed no sign that they were aware of a Jerry's presence. They moved progressively into a big arc around the fleeing elk. The wolves appeared to be pacing their prey, driving the beasts deliberately toward the top of the ridge.

Jerry squirmed further down in the snow. He could feel his heart pumping heavily and the sweat forming inside his bulky coat. His body was producing adrenaline and coursing it through Jerry's veins with the force of a fire hose. His heart rose to his throat and he no longer felt cold. Instead, he was hot.

Suddenly he wished he could call a time-out and take off the confining clothes he wore and be free in his movement. But there was no time. The elk were within a hundred yards, and the wolves were less than fifty yards behind them. The drama of nature was moving steadily up the slope of Elkhorn Creek toward a climax with the waiting hunter.

Then abruptly everything stopped. The elk froze in place. Jerry watched as the big bull stood as still and erect as a park statue. The tense cow did likewise. The only movement was the spouts of vapor forcefully thrust from flared nostrils.

The wolves hesitated, appearing to be taken by surprise by the sudden stillness. Then to Jerry's astonishment, the elk turned back on the trail. They headed away from the hunter's blind and right for the big white wolf that was the closest. The bull began to snort with force and moving deliberately that signaled the end of flight and the will to fight.

Jerry knew that a battle for survival was about to begin, moving quickly away from his position. If the elk and the wolves crossed back over the Highway 93, and into the tree cover, Jerry knew his chance of getting a clear shot would go with them. He had to make a decision and make it fast. Shoot now at one hundred fifty yards or wait. If he waited, he would have to reveal his position and, most likely, lose his opportunity.

Jerry hastily squinted through the scope. The rubber eyecup cradled his head and steadied his line of sight. At least a dozen targets moved about with frantic energy in the snow. Jerry couldn't decide which one to take. Then, filling the lens, he spotted what he knew must be the alpha male. The big wolf had gray shoulders that gave way gradually to a dark, almost black, hindquarter. He was splendid and moved about with a calculated stride that suggested authority.

It was time.

Jerry tried to mentally compensate for the extra distance. He had never practiced at this distance. A hundred yards was his comfort range, he never attempted anything longer. With the scope filled with the gray/black wolf, Jerry squeezed the trigger as softly and smoothly as he could. The rifle responded and the butt harshly buried itself into padded fabric on his shoulder.

The impact of the hand loaded 150-grain Swift A-Frame bullet spun the big male in the air like a child's top. Soundlessly, the wolf buried its nose into the soft powder.

Frantically scrambling free from his snow blind of sticks and snow, Jerry stumbled through the powder towards the target. The other animals had incredibly disappeared as he reached the fallen wolf. Within ten feet, he abruptly pulled up, suddenly realizing that the dangerous creature might still be alive.

Jerry took a cautious step closer to the magnificent animal. He stood motionless for almost a minute and gazed keenly at his trophy. He couldn't believe it; couldn't believe what he had done.

Joy began to take over his awareness. He now regretted that he was alone—had no companion to share his triumph. The obligatory hunter's pose with gun at side and the kill lying as if asleep was part of the experience. He wanted Sarah to see him as the great hunter—the surgeon by necessity and the champion by instinct.

Jerry took out his cell phone and switched it to camera mode. He quickly recorded three frames of his trophy. Then holding the phone as far away from his face as his arm would reach, he displayed a wide toothy grin and made a self-portrait.

Jerry panned the area all around and snapped random shots, making sure he got one in the direction of the blind. As he put the phone back into his jacket, he noticed the radio collar the animal wore mostly obscured in the animal's thick winter fur.

"Damn it," Jerry muttered. It was a complication that he didn't want. He wondered if someone was monitoring the wolf right now.

Custer County sheriff's report & incident log
11:20 a.m.
A wallet was reported
lost in the Mackay area.

FOUR A CASE FOR SKINNING

THE DEAD WEIGHT OF THE BIG CARNIVORE was a struggle to move. Jerry's breathing was labored and quick as he awkwardly hoisted the carcass up by its hind legs into the low branches of a dead fir tree. The effort made the sweat trickle down his back so he removed his heavy coat and unloaded his rifle. Jerry leaned the gun against a fallen log.

The morning sun fought a battle with the thick unsettled clouds but was warm and brilliant when it won the tussle. The chilly air gave way to a pleasant temperature, and the absence of wind made the ridge ideal for the task that Jerry faced. The rules for hunting wolf required that the successful hunter report his kill within twenty-four hours. After that, he had five days to bring the hide and skull to a Forest Ranger station. As he admired what he had done, Jerry took a wolf tag from his inner shirt pocket and dutifully recorded the month and the date of the kill by tearing out the appropriate triangles on the document.

Jerry had never skinned anything this big before. He reached into his shirt pocket and took out a piece of paper. *Care of Pelts: Case Skinning Coyote and Fox* was the heading on the pamphlet. From under his shirt, he retrieved a heavy leather scabbard that protected his custom knife.

Like the rifle, he had it made special by Crandall Knives. Crandall called the blade the *Little Game King* and the maker assured Jerry that the knife would do its job with small and big game alike. It was as sharp as the surgical blades that Jerry was used to. He easily made the first cut.

He sliced forcefully completely around the rear legs just below the hock. The steel made it easy to cut precisely down the two legs to the anal opening and to carve around it cleanly. The regulations required that animal's sex be verified, so Jerry left the big wolf's maleness intact. Jerry had to pull hard to get the hide down the two rear legs, but the flesh was warm and the skin came off smoothly without tears. The next step was to remove the tailbone. That required another cut along the bottom of the tail, but Jerry easily made that cut as well.

Jerry, lost in his work, failed to see the movement in the tree cover behind him and continued by cutting around the front legs about two inches below the elbow. From there he slowly worked the hide down and over the body turning it inside out as he went. Finally, he reached the imposing head and meticulously skinned around the ears and the eyes making sure he didn't cut the eyelids. He left a hole in the hide where the eyes stared into nothingness. He was almost done and reached his knife inside the mouth and cut through the inside of the lips. At last, he severed the nose cartilage free and pulled the intact pelt from the warm carcass of meat that gave off a slow rising steam in the cool air.

Jerry spread the fresh hide on the snow and marveled at its beauty. He picked up the radio collar and again wondered if some wildlife biologist or game warden was monitoring his location. The thought of the technical world and the wildness of the wolf roaming the northern Rockies together in a way disturbed him.

'Is a wolf wired to the society of man still wild? Why can't a wild wolf simply be a wild wolf and do what wolves have always done?' he thought to himself.

Jerry let the thought escape and stared at the raw body hanging from the tree, rudely exposed to the cold. He made the choice to roll the radio collar up in the hide and tie the bundle with a piece of cord. No way did he want to lose the device and have to explain the loss to the wildlife wardens.

The sky had become dark in the hour it took to skin the kill and now the first flakes of a new snow drifted preemptively across the high ridge. Jerry figured he'd better pack up and head down the slope to his Toyota before the storm began in earnest. He could see it was moving deliberately from the west.

Jerry picked up the soft still warm pelt and secured it under his right arm. He picked up his rifle and, as he straightened up, the distinctive whiz of a bullet flew past his ear. Jerry instantly knew what it was and the surprise sent an electrical shock through his body. Before he heard the report of the gun that had fired the round, another shock struck him deep in his chest. He knew what that was too. The pain was brutally sharp and sudden, causing the air to rapidly vacate his lungs.

The lonely hunter stood frozen in time for a long second and then, in slow motion, slumped to his knees without a whimper. As he sank, the stunned man reflexively hugged the soft trophy pelt to his chest like some child's binky. Jerry's superb custom rifle slipped from his hand and landed back into the soft snow, disappearing at the base of the tree just below where the remnants of the trophy wolf swung with the freshening wind.

Gerald B. Cahalan never looked up, he simply dove head first into the new powder, breathing out heavily before his face disappeared, like his rifle, into the immaculate whiteness.

From somewhere high in the Big Lost River Range a wolf howled. First one and then another joined in the chorus. Most hunters in these mountains would recognize the call. They would recognize it as a call of gathering.

Custer County sheriff's report & incident log
10:33 p.m.
The deputy on duty went to hunt
for a drunken driver near Stanley.

FIVE   HOT CHIHUAHUA

SHERIFF CHESTER A. TILGHMAN RECLINED DANGEROUSLY in his swivel chair as he pitched peanut hulls across the room in the direction of a big mouth wastebasket. The target sat under a large cork wallboard that was littered with a hodgepodge of wanted posters attached in no particular order with a rainbow of colored plastic stickpins. The warrants for arrest represented every kind of villain that the rule of law could account for. Sheriff Tilghman had put their kind in jail in Custer County, Idaho for well over thirty years.

An unusually ugly and mostly hairless, sand-colored Chihuahua the sheriff called Hot Sauce rested undisturbed in his lap. The tiny dog had a permanently arched backbone that made him look like he was always about to pee on something. He chewed aggressively on an oversized milk bone biscuit from a supply the sheriff kept handy under his desk. A red bandana loosely tied around the animal's neck made the small dog appear even smaller than he really was.

The crumbs Hot Sauce produced in abundance littered the sheriff's blue jeans and found their way into the lawman's pistol holster and onto the floor. The big lawman didn't seem to notice. He was too busy giving one-word responses to the questions the caller was asking while holding his cell phone in one hand and launching hulls with the other.

As he let fly another missile toward the cylinder and said yes into the phone, he glanced out the window and noticed that the mid-afternoon traffic, passing in front of the Custer County Courthouse, was especially light. He figured it was the early season snow that kept most folks off the roads. The same lack of activity was apparent on Linda Davenport's 911 call board too. It had been silent for most of the afternoon. The pretty young dispatcher passed the dead time reading a *Wild West* magazine that had been gathering dust on the reception table for nearly two years. Tilghman enjoyed these quiet times in the sheriff's office more and more as he got older. The sheriff's step had long lost a spring or two and the peace was welcomed.

As the sheriff's yes and no conversation droned on, the afternoon sense of peace was abruptly shattered as Deputy Charlie Two Leaf noisily crashed through the front door. Without waiting for the sheriff to finish his phone business, Charlie began to animate wordlessly something about a body. He filled in the lack of audio with hand signals but the sheriff was having trouble deciphering the deputy's wild arm movements. Without bothering to say goodbye, the sheriff flipped the lid of his cell phone closed and stood up. Hot Sauce, along with a half-eaten biscuit and assorted peanut hulls, tumbled to the multi-stained linoleum floor.

"What the hell Charlie? What's got you in a lather?" The sheriff brushed the hull remnants from his lap as he spoke.

The chief deputy continued to mouth silently his news before he realized he could now speak aloud. Charlie caught himself in mid-sentence, "...some hunters have just reported a body to the Forest Service Ranger Station down in Mackay. They say it's a bloody mess. The ranger is on his way to the scene. They don't know whether it's on Federal land or not at this point."

Charlie paused long enough to quickly grab a cup of the black mud that was left in the coffee pot. He took a sip, made a face and returned the cup to the table.

"Did the hunters know what happened?" The sheriff began to straighten his clothes and tuck in his shirttail. The two men exited the sheriff's office and moved towards the dispatcher's station where Linda had thrown the magazine back toward the table and was sitting as straight as a lamppost recognizing by the deputy's agitation that something was up.

"No. They just said there wasn't much left."

"Wasn't much left. What the hell does that mean?"

"Well they said that there wasn't a face with the body. The body was pretty much chewed up too. You know gutted. The hunters said wolves had got to it."

The sheriff's cell phone began vibrating and playing an Irish jig simultaneously. It made Tilghman jump. He answered it and listened for a moment then told the caller that they were on their way. The sheriff scooped up Hot Sauce and tucked him in the crook of his left arm. He and Charlie quick stepped out the side door and climbed into the sheriff's Jeep Cherokee. Charlie always drove when the two men rode together. The deputy tried flipping the switch for the siren but it didn't work so they headed south down Highway 93, in silence.

The sheriff continued to eat peanuts and threw the hulls over his shoulder into the back seat. Hot Sauce stood on his hind legs in the sheriff's lap, bracing his front paws on the dashboard. The small dog looked down the highway as the sheriff told his deputy to slow down on the snowy roads.

Custer County sheriff's report & incident log
8:40 a.m.
*Deputy responds to a report of a
reckless driver on Trail Creek Road.*

SIX   RED SNOW

YELLOW CRIME SCENE TAPE WAS HAPHAZARDLY LAID ON THE GROUND in a large circle around what appeared to be a body half buried in the snow. It was on a lower elevation plateau of the Big Lost River Range about half way up the Elkhorn Creek trail. As Sheriff Tilghman and Charlie Two Leaf struggled up the trail, the sheriff could see two groups of men up ahead. Those in one group were dressed in Forest Service uniforms and hovered just inside the tape near a dark mass contrasted in the snow. The sheriff recognized the head forest ranger for the Challis National Forest; it was his friend Rick Clyde. Off to one side, standing under a small clump of scrub trees, were three other men. Tilghman noted that two of the men were obviously hunters. The other person had his back to the sheriff but he thought he recognized the long gray braid that hung past the man's waist.

"Well hello Sheriff. You sure got here quick for an old man," Forest Ranger Rick Clyde said with a slight grin on his face. The two men hadn't seen each other for almost a year. They had had been friends from the time Rick had transferred from Klamath Marsh Wildlife Reserve four years ago. Light snow continued to fall, and there was just enough of a mountain breeze to make things a bit uncomfortable. The ranger moved around nervously with his hands in his pockets and his face pulled as far back in his hooded jacket as possible.

21

Tilghman did not acknowledge the ranger's humor. "What's this mess Rick?" he asked, pointing to the red mass in the white snow.

"Not exactly sure. My guess, it's what's left of a hunter." The ranger pushed back his hood a bit, revealing a full head of thick blond hair. "We got here about two hours ago. As close as I can tell we're just off Forest Service boundaries on BLM land, but I figured you'd claim jurisdiction regardless, so I didn't want to make too big of a mess. We've tried to keep things as close to the way we found them as possible."

"Thanks." The sheriff turned and whispered something to Charlie Two Leaf and his deputy moved off toward the three men standing by the trees.

"Rick, what do you think happened here?" Tilghman asked as he started to walk around the tape. He noticed that the ground around the body had been tracked heavily. So much for a clean crime scene he thought.

"Don't really know. The only time I've ever seen anything like this was about ten years back when a cougar ambushed a woman from Portland as she was hiking up near Borah Peak. The big cat had his way with the body for so long that by the time we found her there wasn't much to pick up. Same as now. I reckon you noticed most of the face is gone?"

"Yeah, I noticed. Any sign of foul play?"

"Not that I could tell, but we haven't taken much of a look yet. Like I said, we wanted you here first. It's going to be tough to find anything in all this new snow. If we don't get a thaw before the real winter sets in, it will be spring before we find anything up here."

"Let's brush back some of the snow and get a better look."

The two men knelt by the corpse and began to carefully clear snow from around the remains. Most of the stomach was missing and the chest was laid open, exposing ribs on both sides. What was left of the facial tissue was devoid of any recognizable features. What clothing was still on the body was in shreds and caked with blood.

One of the victim's boots had been chewed up. Something about it caught the sheriff's eye. At first he thought it was snow, but as he brushed at the powder it stuck to his gloves.

"Rick, what do you make of this? This looks like some kind of white powder."

"Taste it sheriff, see if its coke."

"Hell with you ranger, damn stuff might be strychnine for all I know."

Tilghman motioned for Charlie to bring an evidence bag. "Put some of this stuff in a bag for me Charlie."

The sheriff stood up and rubbed his gloves together to dislodge the powder. He studied the body for a moment.

"I'm glad I didn't eat breakfast," he quipped. "We'll have to get this body to the Coroner's office down in Boise. I'll get Marty Smithson up here to give us a local coroner's report for the record, but I can see right now we can't handle this locally. I'll get a hold of the state boys when I get back to Challis and let them know what's headed their way. What are the chances of getting a helicopter up here?"

"Can do Chester. I'll get on the radio. The ranger looked back at the other group of men. "Something else sheriff."

"Yeah?"

"If this hunter was killed by wolves, there is going to be hell to pay. It's just the kind of incident that will send the anti-wolf boys in orbit all over the state. The KWiI has been waiting and hoping for just this kind of incident so they can call for the destruction of every wolf pack in the Northern Rockies."

"So you think this mess is of the wolves making?"

"I don't know. I doubt it. I'm just thinking where this might lead. Two or four-legged wolves, either way this one is going to cause a stink. There is just too much blood and guts here not to."

"You're probably right."

Tilghman looked back towards Charlie and the other men. "Is that who I think it is?" The sheriff nodded in the direction of the man standing apart from the hunters with the long gray braid.

"That's him."

"I thought we ran that mountain scoundrel back across the line to Nevada."

"We did, but they ran him back." Rick laughed at his joke. "Yes sir, that's Wishful Wicks in the dirty flesh himself."

"Wishful Wicks," Tilghman repeated sarcastically. "The only thing wishful about that man is all those who wished he would disappear. Tell me Rick, how is it that when there is trouble in this county that critter seems to always be handy?"

"You got me Chester. I've run the man out of the Challis Forest a half dozen times for panhandling to hikers and tourists. He just keeps coming back. And get this. The latest story is that he has taken up with the Chilly Buttes gray wolf pack."

"What!"

"You heard me. Mr. Wishful Wicks moved right in and set up camp in their range. You have to say one thing for him though; he is a mountain man from the old school. He could live under two sticks tied together with cat gut."

The sheriff took another walk around the remains. "If the wolves mauled this man—I guess it's a man—would it be the Chilly Buttes pack that's the culprit? Are there any others around?"

"No others around. That pack has been established solid over this range for about three years now. We track them all the time within the forest boundary although the state Fish & Game folks are responsible for the monitoring. The Chilly Buttes pack is led by a large white female from what we can tell, and she wouldn't let any other wolves in her territory without a fight to the death."

"Alright. Let's go talk to wolf man. I can't wait to hear this story."

The two investigators shuffled through the snow towards the men. Tilghman looked back over his shoulder.

"Rick, any sign of the hunter's gear, you know the rifle, personal effects or anything else?"

"No, but I haven't really looked. Like I said, if it's buried in the snow it's going to be tough to come up with."

Tilghman looked around at the ranger. "Right, especially since Wishful Wicks got to the scene first. You know what I mean?"

"I think I do." The two men continued toward the men standing under the tree cover.

"Rick I'm going to take Wicks to one side and see what I can find out. You do the same with the two hunters. Let Charlie stay with you. I want to get the story told twice."

"You know I can't do it in an official capacity..."

"Rick, I know that but they don't. Don't stir the pot; just smell the soup for me."

"I can do that."

Custer County sheriff's report & incident log
8:40 a.m.
Mackay ambulance and a
deputy responded to a tractor accident.

SEVEN WISHFUL

HOWARD JASPER WICKS CAME FROM NOWHERE and appeared to be headed in the same direction. Sheriff Tilghman had put the itinerant, known all over Custer County as Wishful Wicks, in jail so many times that Wicks had a favorite cell—he preferred cell 4. The drifter's offenses were never serious—vagrancy and panhandling down by the saloons on the west end of town mostly. There was the one petty theft charge that Samuel Bevens at the Wagon Wheel Café had brought against Wishful. Sam had caught him stealing his newspapers out of the open rack on the sidewalk. And, there was the time Wishful urinated on the county courthouse grounds in protest. He was always protesting something or someone.

Tilghman had lost track of Wicks when he suddenly disappeared from central Idaho. The sheriff wasn't unhappy to see him go. The man was a constant source of irritation. Tilghman didn't think he was a particularly dangerous sort, although Wishful had once boasted that he had killed a man in Ft. Worth. He said he had strangled him like a new puppy in a fight over a pretty woman. The sheriff, out of curiosity, made inquiries to the Texas Rangers, but there was no record of Wicks or his claimed bad deed.

Even in the open mountain air, the sheriff began to get a whiff of Wishful as he approached him.

"What are you doing here Wicks? Did you have a hand in this?"

"Sheriff, Sheriff, Sheriff. My fine Sheriff. That I did. Me and my friends did the feller in and chewed up his beautiful little head and spit it out in the snow."

"Well that settles it then. Case closed." Tilghman responded quickly without a smile. "Charlie, put the cuffs on Mr. Wicks here and let's get back to where it's warm and cozy."

"That's fine with me Sheriff. I haven't had much to eat lately...is, is my room ready?"

"Shut up Wicks and tell me what I need to know. Did you find this mess?"

"I did. Still warm were the bodies. The hunted and the hunter alike were still steaming my investigatory friend."

"What brought you to this ridge anyway?"

"Oh, just following my associates in the snow lookin' for a handout."

"Your associates? What associates? The camouflage brothers over there? Are those boys your friends?"

"Oh my no! Sheriff. Oh no! Those lads were merely the vehicle to communicate to the world in which you live and work. My friends are the wolves. The wonderful, wily wolves of the wilderness. Now, I'll tell you; there's true friendship. They share their hard won bounty with all needy scavengers."

"Where are you living nowadays?"

"Here Sheriff. Right where you stand now, in this great and beautiful land above a civilization that is corrupt and doomed to extinction on the morrow."

Tilghman had had enough. He motioned for Charlie to leave the ranger and come over to where he and Wishful were standing. "Deputy, we're taking this wild man back with us to Challis as a material witness. Make sure he stays available until we are ready to leave." Tilghman moved toward the ranger and the hunters.

"Oh, don't worry my friendly sheriff," Wicks called out as the sheriff walked away, "ol' Wishful is ready for a little vacation and a restful night's sleep in your wonderful facility. I'll be right here with my friend Charlie when you need me. Right here I'll be."

Custer County sheriff's report & incident log
8:40 a.m.
A caller reported having lost a tool box,
but then found it.

EIGHT THE BROTHERS ELDER

THE TWO EXPLAINED THEY WERE BROTHERS. They were both tall and lanky. The one who stood nearest to the sheriff identified himself nervously as Harry. The one with the almost goatee, Harry's twin, introduced himself as Henry.

They were two peas in a pod, each clothed in the identical hunter's regalia. The only things that didn't match were their hunting rifles.

"Okay boys; let's hear your version of what happened here." Tilghman began his inquiry with the notion that he knew these young men.

"Sheriff we just told the ranger what we know." Harry glanced nervously at Henry for confirmation.

"I know you did but why don't you tell me too. You see the ranger may not have gotten his facts right. Let's start with you telling me where you're from?"

"Yes sir. We live up near Arco. Our daddy is Sensible Elder. We've been up here a couple of days, hunting elk and wolf. Got a camp back over the ridge about a quarter mile."

"Any luck?" the sheriff asked.

29

"Some. No wolves yet but we got a big bull just this morning. He was running with a cow. Man did he have a nice rack. He's hanging back…"

"At the camp?"

"Yes sir, at the camp."

"The sheriff walked closer to Henry and put his hand lightly on his shoulder. "Henry, why don't you tell me what brought you to this horrible scene."

Henry fretfully looked at his brother and then at the sheriff.

"Come on, let's hear the story," the sheriff spoke calmly but with sternness. Tilghman knew how to play this game. He knew when to be lawman and when to be something else. For the moment, he was something else.

"Well Sheriff, you see, like Harry said we was huntin' not too far from here early this morning. It wasn't that long after sun-up when we heard a big gun report. That was the first we knew about any other hunters around. Didn't think much of it at the time. This time of year there is a bunch of hunters in this country. Well, we went on about our business. Then about two hours later this feller, that one over there, the rough lookin' one with the braid, came runnin' up to our campsite shoutin' at us to come see."

"Did he say what he wanted you to see?"

"Yes sir, he did. He said the wolves had killed a feller. He wanted us to get word to the ranger or somebody."

"Did he say how he happened to be up here and discover the body?"

"No. But he did say something kind of stupid though."

"Kind of stupid? What was that?"

"All the time we were coming over here he kept muttering something about how he and his friends had killed a hunter. He said that more than once." Henry tried to make eye contact with Harry but Harry was looking at his boots.

"What did you make of that Henry?"

"I, I don't know. He's a strange one for sure. I was nervous coming here. I didn't trust him, no sir, not one bit."

Tilghman turned to Harry. "Is that how you remember it too?"

"Yes sir, just as Henry says."

"Henry, what did you find when you got here? I need you to be very specific and don't leave anything out. Do you understand?" Tilghman looked deliberately at both Elder boys in turn, raising his eyebrow slightly.

"Yes sir, I sure do." Henry took a step back from the sheriff and turned to point at Wishful and deputy Charlie Two Leaf. "Well we followed his tracks. You could see where he had plodded through the snow to our camp. We just followed those tracks back here. As we came over that ridge, the one just back there," Henry turned and pointed back to the east, "I could see something dark in the snow just at that tree line. Right above it was the skinned wolf hanging in the tree. That feller was almost jumping in the air. He kept saying 'See I told you so, I told you so. We got him for sure, we did.' It was spooky Sheriff."

"Did you see any sign of the Chilly Buttes pack of wolves around?"

"No. It was very quiet. The snow had dusted everything white so we really couldn't tell much about the body." Henry hesitated for a second.

"What is it Henry? Is there something else?" the sheriff prodded.

"Yes sir." Henry again looked at Harry. "I thought it a bit strange but then didn't pay it much mind either."

"What's that?"

"There wasn't any gear around. I mean nothing—no rifle, no clothing, nothing a hunter would carry. It was as if the area had been cleaned. The only thing was the hunter's body in the snow and the wolf carcass hanging from that branch."

Sheriff Tilghman turned abruptly towards Harry and surprised him with his question. "Harry what do you make of that?"

Harry looked again at Henry and at first didn't seem to understand the question. "About what, Sheriff?"

"About no gear around the hunting site."

"I don't know. It don't make no sense like Henry says. No sense unless someone took the stuff."

"You mean stole the hunter's gear?"

"Yeah, I guess."

Tilghman paused. He looked back at the yellow tape and then back at the brothers. "I've got one more question for you before I let you head back to your camp. Do you think the wolves in that pack killed or mutilated that corpse over there?"

Harry looked toward Henry and raised his eyebrow. Henry spoke first.

"Well Sheriff they can be mighty dangerous creatures. Every since those easterners pushed for putting the gray wolf back in these mountains some folks been saying it was only a matter of time before a wild pack got hold of a man."

Tilghman let himself smile slightly, "So you think the wolves could have attacked and killed this hunter?"

"I don't know. I reckon it's possible. I've heard of coyotes killing a hiker before and coyotes ain't near the danger them wolves are. No sir, not near."

"What about you Harry. You think they could have done it?"

"Wolves can bring down a buffalo bull and cut him up like a shop butcher. I don't see no reason they couldn't do the same to a man."

"What about the gear? Do you think the wolves carted off the hunter's gear?" The sheriff asked the question with a serious tone.

Harry and Henry both grinned slightly and shook their heads no.

"Okay boys, that'll do it for now. You know that we most likely will need to talk with you both again so let's have your contact info."

As he wrote down their address and phone number the sheriff remembered who these brothers might be. "You boys any kin to Rave Elder?"

The brothers looked surprised but both nodded yes. "He is our daddy's brother," Henry said.

"You're free to go. Just keep yourselves available."

"Yes sir." The Elder boys didn't seem to know what to do and made no immediate move to leave until Tilghman turned and began to walk away. Suddenly, the sheriff paused and turned back.

"You haven't seen your uncle lately have you?" he asked.

Harry and Henry glanced at each other and then back toward the sheriff. "No sir."

"Okay then."

Sheriff Tilghman motioned for Rick to rejoin him, and both men walked slowly back to the body and talked. The brothers trudged toward their camp in the same snow tracks that had led them to the scene.

Custer County sheriff's report & incident log
8:40 a.m.
Deputy Quick responded to a report
of unlawful entry in Mackay.

NINE THERE ARE NO SECRETS ANYMORE

"WHO IN THE HELL IS THAT?" Tilghman was watching a short energetic man in tall rubber boots work his way up the Elkhorn trail. As he got closer, the sheriff recognized him. He couldn't believe it.

"Hawk, what in the love of Pete are you doing here?"

The newcomer was breathing heavily and had difficulty answering. He momentarily bent over to get his breath. Finally, he straightened up and smiled broadly. "Hi there Sheriff. How are you?"

"Never mind how I am. What are you doing here? No wait a second; I know what you're doing here. How did you find out about this so soon?" Tilghman shook his head and looked at the ranger with an expression of "what next?"

Ignacio Hawk was a reporter for the *Salmon River Sentinel-Reader*; had been for just over a year. It had been Hawk's first reporting job out of college. He had graduated from the School of Journalism at the University of Nevada, Reno. The sheriff nicknamed the young reporter "Scoop," because he made the courthouse his second home.

Hawk, as everyone called him, was aggressive and took his job seriously even though his paper was a small backwater press.

He showed signs of becoming a good investigative reporter and the sheriff liked him, although he took pains not to show it.

"We got a call at the paper this morning and..."

Tilghman interrupted. "About what happened here?"

"Yes sir. The man wouldn't identify himself but he told the editor *there was important doings,* that's how he put it, *up near Chilly Buttes.* He said that if we wanted to get the story first hand we had better get there quick."

Hawk pulled his hood around his face and tucked his camera inside his parka. "Oh, he also said that it was proof that *them damn wolves,* again his words, *should be put back on the extinction list in Idaho.*

Tilghman and the ranger looked at each other quizzically.

"He didn't say where he was calling from, but we knew by the number that the call had to come from up near Arco or there about. Tried to find the number in the book, but it wasn't listed. What's going on here?"

Hawk took a few steps toward the yellow tape but the sheriff stepped in front of him.

"Hold on. I'm not through with my questions yet." Tilghman turned to the ranger. "Rick can you send your man back up that ridge and tell the brothers to get back here on the double? We may have a few more questions for them."

"Can do, Sheriff."

The reporter again craned his neck around the sheriff trying to get a look at what lay beyond the yellow crime scene tape.

"Is that a body? Who is it? Is that a wolf hanging from that tree? What happened here Sheriff? Can I get some pictures?"

"I thought I was going to ask the questions. We're trying to figure this one out ourselves Scoop. All we know now is that we have a body. Maybe I should say a piece of a body. Don't know how he died or what happened after he died. We don't know who he was. The fact is what we don't know outruns what we do know by a mile." Tilghman looked back toward the ridge. He wanted the Elder brothers back here at the scene.

"I can't tell you what to write, but I do need to make something clear. Given the nature of this situation, I strongly encourage you not to sensationalize the story. Don't make any assumptions. Folks around these parts are on a short fuse when it comes to the wolf packs in Idaho. Some are pretty dang close to forming vigilante groups to hunt down and kill wolves. You follow?"

"I follow but I can't promise anything Sheriff. I have to let the story go where the story will go. You know that."

"I do. But try to use some good judgment. Don't throw gasoline on the fire—got it?"

"Okay, no gasoline—maybe a bit of kerosene." Scoop grinned hoping he could get the sheriff to relax a bit.

The ranger sent to fetch the Elder brothers came back over the ridge at a trot. "Sheriff they're gone. The brothers have broken camp and left."

"Great. That's just great." The sheriff stared across the ridgeline for a moment. "I know where to find them." He turned back toward Ranger Clyde. "Rick how do you think the message got out about this so quick?"

"Chester, I'm thinking the same thing that you are. Had to be a cell phone call. I don't think Wishful Wicks had one, but I bet the brothers do."

The sheriff looked at Rick and then at Hawk. He didn't really want to ask this next question in front of the reporter, so he told the reporter to stay put for a minute. He took Rick by the arm and led him over to the body.

"What's on your mind Chester?"

"Do you think the victim was carrying a cell phone? I know we haven't found one but wouldn't it make sense that he would have one with him?"

"I think you can pretty well bank on it."

"What about the hunter's vehicle? Shouldn't it be fairly close by?"

"Yeah, We did pass a yellow FJ Cruiser parked in the Chilly Slough turnout just up the road. I can't say for sure, but I'd put money that it belongs to this poor fellow."

"Rick, I am going to need some help from the Forest Service. I know you don't have to do this, but I need this place secured. There are too many unanswered questions, and it looks like the answers are here buried in the snow. Can you put a man here and maybe near the car until I can get some help lined up?"

"Sure, if we can get our reporter friend not to publicize that the Feds are stepping over the boundary. Yeah, I can help for a few days."

"Good. I'll see if I can get Scoop to work with us."

Tilghman headed back to the reporter knowing he was going to have to give up something up to get the young man's cooperation.

"Okay, Scoop, before you begin with the questions I need something from you."

"What's that?"

"I need you to agree that you include what I'm about to tell you in your story."

"Okay, I can do that."

"We found a cell phone in the snow a little ways from the body. We think it belongs to the victim. We're not for sure, but I took a look at the pictures on the phone. Well, let's just say it might help us get to the bottom of this. You can quote me on that. That's what I need you to make sure gets in your story. Can you do that for me?"

"What are the pictures of?"

"Never mind that. I promise you'll be on the inside looking out on what we learn."

Tilghman went through what he knew with the reporter. Satisfied, Scoop trudged back off the plateau saying he hoped to get his story in that evening's edition. As Scoop cleared out, Rick walked up to the sheriff's side.

"What phone? What pictures? Did I miss something?"

"No." Tilghman kicked around some snow for a second. When he looked up he said, "Just casting a fly in the river is all. Hoping something might jump out of the bushes at it."

"You know Chester, for an old worn-out sheriff from Podunkville you can be pretty cagey at times."

"We've got ourselves a mess here Rick. And I don't mean just the poor soul lying over there in the cold snow. Everything I have seen or heard today points to trouble down the road. From Wishful Wicks to the brothers Elder, to that skinned wolf carcass hanging in that tree, to the missing pieces of evidence. This is a rank stew that I'd just as soon not stir, but I don't guess I have a choice now, do I?"

"Well, you could hand this one off to the State Police. In some ways, they are better equipped to bring this to a resolution. They may take the case away from you anyway once that stew you're talking about begins to heat up."

"They may try. But, this is my jurisdiction; my county, and I've always seen after it. I'm not about to give it up now. Anyway, if this is a murder then I'm betting that it was home grown. I know these people in this county pretty well. I know the bad apples that live here and the ones that are headed to the discount bucket. I don't like bad people. Whoever or whatever did this thing,"

Tilghman turned his line of sight in the direction of the yellow tape, "has to be caught. We can't tolerate such deeds in Custer County."

"You're right Chester. I'm set to help out however I can."

"Thanks Rick. We're going to have some tough times before this is done."

The snow had started up again as a medical helicopter came in low from the east. The blades created a blizzard, whipping up the new powder as it settled a hundred yards from the remains of Gerald B. Cahalan.

<u>Custer County sheriff's report & incident log</u>
12:40 a.m.
A caller reported an
abandoned vehicle in his drive way.

TEN ANOTHER KIND OF WILD LIFE

THE LECTURE HALL WAS NOISY WITH CHATTER as Professor Victoria Wilds briskly walked into her undergraduate biology class. She was her customary five minutes late; it was her trademark. Students sometimes complained to the department chair but the professor had tenure and she paid little attention to the pettiness of the protests, especially from undergraduates. Wilds hated these big lecture halls filled to capacity anyway. Money makers for the university, she called them. To her this was not a place where learning took place. Being late was her ongoing protest.

Wordlessly she took her place behind the podium, not bothering to look up. She stood on her toes to push her five-foot-two frame a little taller as she arranged her lecture notes, finally looking out into the auditorium at the sea of anonymous faces. Most of the students were beginning to open their notebooks.

Wilds stared at the class until the roar reduced to an uneasy rumble. The semester was winding down and the professor was grateful for that. She was dreading the next several weeks. The incoherent ten-page papers she was going to have to grade depressed her. It wasn't enough that the writing was bad but having to accept the papers and give them a passing grade grated on her nerves.

Failing a student had become impossible. Unless they committed a felony or mugged her in the middle of class, a "D" would be the lowest grade she could assign.

She remained silent until all but one or two were quiet and paying attention. "Are there any questions before I begin today's lecture?" she asked flatly.

A hand went up in the back row. From the lectern, the student was rendered unknown by the separation to the back row. The female, Wilds thought her name was Annie, Annabel, or something like that, shouted her question.

"Professor, do you have our mid-terms graded?" Wilds looked at the class with no one in particular in focus and answered.

"The short answer is no."

The professor didn't wait for a follow up. It was a subject she did not care to discuss in class. She was feeling guilty — the papers were three weeks late.

"Any others? Good. Today I will continue our discussion of the reintroduction of the gray wolf to the Northern Rocky Mountains. In particular, the reintroduction to the state of Idaho."

She adjusted her notes, "From your assigned readings and the last lecture, can someone tell me the year and the number of wolves that were initially reintroduced into central Idaho?" Wilds waited.

After an awkward moment, she decided to forego the question and answer approach, she didn't like it anyway. Just give the damn lecture and be done with it.

"All right then, the year was 1996, and the number was 20. Twenty Canadian gray wolves were tranquilized, intensively inspected, marked, and transported to central Idaho for a hard release into the wilderness of the state. Now for those that need reminding, a hard release is one in which the animal is immediately released from the transport cage into the wild. There is no transition, or what is called a soft release, as was done in the case of the reintroduction of the gray wolves in the Yellowstone in Wyoming."

Wilds glanced furtively at her watch that she had removed from her wrist and laid on the podium next to her lecture notes. She privately sighed — more than an hour to go.

"I am going to give you a quick outline of the events leading up to that 1996 release. I expect you to fill in the details from your readings that I again remind you, have been assigned. There is one point I want you to understand well."

Wilds paused for effect. "The reintroduction of the gray wolf into the western region of our country, from its initial inception until today, is extremely controversial. In the last ten years, science has firmly established that the biology of the process is sound and effective. The re-establishment of the wolf into areas where they were native 60 years ago has been an overwhelming and unequivocal success."

"However, the social and political issues surrounding the effort are another matter. There continues to be a strong and considerable negative reaction to the wolf in the three states where they have been biologically re-established. Moreover, it appears that this reaction is not likely to diminish in the near future. However, I would remind you that in this course the focus is in the biological process and not the political or social issues. Having said that, I also believe it is important that scientists ground their work in the realities of the society in which they live. Thus, one cannot ignore the political and social issues you will encounter in your assigned readings."

A hand went up. Wilds ignored it. "But, you can relax. I will not emphasize that on the final exam."

Another hand went up near the rear of the hall. Professor Wilds ignored it as well.

"This wildlife saga started in earnest in 1974," she began, "when four subspecies of gray wolves, identified scientifically as *Canis lupus*, were given the protection of the Endangered Species Act. We are most concerned with the gray wolf of the Northern Rocky Mountains. Also listed was the eastern timber wolf, the Mexican wolf in the southwestern U.S., and the Texas gray wolf. I know that I said the biology aspect was the most important to our inquiry, but I want to briefly make you aware of the political nature of the reintroduction process."

"During the 1980s there were many field studies conducted in Idaho that sought to document the presence of wolves. These studies were largely intended to promote the re-establishment of wolf packs that were migrating into Idaho from other states and from Canada. This prompted the State Legislature to place restrictions on the fish and game agencies, forbidding them to continue recovery efforts unless it was expressly authorized by state statute. In other words, political interests in the state did not care to have the wolf reintroduced to Idaho whether that reintroduction was by natural processes or by the intervention of man."

"The national climate in favor of the wolf began to build in the 1990s as the Congress of the United States by legislation authorized a National Wolf Management Committee. The purpose of this committee was to develop a plan for gray wolf reintroduction for Yellowstone National Park and the Central Idaho wilderness area. By July of 1993, a plan was developed and a draft Environmental Impact Statement was created. The scene was set to bring the gray wolf back to the wilderness of Idaho."

"All of this planning and work was brought to fruition in January 1996, when, like I previously pointed out, 20 gray wolves were released into Central Idaho. From that early nucleus, the number of wolves has grown to over 1,600 wolves today. The success of this biological program of reintroduction has had the gray wolf delisted from the protections of the Environmental Species Act. Idaho State Fish and Game people now conduct the management of the wolf population. One result of this transfer of authority over the gray wolf has been the reestablishment of a wolf-hunting season in Idaho. I might add that this action has provoked a considerable outcry from many environmental activists, while at the same time drawing an equal cry of support from hunting and ranching interests in our state."

Wilds noticed, as she continued, the furious note taking occurring in the first three rows. As she let her gaze extend deeper into the classroom she smiled to herself; note taking seemed to be a function of nearness to the lectern. The farther away the less of it was observable. As she finished her lecture, she scribbled a reminder in the margin of her notes to see if the test scores correlated with the seating pattern. Her guess was that it did.

With the class concluded, Wilds was grateful she had no students staying behind to ask questions. Most of those that did, she knew by long experience, tended to be either sycophants or whiners, and she disliked both varieties. She was anxious to get back to her office. Given the question in class about the midterm exam she figured she'd better get the grading completed before the next class session. Being late for class was one thing, failing to grade papers was another.

Custer County sheriff's report & incident log
12:40 a.m.
Deputies responded to a
domestic violence complaint in Arco.

ELEVEN   A 'C' IS NOT THAT BAD, REALLY

AS WILDS PASSED THE DEPARTMENTAL CHAIRMAN'S OFFICE, Dr. Jon Grayson waddled out of his office and stopped her.

"Good morning Victoria. How did class go this morning? Did you make it on time?" The Chairman raised his right eyebrow slightly and smiled through a bushy white mustache.

"Close enough Jon."

"Have a message for you. It came in last night on the departmental answering machine. Seems it's from a Sheriff Tilghman up in Custer County. Did you rob a bank or something?"

The slightly stooped leader of the Biology Department was particularly playful this morning and Victoria, as she always did, humored the old man.

"I guess they finally caught up with my chop shop operation. Give me the number and I'll call him before my next class. By the way, Jon, any word on my sabbatical request? I could use a leave from the grind."

Wilds began to back away not expecting an answer but Chairman Grayson surprised her.

"As a matter of fact professor there is word. The dean approved it yesterday afternoon. I was going to come see you later today. Congratulations, you have earned a bit of a rest for sure."

"Thanks, that's some good news."

Wilds picked up the three student messages from the box next to her office and pushed open the unlocked door. She had to weave her way around the stacks of books scattered about in the office. The desk was also almost invisible under a mixture of term papers, textbooks, magazines and trade journals. She pushed the litter to one side to clear a area of desktop and sat down. The professor stared at the message. It read, *Dr. Wilds I am Chester Tilghman, Sheriff of Custer County. I would appreciate a call as soon as possible. It is urgent. Thank you.*

She picked up the phone and dialed the number then leaned back in her swivel chair.

"This is the sheriff's office. How can I assist you? Linda answered."

"Hello. My name is Victoria Wilds. I am calling from Boise State University for Sheriff Tilghman. I received a message to call him."

"Yes, he is expecting your call. Just a moment please."

While Wilds waited for the sheriff to get on the line, she watched the mid-morning activity on campus from her office window. The day was agreeable with a brilliant sun.

"Dr. Wilds, thank you for returning my call so quickly. I hope you are doing well."

"Yes sir, I am."

"The reason I called you is I have a bit of an investigative problem in my jurisdiction that I think you can help me with. Do you have a moment for me to explain, or should I call you at a more convenient time?" Sheriff Tilghman made an effort to be as polite as possible. He needed the biologist's help.

"I've got about 30 minutes before my next class Sheriff. What can I do for you?"

"Well Dr. Wilds..."

"Before you begin may I ask why your name seems so familiar?"

"Well, about three years ago I was feeling the urge to get a bit more education and I signed up for one of your internet classes. Your expertise left quite an impression on me.

"Chester Tilghman. I do recall your name. What is it I can help you with Sheriff?"

"Well I've got somewhat of a mess on my hands. We had a hunter killed two days ago up near the Challis National Forest in our county. He was a permitted wolf hunter. We found his body badly mauled by wild animals. If we hadn't found his car nearby, we would have had a very difficult time figuring out who he was. All of his belongings were missing including any identification other than a hunting permit." Tilghman hesitated anticipating a question.

"You think wild animals did this?"

"Well, that's part of the dilemma. You see we're not sure at this point. The body is in Boise at the State Coroner's office. We're waiting for the results of the autopsy. There wasn't a whole lot left of this guy, and that gets me to why I called you. I need an expert in wolf biology and behavior to take a look at the remains."

"Sheriff I am flattered you have called me, but there are certainly very competent wolf experts in the state and federal offices. Jonathon Bunch over at Fish and Game is good, very good."

Tilghman sighed slightly, "Yes I know, but I need someone that does not have an axe to grind. As you are well aware, the wolf reintroduction in Idaho has caused a good deal of turmoil. It has brought about a side-taking attitude that has pretty well drowned out the more moderate voices. I need a neutral voice to give me some advice and counsel. You see, I think this old county sheriff might be getting in over his head."

"What makes you think I am the voice of neutrality?" Wilds didn't wait for a response.

"You will need to clear the way with the coroner before they will let me view the body. I would also like to make contact with a couple of other wildlife experts that might provide us some insight. Would that be all right?"

"That's more than all right. Your help is going to considerably cut down on the amount of Rolaids I have to chew."

"Today is Friday. Why don't you give me the weekend and I'll touch base with you on Monday. How is the best way to reach you? At the office number?"

"No, let me give you my cell number so you can get to me wherever I am."

When Tilghman hung up, he felt the need to talk. He walked out into the office to find Charlie Two Leaf. It was relief to get outside help and the sheriff wanted to boast a little to his deputy.

Custer County sheriff's report & incident log
4:40 p.m.
A 911 drill was performed.

TWELVE   RAVE ON

FRED STANTON SAT AT HIS FRIEND'S TABLE in the ramshackle farm house on the north side of Arco. His hand gripped tightly a short glass of Bushmill's. It was his third and he was feeling a bit of the Irish glow.

The whiskey smoothed the edge, but his friend's anger made the room feel ragged. Rave Elder was on one of his rants and when the old rancher was on a rant he was a scary thing. Fred knew full well what damage Rave could do when he was drunk and mad at the world in equal measure.

The last time the two came together, Rave had nearly killed a poor young man in the Round-Up bar in Challis. He would have, if Fred hadn't pulled him off. The young man's sin was professing a love of nature in general and the wild wolf in particular. In a moment of ill-advised naivety among strangers in Idaho, he admitted he was a field technician for the *Citizen Advocates for the Wolf*. Rave seized on that information like a shark does a halibut and vented his anger in a bloody and ugly way. Sheriff Tilghman had put the old man in the jailhouse, but the victim refused to press charges and Rave went home to his sheep the next day.

"I'll be a slick three-legged flopped eared mule before I let some smooth-talking easterner tell me that I can't shoot a mangy wolf that is bloodying my livelihood. If the damn greeny types

49

hadn't put those killers back in Idaho, we wouldn't even be having this conversation Fred."

Rave Elder was near to shouting at his drinking mate. The hot blood was rushing to his face, and he had grabbed his long gun off the rack and was waving it around like a flag. Fred was sure the man was about to explode.

Fred took another big sip of his whiskey and pretended not to notice the urgency in Rave's voice.

"Rave you're just upset 'cause you lost those sheep last month. You know as well as I do that the wolves are here to stay in Idaho. And I'll tell you this, having a rifle ain't going to be enough to make any difference. Why don't you put that big gun back in the rack and let's take another taste."

"Fred you're a goddamn traitor from New Jersey. That's what you are. If we follow the path you're on, there won't be any sheep ranchers in central Idaho in a few years. Hell's fire and damnation, the family ranch is being attacked just like the wolves are attacking my sheep. If we don't wake up soon, your son might as well pack it up and head to Seattle. Open some fuckin' curio shop or some such touristy thing or another."

"Rave you got paid for your losses didn't you?" Fred made another attempt to calm his friend but Rave was having none of it.

"Paid? What does a few hundred dollars mean when you've just got to sit on your backside and watch your livestock get eaten and the land you've always grazed taken out of production to satisfy some goddamn slick talkin' easterner's sense of the way the world should work? Hell with you. I for one intend to fight until they throw dirt in my face. That I do."

"Fight with a gun Rave? Now that's a dead-end route, I can assure...."

"Dead-end it may well be but my family's been on these lands for five generations. They fought and bled to carve out a life here and I'll be damn if I'll be the one to give it up."

"I know how you feel. I feel the same. But there is a way to do it and a way not to do it. You interested in hearing my opinion on the right way?"

Fred took another sip and waited. There was a long awkward silence in the kitchen.

"Well let's hear your point, goddamn it. You always have been the one with words about you. Most of them coated with a bit of bullshit if you want the truth about it."

Rave drained his glass and reached for the almost empty whiskey bottle.

Custer County sheriff's report & incident log
7:10 p.m.
Tilghman checked out a possible case of trespassing.

THIRTEEN BAD DOGS RUNS FREE

IT WAS A CHILLY TUESDAY NIGHT but the heat in the crowded City Hall made everyone shed coats and scarves. There was a low buzz throughout the chambers. Hector Lioncamp moved from the rear of the room toward the podium. He looked out on the crowd for a moment and then tapped at the microphone with his finger. The room quieted obediently. Lioncamp cleared his throat.

"Good evening everybody, I am..." the sound system reacted with a harsh squeal and Lioncamp backed off. He hesitated but then cautiously continued.

"I am very happy to see so many people turn out for our discussion tonight. My name is Hector Lioncamp and I am the director of the *Kill Wolves in Idaho*. As most of you know, the KWiI organization was formed several years ago to combat the reintroduction of the gray wolf in the region of the Northern Rocky Mountains and specifically in our state of Idaho. I am here tonight to report on our situation, which I am sorry to say is becoming more critical by the day. We're losing the so-called *wolf wars* my friends."

The low buzz of private conversations finally ceased as Lioncamp shuffled his notes on the podium and cleared his throat.

"I know most of you here tonight are already members of KWiI, but if you're not I am going to plead with you to join your voice with so many others calling for justice in our state. For too long now, we have had to watch as people and organizations from around the country have demanded of Idahoans that we indulge in their fantasies of what nature and natural environs should be."

"These groups and individuals have had their way with our land and our people for over a decade when it comes to the gray wolf. We have had that bloody predator forced on us even by our own Fish and Game people who continue to support the greenies against all evidence and reason. Their policies are clearly set against the ranchers and the hunters of Idaho. They encourage the increase in wolf numbers while turning a blind eye to the predation on our livestock and elk populations by that marauding menace. And that's not to even mention the ever-increasing fees for hunting permits and tags."

Lioncamp paused for a moment to let the crowd react.

"I for one am here tonight to tell you that we are about at our wits' end as to how we can reverse the consequences of the reintroduction of these bloody carnivores to our land; animals that our ancestors wisely eliminated."

Lioncamp again paused and sipped at a glass of water. As he returned the glass to the table, he motioned to a man in the back row of the meeting hall to dim the lights and switch on projector connected to a nearby laptop computer.

"Ladies and gentlemen I'm going to take a few minutes to present the latest facts that we believe overwhelmingly support our position that the gray wolf must once again be hunted and destroyed; once again removed from the mountain streams and the lush valley pastures of our state."

Lioncamp progressed through his slides methodically. He made sure to linger over graphic photographs of wolf depredation of sheep and cattle from all over Idaho, along with testimonial quotes from the ranchers who had lost animals. Then he displayed numbers depicting the drastic reduction in elk and deer populations on their customary ranges. He clicked through pictures of partially eaten carcasses of both wildlife and domestic animals. His next graphic was of an elk cow that had her birth sack ripped open and the two fetuses she carried drug from her body with only the hearts consumed.

"I know for many of you this horrible image is very disturbing. I apologize for leaving it up on the screen, but I want to make sure my summation is sufficiently clear before I open this meeting up for discussion."

"All the members of KWil are very tired of hearing the claim that the wolf only kills what he needs to survive. The kill I show you here should put to rest that simple notion. It is a notion held by people who live far from our state. People that reside safe in their apartments and homes in the urban areas far from this reality."

"Moreover, I submit to you that this has always been the case from the earliest days of the settlement of the West. It has always been the folks who daily confront the reality of the wildness this land presents that also have to deal with the remote, detached minds of people who have no clue as to what daily life is really like in the West."

Again, Lioncamp paused to take a sip of water. Still holding the glass, he turned and took a long look at the bloody image on the screen. Finally, he clicked for the next slide in his presentation. It was a bullet-point that set the tone for the open forum.

"First, the fact is that a majority of the rural residents in our state did not want the wolf returned in the first place. But that's history now. That is water under the bridge. The facts on the ground dictate our future course of action. After having lived with the wolf now for over 12 years, I think we all have the evidence we need to do what we need to do. The environmentalists and their legal hatchet men and the remote politicians have had their way far too long in my judgment. It is time that we have our say on how the wolf is to be managed."

There was a chorus of agreement arising from the crowd. Lioncamp let the enthusiasm continue until it died out slowly. He was encouraged by the crowd's participation.

"Our ranchers, our hunters, our herds of elk and deer have borne the true brunt of the reintroduction of the wolf on our lands. All of this has served to drain our rural economies in a tough economic environment that we find ourselves now dealing with. Of course, the rural economy is never considered by the greenies in their cities. They don't know what it is like to have to sit during the long nights to watch out over a herd or a flock during the season when their animals are having their young. They don't understand the heartbreak for a rancher who goes out in the morning to discover 100 or more of their animals, their livelihood, killed with their throats ripped out in what appears to be done for nothing but the sport of the kill. The city dweller can walk their dogs along their ordered and protected streets with no fear that wolves will viciously attack their loving pets. They don't have a clue what it feels like for a parent to watch a child who has trained and loved a horse heartbroken when that animal is brutally taken down by a pack of wolves and disemboweled."

"I know that some of you have hoped that we could find a solution to our troubles with the wolf through an annual wolf hunt. The argument goes that if we can control the population, as we have the bear and the cougar, we can live with this predator. I can agree with that notion to the extent that this is our best hope at present. However, let me caution you in your optimism. In my judgment, even if we do have a wolf-hunting season it will have limited effect on the overall populations. Why? Several factors mitigate the overall success of hunting wolves by individual hunters. First, the terrain where the wolf holds sway is steep, thickly forested and remote. It is an environment extremely difficult for a hunter on the ground to get within range for a clear shot at the wolf who is extremely adept at avoiding man. And, at the rate that the wolf multiplies, this method of hunting will have limited success. So most of the animals taken in this way will be incidental kills by hunters out hunting other game.

"So what are we left with? What are our choices? What can we do to protect our property and maybe our very lives? I want to hear from you now. I want to hear from those of you who I know have dealt with the wolf on a daily basis for over a decade. I want you who are on the front lines of this struggle to speak up."

Lioncamp again motioned to the rear, the lights came back up and the projector went dark. A hand went up on the middle row of the meeting hall. He acknowledged a woman in the rear of the chamber and the short plump woman rose to speak.

"Mr. Lioncamp my name is Harriet Smithson. I live about ten miles from here up in the Copper Basin. My husband and I raise sheep and miniature horses. Last month we lost two of our horse breeding stock to wolf depredation. Up until then my husband and I were divided on whether the wolf reintroduction in Idaho was a good thing or not. My husband was for them and I was against those killers. After that night, we no longer disagree. We both want those vicious animals out of our lives and out of our state. What can ordinary people do in the face of what you have said tonight? It seems to me that we are in a hopeless battle for our future."

Several members of the audience responded in agreement and all eyes turned towards Lioncamp. He called on another participant.

William Brady introduced himself. He described for the audience how he had lost two of his pet llamas to wolves up on the Wide Mouth Creek. "You know for years I have let them llamas roam around the woods," he said. "I never seen the need to keep them cooped up in a pasture or nothing like that. But then, them out-of-state people brought in the wolf and now I've lost two just in the last six months. I put my last one up, I'll tell you that. I ain't feedin' no more wolves."

As Mr. Brady sat down three more hands went up among the crowd. Hector Lioncamp called on a young girl in the back row. Her story of her dog Brandy, taken by a wolf pack in her back yard, brought some in the audience to tears. It was a good night for the KWiI and its director.

Custer County sheriff's report & incident log
7:10 p.m.
Constance Quick checked out a fire near Highway 93.
It proved to be a camper's and was well supervised.

FOURTEEN NOT UNDER MY TENT YOU DON'T

LIONCAMP BEGAN PACKING UP HIS GEAR. His yellow pad sign-up sheet displayed the signatures of ten new members for KWiI and with the names came over $3000 for the cause. He could feel the energy that was flowing around his efforts to turn the tide against the reintroduction program. There were still a few people milling around in the foyer outside the meeting room, and Lioncamp was ready to begin carrying his gear outside when two men broke free from the bunch in the back of the room and approached him.

As they did, the taller of the two stepped forward and extended his right hand. "Mr. Lioncamp, I wonder if we might have a word in private with you."

He looked up and smiled at the strangers. "Certainly, what can I do for you gentlemen?"

"Well, it might be more what we can do for you. My name is Rave Elder and this is my ranching friend Fred Stanton. We're both from around these parts and we both joined up with your organization tonight and put some money in the kitty."

Lioncamp looked at both men in turn and nodded his appreciation.

Rave Elder pulled out a chair from behind the presentation table and invited the director to take a seat.

"Mr. Lioncamp," he began, "the folks from these parts certainly agree with all that you have said tonight. And, if I might say, we are all very supportive of your efforts to rid our state of these pests and killers of our livestock and our game animals."

"That is really good to hear Mr. Elder…"

Rave interrupted, "But we think there is much more going on with this wolf thing than you are letting on." Rave turned a quick look toward Fred who seconded his agreement with a nod.

"You see we have given this considerable thought in the last ten years, ever since them federals and their green allies began taking over our lands and our state officials. Ever since, they began to tell us folks in Idaho how to run our business and our state. To put it bluntly, we have come to believe that their agenda is not simply the wolf back in its native habitat but something far greater," Rave Elder paused for effect.

Lioncamp did not answer Elder's assertion but leaned back in his chair and slowly moved his head up and down inviting the big man in the dirty cowboy hat to continue.

"Mr. Lioncamp I'm going to ask you a question, one of them what you call it, them hypa…"

"You mean hypothetical?" Lioncamp volunteered.

"Yep, that's it, one of them hypothetic questions. What if the real goal of the outsiders, these urban foreigners and their in-state lackeys, was really to eliminate our way of life out here in the West? What if what they really wanted was to come here and change the values that our people have held ever since we carved our future out of the wild and untamed wilderness that is now the great state of Idaho? What would you say to that Mr. Lioncamp?"

"Mr. Elder I would say that your proposition is not new to me. I have heard this same notion expressed in several areas of our state by folks from many different walks of life. Do you want to elaborate on your version?"

Rave Elder leaned forward in his chair letting the front legs come down hard on the concrete floor. "Yes sir, elaborate, as you say, I will. You see, I've got an idea of what is really going on here, the real goal of these people and how they think they're going to carry it out. Their real goal is to eliminate the private ranches and livestock producers in and around all of the wilderness areas. And then, once they accomplish that, their next target will be the hunter and his guns. You see, and then the land will only belong to the environmentalists and the so-called naturalists. They will own it and have the state and the feds run it for them."

Fred Stanton sat quietly to one side even though Lioncamp occasionally looked in his direction. Lioncamp turned back to Rave Elder.

"Mr. Elder I must say that your notion of what these outsiders are really about is not one that I can disagree with, but I'm not sure that it is the correct one. On the other hand, let me put it this way, I'm not sure it's a strategy or goal that we can fight directly in public. Do you understand what I mean?"

"I think I do. You mean that we'd look like a bunch of radical Limbaugh right-wing crazies if we came out with that kind of talk. Is that it?"

"Pretty much."

"Well maybe you're right but let me lay it all out, how it might work. Then we can discuss in a most serious fashion what we have to do. Alright with you?"

"I suppose so, go on."

"Okay, if I wanted to eliminate the hunter for example. What would I need to do? I can't directly eliminate the hunter or his guns or his desire to hunt. That's impossible. But, I could come up with a scheme to eliminate the thing that brings the hunter to the wilds. And what might that be? Obviously, the game animals; the deer, the elk, and so on and so forth. Do you follow my point?"

"Go on."

"Well, how do I go about that task? It's not as hard as you might suppose. First, I would need to bring into the territory an efficient and vicious killer. Someone or something that can do the job without me having to take responsibility. My tool of extermination would also have to be untouchable. That is, my efficient killer of game animals would be beyond control itself. That is to say, would have no natural enemies."

Elder slid to the front edge of his chair before he continued. "Then to help me along in my task I would need to get the law on my side. That would allow me to do what I wanted with all of the force that the law can bring. So, now what I have is a very proficient killer of the game animals at work in the forests and valleys all over the state."

"Of course you mean the wolf, right?"

"The wolf, that's exactly what I mean. You said as much yourself in your well-thought-out presentation tonight. The wolf is a most efficient killer. How many photographs did you display that showed just how efficient the wolf is at killing? Often with little regard for consuming the carcass but only for the sake of killing. How long before this rate of killing depletes the wolf's food source and then he turns to domestic livestock to survive. You showed us that outcome very well tonight too, that you did. And, we heard from many folks such as that lady Mrs. Smithson and that other cute little girl, who have lost domestic livestock or household pets to the vicious wolf."

"And what about the man who tries to protect his property, who tries to defend his rights as a land owner? What about him? He finds the full force of the law used to beat him down to the ground. Make him fearful to defend himself. Hell's fire, them environmental bastards have got a reward program going so that anyone can turn in a person for killing one of those mangy critters. Everybody here tonight knows of that fellow over in Cameron County that killed a wolf that was harassing his sheep, and we know what happened to him. He got six months in jail and a $10,000 fine. Now you think about that. A $10,000 fine. That'll put the fear in you now won't it?"

"The fact of the matter, Mr. Lioncamp, is that these people have devised a plan that is almost fool-proof. You have to give them credit for their genius. With no game, there is no need for the hunter. With no hunter, why do you need a gun? With no way of making a profit on the land, then the rancher moves out and off the land. Now is that genius or what?"

Rave Elder again leaned back in his chair. He folded his big arms across his chest and looked over at his friend. They both smiled slightly and looked back at Lioncamp.

"Well, that's quite a picture you paint Mr. Elder. If you are correct, the ranchers and the hunters in Idaho are in for a great struggle."

"That they are Mr. Lioncamp."

"You know that we, I mean the KWiL, are actively fighting the unregulated distribution of the wolf and his packs in the state of Idaho. We are fighting for a greatly expanded hunting season for the wolf. And this will be the first year of a legal hunt in our state since the wolf was forced among us. Although, as I said, this is not the complete solution. We think that an open season on any predator that crosses into private space or threatens any private property is in order as well, to help control just the outcome you predict."

Lioncamp paused to let Rave Elder respond but the old man sat quiet.

"Also we are, with the help of the contributions from folks like those here tonight, ready to mount our own legal assault on the uncontrolled wolf populations. In fact, our ultimate goal is to have the entire question put on a statewide ballot seeking to get the people to speak—to call on our Governor to demand that the feds reduce wolf pack numbers in our state."

Rave Elder took a deep breath and let it out slowly. "Mr. Lioncamp you can save the political speech and all that about them politicians at the State Capital. Fred and I have heard it all before. If they had been any good to us, they would have stopped the whole thing before it ever got started."

"Let me tell you what we are prepared to do and why. First, the only way we are going to stop this madness in Idaho is with a bit of madness of our own. Look, the greenies and their allies have all of the cards in the deck. They have the expertise to argue in ways we can't imagine. They have the money that comes from thousands of sources that we can only dream about. You're little take here tonight wouldn't pay the cab fare for one of their lawyers in Washington. They have the Congress and the President on their side. They've got every bureaucrat in Washington with pretty little pictures of wolves on their walls and stuffed fuzzy wolves for their little nieces. They have the press eating out of their hands, just waiting for the next lawsuit. And, of the utmost importance, these people have every wildlife advocate from the *National Geographic* to the *Citizen Advocates for Wolves* ready to portray us in Idaho as Neanderthals intent on destroying the earth and mankind along with it. To hear them tell the tale we invented global warming and baby seal hunts. And you're going to deal with these people and those odds with a vote of the people. Forget it my friend."

Rave Elder stood up. "Mr. Lioncamp we may very well be little people in the eyes the world, but I'll tell you this; before we are through our voices will be heard. And they will be heard loud and clear. That I promise you."

"All right Mr. Elder. You have made your point." Lioncamp also stood up and started to pick up a piece of his equipment.

"Wait Mr. Lioncamp, hold on. I didn't mean to be so harsh but we are fed up with being beatin' to a bloody pulp. We've got a plan. I ask you to listen a bit more, and then if you're still ready to leave we will help you load up and I'll give you another check for a thousand bucks. Deal?"

Lioncamp eased the projector back down on the table and turned to face Rave Elder. "Mr. Elder I'm tired. It has been a long day and I have traveled for several hundred miles and given three presentations. I will sit back down and give you fifteen minutes to hear you out and then I will be on my way."

"Okay then. Here is the bottom line. On the present course we have taken to fight the wolf in our state and the people who would run us off our own land, in my judgment, we are doomed. So, we have to come up with an alternative; an alternative that has some chance of success. Now you might ask what constitutes success. Well, to hear you talk success is measured in increased hunting privileges to control wolf numbers. For my friends and me, success is the total and final removal of the wolf. First from the state of Idaho and then from the entire Northern Rockies. That, Mr. Lioncamp is what we aim to accomplish."

Lioncamp leaned forward in his chair. "Now that's what I call a tall order of business. You are going to have to give a good idea of how you intend to accomplish your version of success. As I see things, the wolf is here stay."

"Yeah, and that is why we are here. We have to change your mind because you have put together an organization that will be vital if we are going to pull this off. We need a way to reach a much larger audience once we get things going our way. But wait, I am getting ahead of myself."

"What we think will have to happen before we can be shed of the gray wolf is that we will have to turn the majority of people against the reintroduction. I'm not talking about just these rural folks like we had here tonight. No sir, I mean we have to turn all of the state and many in the entire country against the wolf. We have to do a great job of marketing so to speak. Just like the greenies did over the last two decades getting the wolf out of Canada down here. How we get that job done is not a simple quick fix but a steady long term effort that begins now."

Lioncamp looked at his watch and started to speak but Rave Elder began again. "And this is how we start on that trail. I have a friend who is a good tracker. He has been following a particular wolf pack around for the last six months. He is also a darn good photographer. He has some very good photos of wolves getting really close to populated areas. One picture in particular is important. It shows a black wolf and several of his pack members within a half-mile of the Salmon High School. These wolves seem to be scouting out the school. Now this kind of thing I want to start to publicize. I want mothers to start thinking about the possibility that a wolf will attack a kid—their kid. I want them to imagine a wolf chasing and bringing down a child the way they do an elk. Mr. Lioncamp that is the way we fight fire with fire. That is the way we can begin to turn the tide against the wolf and in our favor. It is this long-standing fear of the wolf that we reintroduce into this argument."

"You know that the wolf advocates, Mr. Elder, have pretty much been able to counter that traditional fear over the last several years. Some of the films that have been rather popular have depicted the wolf packs as just another wild creature living and raising their young like any other animal. They have been very successful in this campaign. Do you really think you can overcome that momentum with a few pictures of wolves near schools?"

"No I don't. Not with just pictures. Let me lay it out simple for you. The day that a wolf pack does what most of us believe will eventually happen; then we will see the Disneyland attitude to that vicious killer change among the general population. And, what day is that? Simply it is the day when the wolf stalks, kills, and devours a human being. That day we will gain the initiative. We will then be able to rouse public opinion in our favor. From that day we will have the argument to get our public officials to begin re-thinking their attitudes to regain a backbone sufficient to resist the hair-brain schemes that come out of Washington, D.C."

"Wait a minute Mr. Elder," Lioncamp hesitated. He was, for a second, unable to put into words what he was thinking. "Mr. Elder, Mr. Stanton I don't want to jump to conclusions here, but do I understand you? Are you suggesting..."

"I think you understand me Lioncamp. We are in a war in this state—a war that we are losing. A war that if we don't win, all that we have is in danger of disappearing forever. In war you have to fight to win or you will surely be defeated. That's a big part of the problem in this country now-a-days. We don't have the gumption to fight to win. To take and inflict casualties. To kill the enemy in sufficient numbers so he loses the will to fight back. We have lost our toughness. The toughness that won this country in the first place."

Hector Lioncamp stood from his chair and again began to retrieve his equipment. He didn't offer any comment.

"Lioncamp, as I said. We are going to make ourselves heard. Now, if you walk out on me right now I will consider you and your group a hindrance to our purpose and mission. Is that I how I read it?"

Hector Lioncamp turned to face Rave Elder clutching his projector in his arms. "Mr. Elder, I am passionate about what must be done to overcome the assault that is being waged against our life here in Idaho, make no mistake about that. Nevertheless, I am a man deeply committed to the rule of law and to justice. If I understand you correctly, if I understand what you are proposing to do, then I cannot help you or your kind."

He turned his gaze to Fred Stanton and then back to Rave Elder. "What you are suggesting to me is the very thing that eventually destroys any worthwhile society. I will not be a party to that."

"Well then, you are, as far as I am concerned, just another part of the problem I have to deal with. You can scratch our names off your roster tonight. I can also tell you that there is a group of men in your organization right now that will pull out and come to work with us."

Rave Elder stood up abruptly. "Hell, I can see we aren't the kind to work together anyway."

"No, Mr. Elder I don't think we are. Goodnight sir."

Lioncamp was shaking slightly as he loaded his equipment into his truck. He wanted to look over his shoulder out into the dark but fought the urge. He wondered what was happening to his state and to his country. For the first time since he had started his campaign against the gray wolf, he felt afraid. He felt that he was losing control of his own organization and its mission.

Custer County sheriff's report & incident log
10:10 a.m.
*Deputy responded to report of a runaway hiding
behind the White Knob Inn in Mackay.*

FIFTEEN   SHAKE THE BUSHES

Possible man killer on the loose?

Ignacio Hawk reporting

*The new snow brought an early season harsh blast of winter to the Big
Lost River Mountains last Thursday and for one unfortunate hunter, the
snow proved to be the final chill. A yet to be identified man was found dead
by other hunters, badly mauled and lying in the new snow where he had
fallen.*

*Sheriff Chester A. Tilghman of Custer County, along with Ranger
Rick Clyde of the Challis National Forest, were the first investigators on
the scene. However, neither official was able, due to the condition of the
remains, to immediately determine the cause of death or identify the victim.
The investigation was hampered further by the new snow that was nearly a
foot deep at the scene. The early snow also made it impossible to do a
thorough search of the area around the body.*

*Sheriff Tilghman said that they had found what they believe is the
hunter's cell phone near the body. Other personal effects were not found.
The sheriff hoped that the phone would reveal the identity of the victim and
possibly offer some clue as to the cause of death. He was especially hopeful
that there would be some recent photographs stored in the device.*

One of the men who discovered the victim is a well-known character in Custer County. Howard Wicks, known by most as Wishful Wicks, is being held as a material witness in the county jail pending further investigation. Wishful told this reporter that he believes wolves killed the man although the sheriff strongly discouraged this idea. Sheriff Tilghman pointed out the unreliable history of Mr. Wicks.

The sheriff said that "although foul play is not to be ruled out, any cause of death or the circumstances surrounding this unfortunate event will have to wait until further investigation can be conducted and a coroner's report is made."

Two other hunters at the scene, those who actually called in the discovery to authorities, were Harry and Henry Elder. The Elder brothers were in the area hunting wolves and elk. According to Harry Elder, the victim's remains were unrecognizable due to the severe scavenging by wolves and other wild animals. Henry wouldn't speculate on the cause of death but did say that "he thought the signs pointed to a wolf attack." It was thought that the victim had made a wolf kill on this first day of the season because the carcass of a large male wolf was freshly skinned and hanging nearby in a tree.

The Salmon River Sentinel-Reader will continue to follow this developing story.

Linda Davenport stuck her head into the sheriff's office. "Sheriff have you seen this?" She held up this week's copy of the *Salmon River Sentinel-Reader* and waved it above her head. The sheriff looked up and motioned her to come in.

"What's that? Let me guess, it must be Scoop's article about the body, right?"

"Well sir, that it is and I think you had better read it right away." Linda laid the paper with the front-page headline so that Tilghman could see it clearly. The sheriff glanced at the bold type and promptly picked up the phone.

Ignacio Hawk came on the line. The sheriff shouted, "What in the Sam Hill did you do? I haven't even read the article but I'm already worked up about it. I thought we had an understanding Scoop. *No gasoline!* Remember?"

"Sheriff read the article," Ignacio tried to interrupt the sheriff's rant but Tilghman wasn't through.

"I don't have to read it, the headline will do. For the folks around here that hate the wolf this is like lighting a fuse in a stick of dynamite. *Man killer* to them means only one thing. *Wolf!*

Hawk broke in. "Sheriff if you will read the article you will see that I am only stating the facts of the case. You said yourself that you're not sure what happened to that hunter. Am I right?"

The sheriff paused briefly. "Scoop, being right is not always the point. Listen to me. We've got a potentially explosive situation here. If we knew for sure that the victim had been murdered, it would be bad enough, but if wolves actually did kill this man it is going to be impossible to contain the anger. I am afraid that some people around here are very close to taking the law into their own hands. If that happens, that poor soul up in the mountains won't be the last to get hurt."

"So you think the wolves did it Sheriff?"

"Damn it! Hawk, I didn't say that. And don't you dare write that. I'm just saying that sometimes the facts simply do not matter. It's the perception that counts. Don't you get it?"

"I'm not in the business of perceptions..."

"Oh! You're not. *Possible man killer on the loose.* What the hell is that?"

"Okay Sheriff, I get it. So give me something new. What's new that I can use? Everybody is hungry for an update. Especially my editor. He's salivating over this story."

"There is nothing new; that's the problem. But, I'll tell you this Hawk. When there is, I want to be the one who writes the next headline. Agreed?"

"I owe you that. Just keep me in the loop."

"Okay, will do."

"Goodbye Sheriff."

"Goodbye."

SIXTEEN   JUSTICE, MY JUSTICE

HECTOR LIONCAMP SAT MOTIONLESS IN HIS PICKUP for well over an hour. He was about three blocks west of the Custer County Courthouse on the main drag, next to the strange diagonal crosswalk that ran from the bars on opposite sides of the street. He was a conflicted man. He didn't have any evidence that would stand up in a court of law or even in a heated argument among friends. But he knew that what he knew had to be spoken. That is, if he was to have any peace of mind. He laid the copy of the *Salmon River Sentinel-Reader* down on the front seat and moved deliberately out of his truck. As he approached the courthouse, he saw the chief deputy exit the building.

"Charlie! Charlie!" he shouted, "Is the Sheriff in his office?"

"I believe he is Mr. Lioncamp. He's working on a new case."

"Thanks."

Lioncamp bounded up the steps and entered the building. He passed the length of the courthouse and exited the back door. The sheriff's trailer and the attached old stone jail were just across the parking lot. As he passed under the elk antlers that hung over the entrance and entered the dispatcher's lobby he ran into Linda coming out of the jail area.

"Hello Hector, how in the world are you these days? We haven't seen much of you lately."

"No not much, been kind of busy with the KWiI group and such. Can I see Chester?"

"Sure Hector. You know where he is, go on in."

"Sheriff Tilghman, you got a minute to talk to me?" Hector Lioncamp asked as he timidly peeked around the door jamb into the sheriff's office.

"No Hector I don't," the sheriff replied gruffly and at the same time smiled broadly. "But I'll make one for you. In fact, I have been meaning to get a hold of you anyway. Got some questions for you. Come on in and have a seat. How about some coffee you old rascal?"

"Yes sir, I could use some, thanks. And I could use a shot of Jack to boot if you still keep it in that top left drawer."

"Not anymore Hector, not anymore," Tilghman replied as he stuck his head outside the door and asked Linda to bring in a couple of cups of coffee. When he sat back down, he moved a pile of papers off to one side of the desk and leaned back.

"You want to tell me why you're here? I assume it's more than a social call."

"Yes, Chester it is. But, I'm not really sure why I am here. I've just got something rubbing a sore spot on my mind that I need to get rid of."

Hector took the cup from Linda and thanked her. He took a long sip and stared into the black opening. Finally, he raised his head and looked long at the sheriff. Tilghman sat still and waited, looking at his long-time friend without expression.

"Chester, I know you are investigating that hunter's death up at Chilly Buttes. Making any progress?"

Tilghman mimicked Lioncamp's behavior and sipped at his coffee before he answered. "Is that why you're here Hector?"

"It might be. Yes sir."

"I guess you've seen the article in the *Reader* then?

"I have."

"Well, to answer your question. No, I haven't come up with much yet. We are still waiting for some reports out of Boise before we can say for sure what killed the poor man. Until we know that, we can't even start down any other trail. Do you know something I need to know? About this case I mean?"

"I'm not sure but something happened at one of my meetings a few days back that is keeping me up nights. It may have a connection to your investigation; I'm not sure."

"Is that right? What was it?"

"Well there were two fellows at my last gathering; they were strangers to me and they said some pretty radical things. One of the men did most of the talking. The other one just sort of nodded his agreement. It was my understanding that they were both ranchers somewhere around Arco. Like I said that was the first I heard of them."

"This fellow," Tilghman interrupted, "what did he look like?"

"He was real tall, sort of dark complexion and wore a big cowboy hat. The other one was short and kind of stubby."

"What was the talkative one's name?"

"He introduced himself as Rave Elder. You know of him?"

"I'll tell you in a minute. Go on."

"Well, after the regular meeting these two approached me as I was getting ready to pack up my dog and pony show and head to Boise. The Elder fellow said he wanted to talk to me about a proposition. They had both joined the KWiL and contributed some money to the fund at the meeting. To cut to the chase Chester, these men were more than disturbed about the way the wolf reintroduction has gone in Idaho. The way they put it, to them it was a matter of life and death. And I mean that just the way it sounds. These were serious men."

Tilghman put his coffee cup on a side table and picked up a small notepad. "Keep going Hector. What did they say then?"

"They said they had a plan on how we could rid the state of the wolf. That plan of theirs is why I'm here. You see Chester, I've got some pretty far-out folks in my organization. I mean some are walking along the edge most of the time. But I can't say any of those are for doing something illegal. They all want to fight and fight hard but inside the law. This Rave Elder fellow, I'm not so sure.

"What he said that night I pretty much dismissed until I read that article in the *Sentinel-Reader*. The one you just mentioned. It was that headline in particular that caught my eye. Something about *Man killer* right?"

"Yep, Hector that one caught my eye as well," the sheriff smiled slightly.

"Well, it made me recall the gist of those two men's idea. Now I want you to understand that they never said this outright, but there was no mistaking what they had in mind. They said the only way to win our fight with the greenies and the feds was to turn widespread public opinion against the wolf. And the only way to do that was to portray the wolf as it has been portrayed until recent times."

"Man killers, right?"

"That's exactly it Chester. That's exactly what they had in mind. But here is where I told them I would not have anything to do with them or what they were hinting at. I had the real impression that if the wolves would not cooperate then they would find a way to force the issue as they saw fit. You get me?"

"You're as clear as the Clearwater River. You say you haven't heard from them since that night?"

"No I haven't. We parted company in a sort of strained way. That Rave Elder feller made it clear that we were in separate corners after that. Tell you the truth, I was relieved when I got out of their range. I ain't a spooky man but that one put a shiver to my backbone. I suspect he's a mean one."

Sheriff Tilghman got up and came around the desk. He told Hector Lioncamp to wait a moment and he left the room. When he returned, he had a folder in his hand. Tilghman sat back down and opened the folder. He laid a photo on his desk and turned it toward Hector to see.

"What do you make of this Hector?"

The image froze the Lioncamp in place. He studied the graphic of the bloody human remains for a moment and then he looked back at the sheriff.

Tilghman withdrew the photograph. "Do you think something like that would make Mr. Elder happy?"

"Well Chester I hope the death of that man wouldn't, but I believe with certainty that if he was killed by wolves, Rave Elder would do a little happy dance. That I do."

"Then you must also think that the headline you spoke of is exactly what those men were looking for, right?"

"Right."

"Okay, Hector I'm going to tell you something that might make you feel a little better about coming forward with this information. But I need you to hang on to this info pretty tight. I'm asking you as a friend not as a sheriff. Do I have your word?"

"Chester we go back a ways and that's part of the reason I'm here. Yes, you have my word."

Tilghman again opened the folder and took out a piece of paper. "I've got two copies of Idaho Fish and Game hunting licenses in my hand. They are both for this year and both are permits to hunt elk and wolves. Now there is nothing unusual about these

76

documents except that they are in the names of Harry and Henry Elder. Both men are from the Arco region. Would it be reasonable to you to assume that these boys are in some way connected to Rave Elder?"

"I believe it would Chester. I can't tell that they are but if there is a connection of blood I would want to check it out."

"Oh, you can count on that. You see what you have told me this morning has changed my whole line of inquiry into this death. It has finally given me something to go on. I am more than anxious now to get the report on the cause of death."

Lioncamp agreed with the sheriff and stood up to leave.

"Chester let me say one more thing before I go. This really doesn't have anything to do with your investigation but it is important for this county and for our state. I've got some folks in my organization that are feeling that no matter what they say or do everything is working against them. They're in the main rural folk, hard working ranchers and farmers and the like. They see the outsiders with their high-priced lawyers and lobbyists and those kind taking over everything they hold dear. They get beaten every way to Sunday. They lose financially, they lose politically, they lose socially and they lose ideologically. Some of them are very tired of losing. If this continues much longer, then the Rave Elders in our state may be more numerous than we would like. That's not a warning Chester, it's just an unhappy observation."

"I know what you're getting at. That is one of the reasons I need to resolve this case as quickly as I can. It's like a festering wound; the longer it stays open the more the flies are going to lay their filth in the sore."

The men shook hands and Lioncamp headed for the office door. He stopped and turned back toward Sheriff Tilghman. "Chester I hope you can keep what I told you in confidence. It's not my purpose to stir up snakes or hurt any of the people in my state. We're all kind of frustrated about this wolf thing."

"Yeah, I know. But you know that's just how things are. They don't always go the way we want or expect. Some of us stay in bounds and play the game by the rules as best as we can. Others... others look for the fix anyway they can, using any methods they want. It's that kind that I have been picking up after for over thirty years trying to protect the rights and interests of your kind. It's a tough job and it's getting tougher by the day."

"Thanks Chester. Good luck with this one. See you soon. Oh, and Chester..."

"Yeah?"

"I never told you, but I really am sorry you lost Maggie. I've never said anything because I was ashamed that I didn't come to the funeral. I'm really sorry though. I know you two were awful close."

"It's alright Hector. And thanks. She was a real peach. I miss her more every day."

"I'm sure you do. Listen, take care with this case will you? I don't like the feel of this one. You're getting a little old to be chasing the bad guys."

"Thanks, I will. I've got Charlie to watch my back. That Indian is a good man."

Hector Lioncamp walked slowly out of the sheriff's office. He stopped to talk with Charlie Two Leaf and Linda as he left the building. When he was gone, Tilghman walked up to the deputy.

"Charlie see what you can find out about the whole Elder clan up in the Arco area. Run some record checks. See if we have any bad guys up that way. Pull the file on Rave Elder too, the one from that fight incident last summer. Let's take another look at that too."

Charlie turned to go but then turned back. "You goin' to tell me what that was about?" He nodded toward the front door.

"Soon enough Charlie—get those records."

Custer County sheriff's report & incident log
11:45 a.m.
*Mackay ambulance volunteers responded
to an ATV accident near Whiskey Springs.*

SEVENTEEN   MOVED ALONG BY A WHISPER

SHERIFF TILGHMAN AND CHARLIE TWO LEAF had been on Highway 93, headed south out of Challis, for almost an hour. Neither man had spoken a word since they started. They would be on the highway another two hours before they got to Pocatello. Finally, the sheriff broke the silence.

"Charlie, what do you think about all this hoopla and fighting over the gray wolf? I mean does it make sense from where the Nez Perce are perched?"

The chief deputy didn't respond and the sheriff thought that he must not have heard him.

Finally, Charlie repeated the sheriff's question, "Does it make sense?" — "No it doesn't, but to be truthful, there's not a whole lot that the white man does that makes sense to the Indian. The wolf is just another in a long, long line of confused thinking the way we see it. But, the sad fact is that we lost most of our voice 160 years ago and so we just sort of keep our collective mouths shut. There's no future in criticizing you folks. You don't have a tendency to listen anyway."

Tilghman was surprised by his deputy's tone. Charlie had never spoken that way before. After an awkward silence the sheriff spoke up. "I'm asking Charlie. Not that I can do anything to change the way the white man conducts business, but I'd like to know your take on this predicament we've gotten ourselves into in Idaho."

Again, the silence was broken only by the road noise.

Tilghman tried again. "In some ways, I'm really beginning to believe that the Cahalan case is as much about the conflict over the wolf as anything else. I mean, I think this man's death on the Elkhorn is somehow tied to that dispute."

Hot Sauce was nervous and moved continually back and forth between the sheriff's and Charlie's laps. Finally, Tilghman had had enough of the fidgeting, picked the miniature dog up, and tossed him into the back seat. The hunched-back Chihuahua let out a sharp bark of protest but quickly curled up on his blanket and settled.

"Well Charlie, you gonna give me some kind of answer?"

The deputy didn't look away from the highway and only nodded slightly. "No, but I'll tell you a story Chester." Charlie rarely called the sheriff Chester but when he did, Tilghman knew they weren't talking any longer as sheriff and deputy but as two men.

Charlie began in a low and calm voice. "There is a legend that is told around the council fires on the reservation each year that I think might help you with your question. The elders call it the legend of Black Wolf's spirit. If you want, I can tell it."

"Yeah sure, I'd like that Charlie."

The deputy pushed his back against the driver's seat with his arms braced against the steering wheel and let out a long sigh before he began.

"In the time when my people where known as the *Nimiipuu*, the real people, and ruled the world, long before the white man ever dreamed of this land, there was a young warrior without a name. What that means to us is that he had no spirit. He was here, I mean in this world, but he was not really here. Only his body walked the paths and hunted the game and lived amongst his people. His parents watched the boy as he grew but even though they followed

81

him closely, they could never find his true spirit. Without the true spirit they couldn't give him his name—his spirit name. As a result, the boy was a loner in his tribe and didn't fit with any others his own age. He hunted alone and spent his time roaming the land in solitude.

"One day the young warrior wandered off far from the lodges, farther than he had ever gone before. But something kept him going, and he didn't turn back. He just kept going. Before he knew it, he was out on the vast prairie with its tall grasses and great herds of buffalo and elk and antelope. Yet he just kept going, wandering farther and farther, as if in a trance, away from his people and from the safety they provided. Then, all of a sudden, the young warrior realized what he had done. The only things he could see that looked familiar, that he knew he could see from his home, were the peaks of the Bitterroot Mountains far in the distance. He turned and with urgency in his pace he headed for them.

"As he moved toward the great peaks he could see the dark clouds forming on high and rolling down the slopes. This told him that a big storm was coming. And he knew it was coming swiftly. The young warrior realized he was in trouble unless he could find shelter and find it right away. But it was too late. The powerful dark storm came crashing all around him. The heavy rain was laced with a biting snow that quickly turned to terrible sheets of cold ice. A deep chill coated his body as the ice stuck to his bare skin on his chest and back. The wind whipped the warmth from his frame and left him shaking as he searched frantically for shelter. But there was none to be found. The young warrior then sensed the spirit of death moving in the air around him. For the first time in his life, he wished he was with his people and, more than ever, he wished he knew his name. It was his spirit name that would tell him how to behave—what to do in the terrible situation he now found himself in. But he didn't have one.

"The young warrior kept moving as best he could but slowly, bit by bit, he was tiring; and thoughts of giving up began to take hold. At last he decided to sit down and curl up into a ball—to simply go to the other side without protest or resistance. Just when all hope had left him, he heard a soft sound at his feet. It was like a whimper. He thought that maybe he was making the sound himself. It came again. Now it appeared to be two or more voices making the noise. It was close at his feet. He could hear it plainly now and the young warrior hastily pushed at the ice and snow hoping to discover the source of the sound below. That is when he saw it—the hole in the ground. The hole was sheltered by a great fallen log. He stuck his ear to it. Clearly now he could hear the calls coming deep from the underground. The young warrior knew these calls. They were the calls of young wolf pups deep in their den. This was the shelter of a mother wolf and her litter.

"The young warrior was colder now too. He had to find cover or the end was near. He pushed his shoulders into the hole and as he got deeper, the hole got bigger. As he pushed harder and harder the opening in the hole expanded with the force of his body. Suddenly he slid down a shaft that led deeper from the surface. As he crawled on, the opening got bigger still but the light was becoming dim; too dim to see very far into the den. Now he could hear the pups calling clearly. The young warrior thought that the small animals must think that he was their mother returning with food. They sounded excited. So was he. He was at last out of the terrible storm and the warmth of the ground was driving the chill from his body. He was again happy to be alive and, for a time, safe.

"He pushed on into the surrounding darkness until he suddenly reached out blindly and felt the soft fur and the squirming bodies of the wolf pups at his finger tips. They felt good to the touch. They were soft, warm, and alive. He could feel at least five pups, maybe more. It was a big litter for a wolf mother. He could hear the storm still raging above and he knew he must stay put or die. The pups wiggled around him. They welcomed their new companion. The young warrior got warmer. He soon fell asleep.

"More than a week went by and the people of the young warrior's lodges had given up hope that the one with no name would return from the great storm that had raged in the mountains. They were sad because they didn't know how to send the young warrior's spirit to the sky. He had no name. Late winter turned into spring and then into summer. Most had forgotten the young warrior. Only his parents stood patiently once a day and looked towards the rugged peaks hoping to at last catch a glimpse of their returning son. But they, too, slowly gave up the notion. And finally his memory became as a shadow and was lost in the brightness of each new day.

"Mother Earth moved through her seasons five more times. Then on a wonderfully warm and bright day, a young woman was down in the marsh gathering camas lily when she was startled from her labor by the sight of a young, solitary warrior coming across the prairie. He was much taller than she had remembered and he was darker. But she knew who he was. It was the warrior with no name. Then as the approaching figure cleared the tall grasses, she saw that he was not alone. Closely behind and to his side were five wolves. All were black and shiny, big and strong and ferocious looking animals. The young girl became frightened and hurried up from the stream and back to the village screaming as she ran.

"Hearing the commotion, the warriors quickly gathered into the center of the lodges anticipating trouble. They strung their bows and prepared for a fight. Then they saw what was causing the young woman's terror. The warriors smiled as they recognized one of their own and put aside their weapons as they prepared to greet the warrior without a name on his return from the faraway mountains. The young warrior was no longer young and he was no longer a warrior without a name. He was full and strong. And now he had a guardian spirit name, his *wey-ya-kin*. He was Black Wolf."

As Charlie Two Leaf finished his story, he fell silent. Once again, there was only the sound of the road as the two continued towards Pocatello. Chester waited. He wasn't sure whether Charlie was through with his tale.

"Is that it? Aren't you going to tell me the moral of the story? How's that supposed to answer my question?"

The deputy answered quickly. "Don't you see Chester? That's what I mean about the white man. You are always looking for the hard lesson, the end of all things. Sometimes my friend there is only the story. That's it. For once Chester don't push the river. Just think on it for a spell."

The sheriff took a deep breath and looked at the mountains slowly creeping by the passenger's window in the distance as the Jeep sped along. He suddenly wondered how many wolf dens might be up on those low ridges. At that moment, he wished he were an Indian; wished he could think like Charlie Two Leaf.

Chester pushed his frame straighter in his seat and looked directly at the driver. "Well, at least you can tell me about this *wey-ya-kin* thing. What's that all about? Do you have one of those guardian things?"

"I do."

"Well, what is it?"

"It's a wolf."

"You've got to be kidding me. You're kidding me right?" The sheriff displayed a large grin thinking he was playing along with Charlie's joke.

"No," the deputy answered without smiling. The father of my great-great grandfather was Black Wolf."

"You mean the Black Wolf of the legend?"

"Yes. You see Chester the legend is a story, one of many among my people. They tell us how the plane that separates humans and the spirits is breeched. How our ancestors came to know who they really were. What their destiny was and how they were to live. My *wey-ya-kin*, my guardian spirit, is that of the wolf. The wolf has nurtured me, has guided me in my adult life. I know the wolf and know how to think like the wolf. The wolf is nature's great hunter. I have the wolf's spirit — the wolf's ways."

After a while, Chester looked at his deputy. "Charlie how come I have never seen this side of you? Maybe you should be the one taking the lead on this investigation — you being the great hunter and all." The sheriff's tone was sincere.

"Maybe I should," Charlie answered. "I can tell you one thing about this case and about the death of Doctor Cahalan."

"What's that?"

"The wolves didn't kill that man."

Tilghman looked at the driver. "What makes you say that?"

"My spirit tells me. The wolves may be blamed and they may pay the white man's price for their nature, but they didn't kill the hunter. The wolves were not the enemy of that man on that day. He came to kill one of them; it was the other way around."

"Maybe so Charlie. We will see."

Custer County sheriff's report & incident log
3:45 p.m.
*Deputies responded to a blown RV tire and
driver stranded near Stanley.*

EIGHTEEN   FEW TOOK NOTICE OR
REALLY CARED

AS TILGHMAN AND CHARLIE TWO LEAF DROVE DOWN Bradforte Road
in Pocatello, the sheriff felt as alien to the place as an Eskimo would
to Florida. The half-circle drives, manicured grounds and multi-
ridged roofs seemed to him unreal, if not unnecessary. The simple
world that was his in central Idaho had no place for the excess that
lined the upper class neighborhood he and Charlie now passed
through.

"That's it Charlie, right there. 2121, see it carved in the
stone? Pull in there."

The deputy cautiously drove up to the front entrance and set
the parking brake. Hot Sauce excitedly hopped around in the back
of the Cherokee. The little dog was ready to hit hard ground after
the long ride.

"Sheriff you want me to wait here or come in with you?"

"You'd better stay here. Take Hot Sauce out for a little relief.
I don't expect I'll be that long. I'm not looking forward to this I can
tell you."

"I hear that. I wouldn't either. Dog and I will hold the fort.
Good luck."

"Thanks."

The woman that answered the door was nothing like the sheriff anticipated. She was a slight woman, not unattractive, but plainly dressed. As she faced the sheriff, her gaze barely reached as high as his badge pinned to his chest.

Sarah Cahalan looked up and smiled slightly as she gently invited Tilghman in. As they moved toward the living room, she offered him a cup of coffee.

They exchanged light conversation for a few minutes, mostly about the sheriff's drive from Challis and the weather along the way. Finally, Tilghman came around to the subject at hand.

"Mrs. Cahalan, I am very sorry about your husband," he began.

The sheriff waited for a response but the slight woman just sat rigid on the couch and faced him. Her blue eyes remained fixed on her guest and her gaze didn't waver. Tilghman wasn't sure she had heard him so he continued awkwardly. He wasn't sure what question to ask first so he just started.

"Did your husband have any enemies, Mrs. Cahalan?" he said softly. "I mean is there anyone who might have wanted to do him harm?"

Finally Sarah Cahalan spoke.

"Sheriff Tilghman, that's an odd question. Are you saying you think he met with foul play?"

"We don't know, ma'am, what happened to your husband. We have to consider all the possibilities. I apologize for the abruptness of my question."

Sarah simply nodded before she spoke.

"Sheriff, my husband was a simple surgeon. He wasn't the type to have enemies." Sarah returned her coffee cup to the saucer that sat on a linen napkin on the table. She looked down for a moment and then went on.

"Well, I suppose there was one person." She stood up slowly, walked to a hutch in the far corner of the living room, and opened a drawer. When she returned she handed a plain black framed photograph to the sheriff and returned to her seat on the couch.

"That's Jerry's brother Mike," she continued. "He is younger than Jerry by about eight years. I'm not sure where he lives now. He did rent a place up near you in Clayton the last we heard from him. Never was too stable. I don't think Jerry has talked to him since the argument."

"Argument?" The sheriff put his cup down next to Mrs. Cahalan's and took his note pad from his shirt pocket and opened the tattered pad to a blank page.

"Yes. It was about three or four years ago. Around Christmas, I think. The brothers got into a violent fight over money here in the house. Mike had come to see us, which he usually did if he needed something. I heard them shouting in the study just after we had finished our holiday dinner."

"You said violent. What do you mean? Did they get physical?"

"A little," she continued quietly. "Mike was taller than Jerry and had lived a pretty rough life. What Jerry called him was 'a man of the street'. Whenever he couldn't get his way with charm he tried to physically get what he wanted. He and Jerry had had a couple of tussles in the past. Nothing too serious, but they frightened me when they happened. I didn't like Mike coming to the house. Jerry told me that Mike had been in jail at least once before that he knew of. It had something to do with carrying a concealed weapon in a bar near Boise."

"How did their argument end?"

"Well Jerry usually relented and gave Mike money. It was usually the easiest solution. You see, Mike had a gambling and drinking problem. When he had some cash, he usually went over to Nevada; he liked to go to Elko. He always told us about the money he won over there. He worked there for a while as a bartender. When his luck played out, he always made it back to Idaho. That's when we usually heard from him. He always needed a stake to get him back on his feet—until his luck changed, he'd say."

The doorbell rang and Sarah got up and went to the front door. Tilghman couldn't see the door from his chair but he heard his deputy's voice so he got up and moved in that direction.

"Sheriff can I talk with you for a second?"

"Charlie we are right in the middle of something important. Can't it wait?"

"No sir, I don't think that it can." Charlie Two Leaf looked back toward the sheriff's Jeep and nervously shook his head up and down.

"Okay deputy. Mrs. Cahalan, would you please excuse me for a second while I attend to this?" The sheriff could see Hot Sauce running along the dash of the Jeep and barking.

"Sheriff we found one of Cahalan's belongings," Charlie said through a slight smile.

"Where? Where did we get so lucky?"

"A pawn broker down here in town got suspicious about a loan he made on a watch and decided to call the State Police. They called us."

"And?"

"Oh yeah, there is something else Sheriff. The pawnbroker said that the same man who sold him the watch said he would be back with some more stuff.

"What kind of watch was it Charlie, did he say?"

Said it was a...a," Charlie struggled with the brand name.

"Was it a Rolex?" the sheriff tried to help.

"No, that wasn't it...it was a...a Carter I think."

"You mean a *Cartier*?"

"Yep, that's it. And the watch had the initials GBC on the back."

"Do we have a name for the seller?"

"Yes, he said the guy got a receipt in the name of Barry Johnson with an address in Stanley."

The sheriff looked at his boots. "You can bet that's a bit of blarney. I've got to get back inside. Charlie get on the phone and talk to that pawn broker. Let him know that whatever he has is part of a murder investigation and he is to put them under lock and key. Got it?"

"Murder investigation?"

Tilghman scowled at Charlie.

"Got it."

"I'm sorry, Mrs. Cahalan, for the interruption. Would you please go on about the relationship between Mr. Cahalan and his brother?"

"Yes. Well, as I said, we hadn't heard from Mike for quite some time. Then about two months ago he called Jerry here at the house. It was the same story. He needed money. Jerry listened to his tale of woe but refused to send him any financial help. He told him if he would come to Pocatello he would help him find a job. Mike would have none of that and threatened Jerry."

"You mean threatened him with violence?" Tilghman leaned a bit forward in his chair and made a note before looking directly at Mrs. Cahalan.

"Yes Sheriff that's exactly what I mean."

"Can you tell me the specific threat?"

"Jerry told me that Mike said he would beat the...out of him the next time he saw him. I don't like to use that language if you don't mind."

"Of course, I'm familiar with the phrase."

"Did Jerry take that threat seriously?"

"Well Sheriff that is the strange part. Usually Jerry shrugged off Mike's boisterous nature. However, this time he seemed to brood over his brother. He kept asking me whether I thought he should give in and send him money. You see Jerry had turned out so much different from his brother. I mean Jerry had a good life, a stable and productive life. His brother had none of that. He was constantly in turmoil." Sarah Cahalan sighed out loud and paused.

Tilghman sat quietly staring at his notebook but not attempting to move the woman on with her story.

"And then the letter came," she suddenly went on.

"The letter?" Tilghman looked askance at Sarah.

"Yes. It was addressed to Jerry but had no return address. It had three words written with crayon, red crayon. *Hunt the hunter.* Those were the words; hunt the hunter." Sarah got up and again went back to the hutch and opened the drawer. When she returned she handed an envelope to the sheriff and sat back down.

Tilghman opened it and could see the three words in red crayon written on a cheap paper stock. There were no other markings on the sheet.

"Did Jerry think that this came from Mike?"

"Yes, he did. He was certain of it."

"Did Jerry say anything about the words *hunt the hunter?*"

"Yes. You see Jerry has always been an avid hunter. He has hunted in Idaho all of his life. It is his one passion in life. His trophies fill our den at the back of the house. Every year he goes. It is his vacation from his practice. Mike was also a hunter but ever since his life came apart he never had the money to pursue the interest. Jerry had asked him to come along on more than one occasion but Mike always gave Jerry an excuse."

"So, this last trip up to the Big Lost Range to hunt wolf was a solo trip as well?"

"Yes. But Jerry said he was going to go over to Clayton during his hunting trip and see if he could locate Mike and invite him to come on the wolf hunt with him. He said he would like to see if he could bury the hatchet with his brother."

"Did he do that?" Tilghman made a note to check out Clayton.

"I don't think so but I don't know for sure. Jerry didn't like to talk about Mike to me. He knew it upset me too much."

"Mrs. Cahalan, would you mind if I keep the letter and the picture for a while? I'll keep them safe for you until after I finish my investigation."

"Sheriff Tilghman you can have them. They are of no use to me. I would like to forget about that man if I can. I just hope he leaves me in peace and doesn't come around for money. He scares me." Sarah Cahalan looked down at the floor as Tilghman stood up.

"Mrs. Cahalan you needn't worry. Here is my card and I want you to call me if you hear anything at all from Mike, anything at all. Will you do that for me?"

Sarah looked up and met Tilghman's eyes with her own. For the first time since the visit began, she revealed a slight smile. There were tears swelling in her eyes. Tilghman suddenly hated to leave the widow. He usually felt little emotional involvement in such situations, but this time, and this woman, touched him. He extended his big hand to the frail woman. She returned his courtesy as she rose from the couch.

"Sheriff, do you think you will find out how Jerry died and why?"

"Mrs. Cahalan I can't promise you that I will, but I can promise that I won't rest until we come to some resolution."

"Thank you Sheriff Tilghman. I trust you will. If there is anything…"

Tilghman interrupted, "I will call. Thank you for this time."

93

The sheriff stuffed his notebook into his shirt pocket and moved toward the door. Sarah followed without speaking.

"One more thing Mrs. Cahalan, what kind of rifle did your husband hunt with?"

Sarah thought for a minute before she tried to answer.

"Sheriff I have to plead ignorance. I don't know anything about such things. I can tell you this. Jerry was probably prouder of his custom rifle than he was of me," she smiled slightly.

"I doubt that. But you did say it was a custom rifle?"

"Yes. He had it specially made by a man who builds hunting rifles in Colorado somewhere. I think maybe in Colorado Springs but I am not sure. I know Jerry waited for several weeks before it arrived. The day Fed Ex delivered the package you would have thought Jerry was a ten-year-old kid at Christmas."

"Did he have any identifying marks put on the stock or barrel?"

"Yes he had his initials engraved somewhere. I am not sure. Do you have Jerry's rifle?"

"No ma'am, not yet but we expect it will show up. I will let you know as soon as I do. And, one other thing. Did your husband own a *Cartier* watch? I promise this is my last question."

"He did. Jerry liked fine things. He would spend whatever was needed to own something custom. The watch was a sportsman's watch. The kind that has all the dials and hands and such. Why do you ask?"

Sheriff Tilghman resumed his walk towards the front door. "I'll let you know when we have anything; anything at all."

Sarah Cahalan followed him closely. "Sheriff, why was Jerry killed in such a way?" she suddenly asked.

"Mrs. Cahalan we don't know that he was killed. We will find out though, I promise."

The sheriff moved quickly towards the Jeep. Hot Sauce was going ballistic inside. The little Chihuahua didn't like to be separated from the sheriff and he made his feelings known when Tilghman climbed back in the Cherokee. The Sheriff and Charlie were circling out of the driveway when Charlie braked abruptly. Tilghman looked at his driver and Charlie nodded toward the house. Sarah Cahalan was standing on the front porch waving for them to stop.

"Hold on a minute Charlie, let me go see what the lady wants.

Tilghman was almost to Sarah when she said, "Sheriff there is one other thing that you need to know about my husband."

"All right, Mrs. Cahalan. What is that?"

"Sheriff he was a very active man. I mean hunting, fishing and other outdoor things; but he was also a very sick man so to speak. I mean physically. You see Jerry had a heart defect—a serious heart defect."

"You mean life threatening?"

"I do. The diagnosis of Jerry's condition put a big question mark around our whole lives. The doctors said he had two choices. He could die young or have a heart transplant. It was that simple and that stark for us. Jerry's name was on a list for a transplant but I knew he really didn't want to go through that. That was part of the reason he was so active. He was trying to live his life quickly."

"I see. Could you give me the name of his heart specialist? I may need to talk to him before we are through with our investigation."

"Yes, come on in for a second and I'll write it down for you. His office is only a few miles from here. Would you like to try and see him while you're in Pocatello?"

"That would help."

"I can give him a call for you now if you would like."

"Thank you."

Sheriff Tilghman climbed back in the passenger side of the Cherokee and looked over at his deputy as they pulled away from the house.

"Things just got a bit more complicated Charlie. I need to go to the doctor." Charlie Two Leaf snapped his head toward the sheriff.

"What!"

Custer County sheriff's report & incident log
3:45 p.m.
*Stanley City officer responded to a report
of an injured elk near Fisher Creek.*

NINETEEN   SHORT CIRCUIT

IT TOOK TILGHMAN MORE THAN AN HOUR of sitting in the waiting room before Dr. T. V. Radavan Putssen came out of his office to greet him. The sheriff introduced himself and told the midget doctor with dark chocolate skin what he needed. Tilghman hovered over the doctor as the two men went down a long passageway into the physician's private office.

"Yes that's right sheriff, Gerald Cahalan had a condition we believe can lead to what is known as sudden cardiac death. In cases of sudden cardiac death, for reasons that are not entirely clear, the heart suddenly stops working. The body is abruptly denied its blood flow. Death follows very quickly after that. We think that at least half of all heart disease deaths are due to this type of event."

"Do you mean he was likely to have a heart attack?"

"Sheriff, sudden cardiac death is not what is commonly known as a heart attack. When a person has a heart attack, what doctors call a myocardial infarction; it is due to a blockage in a blood vessel. This interrupts the flow of oxygen-rich blood to the heart. The result is the death of heart muscle and, if not treated immediately, death. This process is different with sudden cardiac death. With SCD the heart's electrical system malfunctions. A sudden disruption of the electrical impulses that control the rhythm of the heart occurs. Let me give you this comparison. Think of the heart and its workings as a house. Sudden cardiac death is an electrical problem where a heart attack is a plumbing problem. Does that help?"

Tilghman politely ignored the doctor's analogy, "If someone suffers such an attack, what happens then?"

"Nothing very good, I assure you. As I said, the heart has a built-in electrical signaling network. This circuitry controls the rate at which the heart contracts and thus pumps blood throughout the body. If all is well, this contraction is regular, steady, and very responsive to the body's needs whether at rest or active. But in a condition we call ventricular fibrillation, the electrical signals that keep the heart functioning properly go a bit haywire. When this happens, the heart suddenly begins trying to pump blood in a rapid and chaotic fashion. The lower chambers of the heart cease to provide oxygen-rich blood to the body and most importantly to the brain. As a result, the person suffering such an attack will lose consciousness in a matter of seconds."

"What's the chance of surviving this sudden death thing?"

"Not good. Unless the patient is given a rhythm restoring electrical shock, using a machine called a defibrillator, the person will likely die within a few minutes. The odds are about 70% death rate even if they are immediately transported to the hospital."

"And this condition is what Cahalan had?"

"Yes Sheriff, he was diagnosed last year. In his case, the heart disease he suffered was fairly advanced—advanced enough so that we discussed a transplant in the near future. To put it graphically, Gerald Cahalan's heart was a time bomb just wanting to explode. And Sheriff, I understand that he died under somewhat mysterious circumstances while hunting, is that right?"

"Yes, we still don't know the cause of death. The autopsy was inconclusive due to the condition of the body. You see, the remains had been scavenged."

"I don't know whether this will be helpful, but we do know that often these fatal events are brought about by a sudden increase in adrenaline in the body. And, as I am sure you know, adrenaline is the result of a heightened level of excitement. What I am suggesting is that if Gerald Cahalan was experiencing emotional excitement as a result of hunting or physical exertion, then that could have triggered sudden cardiac death in his case. Does this help?"

"Frankly doctor it helps only to the extent it adds another layer of *what ifs* to my work. This case is proving to be more than an old worn out country sheriff can handle."

"Yes, I can imagine. I'm sorry I can't be of more assistance."

"Me too Doc, but I thank you for your time just the same."

"Charlie let's go home," Tilghman said as he slid into the front seat. "We've got us one here Deputy."

"What do you mean?"

"Well, it seems Cahalan could have died of a bum ticker on that mountain. That's what his doctor told me. The man's heart was on the verge of quitting on him."

The sheriff sat silent as Charlie accelerated on the ramp onto Interstate 15 and headed for Blackfoot.

"Unless we get some real conclusions from the coroner, the fact is we may never know what killed Cahalan. Animals could have done it, another human could have done it, or he could have simply died due to, what the doc said, was a sudden cardiac death."

As Charlie brought the Cherokee up to highway speed, Hot Sauce licked at Chester's hand begging for a pet or a biscuit. The old sheriff sat quietly and offered his dog neither.

Custer County sheriff's report & incident log
11:45 p.m.
*Two deputies were called to a West End bar to quell
a disturbance on the sidewalk outside.*

TWENTY-0   THE PREY KILLS THE PREY

"DAMN, DAMN, DAMN AND DAMN! If it's not one report it's ten!"

Jonathon Bunch looked out of his window. He wanted to be anywhere but here and now. The conference table in front of him was littered high and deep with charts, graphs, photos, reports and notes. Bunch and Erin Moss sat around the piles. They worked for the Idaho Fish & Game Department and both were wildlife biologists.

"What about the final numbers on wolf fatalities for the year, are they ready?"

"Not yet," Erin responded. "We're still waiting for a couple of field notes to come in from the Sawtooth and the Southern Mountains. And we can't seem to get anything from the Nez Perce tribe program either."

Bunch's pot was just about ready to boil over. He couldn't get anything finalized and the governor's office was hounding him for the report.

"Alright, give me what you've got so far. What are we looking at for the year?"

"Okay, this is what I have so far. It looks like we're going to come in with about 88 resident wolf packs in the state. The field observers made actual sightings on 430 wolves and made estimates of about 850 wolves in Idaho. We've identified about 15 border packs that are regularly crossing over into Idaho from Montana and

Wyoming. We're not sure if anything is coming from Washington, but my guess is that there is."

"What about breeding packs this year, how they doing?"

"We know of 60 packs that have breeding pairs. From those we've got about 192 pups."

"Okay. What about the deaths this year, what numbers do you have there?"

"Let's see," Erin shuffled into a stack and came up with a report. "It looks like we had 155 confirmed deaths this last calendar year in the state. Of those, agency control and legal landowner kills accounted for 110 deaths. Humans caused another 23 deaths and that includes illegal kills. We had confirmed 18 other wolf deaths from unknown causes and four wolves died of natural causes."

"Let's talk about the down side. What kind of chaos did our wolves create?"

"The reports from the state show 96 cattle, 219 sheep, 12 dogs and one horse foal as confirmed wolf kills during the year. Unconfirmed but probable, I have 32 cattle, 46 sheep and 1 dog killed."

Bunch reached his hand across the table and Erin handed him the figures. "That's a significant increase over last year, right?"

"Oh yeah, and I almost missed this one. Some old farmer lost a llama up near Arco. Yes it is. But we've had a significant increase in wolf numbers throughout the region as well; specifically down in the Sawtooth and Southern Mountain areas where there is a good chance of wolf/livestock conflicts occurring."

"These figures are going to ruffle some folks at the capital, I can tell you that. The ranchers' lobby is going to go ballistic."

"What's new about that? They've been in orbit around Pluto since the program began."

"Well, wait until you hear this. This one will probably send the politicos up in orbit with the ranchers—seems that the Chilly Buttes pack has been causing a little excitement in Custer, County."

"What?"

"It appears a hunter got massacred in the Big Lost River range a few days ago on the first day of the wolf season. Wolves or something mean and ugly chewed him up so bad no one can figure out what happened. The sheriff down in Custer County is running the investigation. And the local press is playing the uncertainty for a little subscription drive. Are you ready for *Man killer on the loose*, for a headline?"

"Shit! Who was the hunter?"

"Some doctor from Pocatello. I pulled his permit—name was Cahalan, Gerald B. Cahalan. Here's a copy."

"Was the guy found in the Chilly Buttes' territory?"

"Right smack dab in the middle of it. It appears he made a kill of one of the radio-collared wolves in the pack. The freshly-skinned carcass was found hanging in a tree at the scene of the hunter's death. But, get this, the pelt wasn't there. Nowhere to be found."

"Do we know which wolf it was?"

"Yeah, it was CB9342, the alpha male. We're going out this week and see if we can find a signal for the collar. Thought we'd lend that old sheriff a hand."

"Isn't Rick Clyde the forest ranger in that territory?"

"He is and I called him this morning. Appears we've got a first-class mystery on our hands. According to Rick, everyone's waiting for the coroner's report on the cause of death."

Jonathon got up and poured himself a cup of coffee. "Anyone think it's foul play?"

"Well, like Rick said, there was hardly enough left of the guy to tell. The curious thing is that they haven't found his rifle or personal effects, you know, wallet, that kind of stuff. They got his identity because they found his cell phone and his car was parked nearby. Rick said the sheriff was in Pocatello talking to the widow today."

Jonathon leaned back in his chair and stared up at the ceiling for a moment. "Erin, you had better call the governor's office and at least give his staff a heads up on this. If the governor gets blindsided on this, you know who he is going to call and chew on."

"You think? Okay, I'll call Dan in his office this afternoon."

Erin got up from the conference table but stopped and quickly sat back down. "Jonathon, you know what the governor is going to want to do when he hears of this don't you?"

"I know. Get the helicopters airborne and go nuke the Chilly Buttes pack, right? This is the perfect excuse. They've all been aching to show the feds something about state's rights for a long time now."

"Right, and something tells me the governor and a few legislators already know about this. That headline in the local rag, if my hunch is right, was enough to set the phones to jingling. I'm kind of surprised we haven't already got a call from the Capitol."

Connie from the director's office stuck her head into the conference room. "Mr. Bunch, the governor's office called earlier and left a message. They would like for you to give them a call as soon as possible."

Both men looked at each other and mouthed in unison an exaggerated, "Great!"

Custer County sheriff's report & incident log
6:45 p.m.
Deputy responded to an unlawful entry report in Stanley.

TWENTY-1 THE FAJITAS HOT

THE DUST SWIRLED AROUND THE JEEP CHEROKEE as Sheriff Tilghman and Charlie Two Leaf drove up in front of the Grab & Scram Convenience Store on Eva Falls Avenue in Stanley, Idaho. The tall sheriff and his short deputy got out of the Jeep in unison and headed for the front door. Bertha Selman in Clayton, who boarded Mike Cahalan, had told them that Mike could usually be found during the day in Stanley. He did part-time work at the Grab & Scram three days a week, she said.

Tilghman, with Hot Sauce tucked loosely under his arm, entered first and headed to the counter that was all but obscured by racks of candy, potato chips and rows of carcinogenic sugary cup cakes. Charlie pulled the door shut against a stiff wind that was blowing directly off the high ridges of the Sawtooth Mountains. As Tilghman neared the counter, a gruff voice from across the store shouted that pets weren't allowed in the store. The sheriff turned towards the source and saw a fat man in a tight tee shirt, with a feather duster, putting cans on a high shelf at the back of the store.

"He ain't a pet, he's my friend and I'm Sheriff Tilghman. I'm looking for a man that I was told might be here."

The store clerk put his duster in his back pocket and came to the front. He looked first at Tilghman and then at Charlie.

104

"You don't look like no sheriff. Where's your badge and gun?" The overstuffed clerk acted a bit nervous as Tilghman moved the front of his heavy coat to one side to reveal his sheriff's shield on his belt. The matte black handle of the Kimber .45 pistol emphasized the authority of the badge.

"I'm looking for Mike Cahalan, is he here?"

"You got some kind of seepena?"

"You mean a warrant? No, I just to want to ask him a few questions. Is he here?"

"He might be and then he might not be. What's he done? He didn't murder nobody did he?"

"Mister, you're beginning to try my patience a bit. If you don't answer my question, I'm going to put this dog on you." Hot Sauce obliged the sheriff with a slow growl and raised upper lip.

The clerk slapped his side and laughed. "Well I wouldn't want any of that. I mean that's quite a police dog you've got there Sheriff. Chewed up a many a criminal I betcha," again he laughed but the sheriff didn't smile.

"Mike's in the back making up some fajitas for the café down the street. I'll get him for you."

"Never mind, you just point me in his direction and we'll find him."

The clerk hesitated but thought better of it and motioned to a door with his feather duster just to the right of the men's room. "He's back there," he said.

Tilghman and Charlie pushed through the swinging doors with 'employees only' painted in black marker on the rectangle glass. Hot Sauce immediately sensed the meat smell filling the hallway along with the stale mops and dusty brooms. Tilghman could see another door just ahead with a pane of one-way glass cracked on a diagonal in the upper half. Charlie pushed open the door and allowed the sheriff to pass through first. Hot Sauce anxiously squirmed in the sheriff's arms and whimpered slightly.

The man standing at the griddle was tall and lanky. He wore jeans and a dirty tee shirt with a large Star of David across the shoulders. His hair was wrapped with a rubber band and hung to the middle of his back. The stringy black strands were laced with gray and in need of washing. He adeptly flipped a spatula full of fajita meat over on the griddle. Displaying no sense of alarm, the cook turned calmly toward the advancing men.

"Hello Sheriff, I've been expecting to see you. Grab a tortilla off that table behind you and I'll serve you fellows a little breakfast. Get one for that tiger in your arms too."

"Don't mind if I do. Charlie, you hungry?"

"As hungry as a black bear standing in the middle of a wild blackberry patch."

"Well then, get us some fixin's." Tilghman put Hot Sauce down and took the tortilla wrapped meat from the cook. He pushed his big mustache out of the way and filled his mouth with the sweet hot mixture. The sheriff chewed the recipe slowly, savoring the rich flavor of the beef cooked in chilies and dabbed with Cholula red sauce.

He swallowed the first bite and bent down to hand his dog a taste. The hairless canine eagerly took the offering and ran under the table to eat his take in safety.

"You are Mike Cahalan, right?" Tilghman asked as he took another bite. "I'm Sheriff Tilghman from Custer County. I need to ask you a few questions if you would oblige. The first might be how did you know who I was and why were you expecting me?"

Mike Cahalan continued at his work for a few seconds and flipped more meat into a large metal flat pan on the right side of the hot iron surface.

"My sister-in-law called me day before yesterday and said you might want to talk to me. She told me about Jerry and that you were trying to sort out what happened."

"Sorry about your brother."

"Yeah, me too. Hell of way to go. Hold on a minute. Let me get the rest of this meat off the griddle and we can go out back and talk. That door right there, I'll be out in just a minute."

Tilghman motioned for Charlie to follow and he extracted his dog from under the table. Hot Sauce continued to lick the sheriff's hand as they took the concrete steps to the rear loading dock.

"Sheriff, I thought you said that Sarah Cahalan didn't like her husband's brother?" Charlie asked as he was finishing up the last of the wrapped fajita.

"That's what I thought too. Obviously, we don't have the full story. Don't bring that up. I'll get around to it soon enough."

Mike Cahalan came down the steps chewing on a tortilla roll of his own. "Okay Sheriff, I suppose you want to know the last time I saw Jerry, right?"

"That's as a good place to start as any."

"I talked to my brother the day before it happened. It was the first time I had seen him in about a year. He surprised me when he came to my shack in Clayton. I guess Sarah told you Jerry and I weren't exactly the best of friends."

"She mentioned it."

"And, I suppose she told you I haven't exactly been a model citizen like my brother. You see I have a bit of a gambling and alcohol problem. Have had since high school. I'm doing pretty good right now but it's been a roller coaster kind of life for about twenty years."

"How did the visit go?"

"You mean did we fight about anything? It went all right, I guess. Sheriff you need to understand something about my family. Jerry was the oldest, the first-born and the pride of the clan. He always played by the rules and without fail; excelled at everything he ever did. No matter what the rest of us did, Jerry was always the example, the guiding light so to speak. I, for one, got sick of it."

Tilghman sat down on the concrete steps and took out his little notebook.

"I pulled out early in life and knocked around the country for awhile. Jerry was carving out his successful practice about the time I was learning how to shoot craps and play blackjack. At first, he was an easy touch when I got a little short. He had the money and I had the habits—especially the habit of fucking up. After a couple of years of that, Jerry finally had enough and we started to fight every time we got together. You might say there was no love lost."

"Why do you think then that your brother picked this time to come for a visit?"

"I know exactly why. He told me. Jerry said he had this heart condition that could put him in the dirt at any time without warning. He said he wanted to make his peace with me in case something happened to him. I knew about it. Sarah had told me the last time we shouted at each other over the phone. The last time I asked for money. Sarah didn't like me around. She never did like me. Truth be known, I never liked her much either. But Jerry didn't know I knew and I guess he just wanted to bury the hatchet."

"So you brothers didn't get into any kind of argument this time?"

"No, just the opposite. Oh, I did ask him for a few bucks. But he didn't give me any. He said those days were over no matter what. We didn't fight about it though. To be honest, I felt a little sad about my brother. I thought it a little unfair that after all of his work and achievement, all of his success, he would be the one to die young. If anything was fair in this life, it would be me, the worthless one, to take an early fall. Wouldn't you think?"

"Mike I've got something here I want to show you." Tilghman reached into his inside coat pocket and took out a watch. "Do you recognize this?" He held it out for Mike to take.

"Well I'll be damn; you country sheriffs do your homework now don't you. It's Jerry's watch. I hocked it down in Pocatello a couple of days back. I needed the money a lot more than I needed to tell the time. Didn't get near what that watch is worth though."

Tilghman held out his hand for the watch but Mike held on to it.

"I guess you know my next question."

"Yeah, I can guess. How did I get it, right?"

"You're batting a thousand."

"Simple story, Jerry gave it to me. He just said he wanted to help me out a little but he wasn't going to give me any more money. So, he gave me his watch. And, like I said, I hocked it. That's it."

"Okay, I'll take that on its face for now. Is there anything else you can tell me about your last visit with your brother?"

"No, like I said we parted company without any rough talk. As a matter of fact, we hugged each other like real brothers for once. I think Jerry had a tear in his eyes but he wouldn't look directly at me when he got in his car."

"Did he tell you where he was going?"

"He told me about the wolf hunt up on Chilly Buttes if that's what you mean? Yeah, and he wanted me to tag along but I told him since he wasn't going to loan me any money I needed to work. He was excited about that hunt. You know as educated as Jerry was, I think he really enjoyed getting a little wild blood on his hands occasionally. There was just something about his passion for hunting that didn't seem to fit the big picture with him, you know?"

Mike finally handed the watch back to Sheriff Tilghman and sat down on the steps. "Sheriff, would you mind if I held your little friend for a minute?"

"You mean this four legged ball of lightning and thunder? No, but watch out he might tear your arm off."

The sheriff handed Hot Sauce over and the dog went without resistance. The fact was the miniature pooch liked strangers. He'd usually growl at them but he liked them—especially those that smelled of fajita meat.

"Do you think he met anyone up there on the plateau where he put his blind?"

Mike stroked the slick skin of the Chihuahua before he answered. "Sheriff he didn't say anything about someone else on the hunt with him. Jerry was pretty much a loner in most things he did. The truth be known, he didn't like a whole lot of company. He was pretty unsociable. I think that's why he liked hunting so much. He liked to get out in the wilderness and be alone with his gun and his gear. He always seemed to have this need to prove something. You might say he was driven in that way."

"One last question—did Dr. Cahalan have any enemies that you know of? Anyone that might want to do him harm?"

Mike paused and petted the dog. Hot Sauce absorbed the unusual attention and kept smelling Mike's tee shirt with the meat stains down the front.

"Sheriff I guess the only enemy that I know about that Jerry might have had was me."

"But you didn't go on the hunt with him, did you?"

"No, I didn't go on the hunt with him."

"Mike I will need you to stay around these parts until we come up with some kind of determination as to what happened. Do you understand?" Tilghman reached out for Hot Sauce and tucked his dog back into its familiar niche in the crook of his left arm.

"I'll be in my shack in Clayton or here at the Grab & Scram if you need me."

"That'll be good. Oh Mike, do you by any chance know a fellow by the name of Wishful Wicks?"

"No, can't say that I do, why?"

"Just thought I'd ask. Okay Charlie, I think that about does it. Let's head back to the county seat. Thanks. I want you to know I am sorry about the loss of your brother. I lost one of my own some time back and it's not an easy thing."

"Thanks Sheriff, no its not. You kind of wished you'd been better at being brothers after it's too late."

"Let's go Charlie. Oh, one more thing Mike. Do you have any Crayolas?"

"Crayolas?"

"Yeah."

"No Sheriff, I don't. Why?"

The sheriff again reached into his pocket. This time he came out with the crumpled note that Sarah Cahalan had given him. "Look at this. Recognize it?"

Mike laughed as he took the paper. "Yeah, I recognize it. I sent it to Jerry. It was a joke between us. Ever since we were kids. It was just a joke."

"You sure? A joke?"

"Yeah Sheriff, just a joke."

"Okay. I'll be in touch if there is anything else."

Sheriff Tilghman picked up a bit of fajita meat as they made their way back through the kitchen. Hot Sauce wiggled like a worm in the bottom of a bucket under the sheriff's arm. As usual, the little dog would get the lion's share.

Custer County sheriff's report & incident log
11:15 p.m.
*Deputy responded to a fight in progress call
at the Hoodoo Saloon in Clayton.*

TWENTY-2   TEA AND SWEET BERTHA

U.S. HIGHWAY 75 PASSES THROUGH REMOTE AND WILD country in Idaho as it snakes its way east to the junction with U.S. Highway 93. The two riders, as was their custom on the road, canned the chatter as they watched the mountains pass to the right and left. Finally, Charlie Two Leaf couldn't resist, he was the first to break the silence.

"Sheriff, did you believe him? I mean about his last meeting with his brother."

Sheriff Tilghman didn't answer right away. He just kept gently stroking Hot Sauce who was asleep in the crook of the sheriff's left arm.

Finally, he said, "You know Charlie I guess I've been at this work for too long. I've got where I don't believe anybody anymore. I'm coming to believe that most Americans would tell a lie when the truth would serve better."

The sheriff shifted in his seat and rearranged his dog on his lap.

"I've got two problems with what I heard today. First, I don't understand why Sarah Cahalan would tell me she didn't want to see Mike again and then let the brother know I was looking for him. When we talked, she seemed to be truly afraid of her brother-in-law. Was that an act? And, second, the story about the watch. No way José. Why would Gerald Cahalan refuse his brother a few hundred bucks, then turn around and give him a watch that is worth five-thousand dollars if it is worth a nickel. I ask you Charlie, does that make sense?"

Charlie played his part, "Nope, not to me."

"Well then how did he get hold of it? That is if he didn't see his brother after their rendezvous in Clayton. Two-day-old fish sitting in the summer sun smells sweeter than this tale."

Tilghman sat back in his seat and looked up at the ceiling of the Cherokee, and let out a big sigh. "Alright Charlie, I want to stop in Clayton when we get there. I want to talk to Mike's landlady again."

"Right Sheriff, we are almost there. I'll try not to miss it," Charlie smiled. "It's one of the few towns in America where the population is smaller than the number on the speed limit sign through town."

Sheriff Tilghman and Charlie parked the Cherokee out front just off the highway for the second time that day and walked to the door of Bertha Selman's white clapboard house. Tilghman could hear the TV at a high volume inside the house as he knocked on the door. There was no immediate answer so the sheriff walked down the porch to look through the front window. As he did the front door opened.

A short, plump old woman stepped clear of the screen. "Well hello Sheriff. Didn't expect to see you again."

"No ma'am we didn't expect to be back. There are a couple of other questions I need to ask you. Do you mind if Charlie and I step inside for a moment?"

"Heavens no Sheriff. You and your deputy come on in. At my age you get two visitors a day and you start thinking you're something special. Come on in."

The inside of Bertha's house was as cluttered as a museum. Tilghman looked around as the trio made their way into the front parlor. There wasn't any wall or floor space that wasn't covered with knick-knacks of every kind, shape and description. Charlie bumped into a table filled with porcelain dolls and the sheriff held his breath as everything teetered. He gave Charlie a stern look and Charlie mouthed, "I'm sorry." The three sat down.

"Mrs. Selman, I need to…"

"Pardon me Sheriff Tilghman. Would you mind if I ask you a question first? It has been on my mind ever since you were here this morning."

"No ma'am, what is it?"

"It's your name that's got my curiosity up. Tilghman. That's a famous name out West now isn't it? I mean, that name goes back a ways."

"Yes it does."

"You wouldn't be related to William Mathew Tilghman would you?"

The sheriff smiled broadly and glanced at Charlie before he responded. "Well that I am. He was my great-great grandfather. How do you know of him Mrs. Selman?"

"Please Sheriff, call me Bertha. Well, I'm a bit of a history buff you might say. I read all the magazines like *True West* and *Wild West*. You know the kind. And you might say we have something in common."

"What's that?"

"Well sir, your great-great grandfather was a famous lawman and my deceased husband's great-great grandfather was a famous outlaw."

"Is that a fact, who might that be?"

"John Selman. Have you heard of him Sheriff?"

"Yes. If my memory serves me, he's the one that killed John Wesley Hardin, the notorious gunfighter, down in El Paso, Texas, I think."

Mrs. Selman became excited and jumped up from the couch and went to a ancient secretary arranged at a cross angle in the corner of the room. She opened the top drawer, retrieved a worn red photo album, and returned to the couch. "Here, Sheriff, is his picture. This is John Selman." Tilghman took the photo and studied the image.

"Sheriff I don't know whether you know this but in those days the difference between an outlaw and a lawman was often hard to tell. John Selman was both. And he was good at both. He just played the cards how they were dealt so to speak. You know?"

"Yes ma'am, I do." Tilghman handed the photo to Charlie. "Bertha I need to ask you another question about Mike Cahalan if you don't mind."

The old woman seemed deflated by the change of tone. "Sure Sheriff what is it?" Charlie noiselessly returned the photo album to the coffee table.

"Do you remember Mike getting a visit from his brother a couple of weeks back?"

"Do I remember Dr. Cahalan? You bet I do. When he came to the door looking for Mike, I swear I thought it was Mike. They look so much alike. He was a nice, nice man; very polite and friendly, like you and your deputy. We visited a few minutes before I told him where to find his brother. His little one-room house is just in the back there. He thanked me and went out the front and around to the back. Mike was in his room. I know because I saw his brother go in."

"Now Bertha I know you probably don't know anything about their visit but…"

"Oh excuse me Sheriff, but I do. You see I'm kind of a busy body as they say, so I went out back to, you know, see what I could see and hear." The old woman offered a grin.

"And, did you see or hear anything? Here is what I'm driving at Bertha. Mike says that his visit with his brother was a good one and that they parted on friendly terms. Does that seem about right to you?"

"Is Mike in trouble again Sheriff?

"Again?" Tilghman glanced quickly at Charlie.

"Well I sure hope not. Those men from Nevada that came to see him last month were not like his brother. They weren't very cordial you might say; very businesslike. The short ugly one shouted a lot at Mike and made him very upset for a time after they left."

"Do you know who those men were?"

"Not for sure. But, if I was a betting woman, which I am not of course, I would lay down odds that they were from one of the casinos or some gambling kind of thing. Not sure mind you, but Mike has told me more than once about his gambling problem."

"Bertha, back to Mike's brother's visit. Everything go smoothly between the two of them?"

"For a while it did. Then right before Dr. Cahalan left they shouted at each other. Mike was real loud. Said something ugly. I can't repeat the words you understand, but his brother left shortly thereafter. Mike followed him out to the car and kept shouting. Then his brother left. Mike didn't say anything to me about it."

"Okay Bertha, one more question. Did Mike leave the house the next morning?"

"The next morning, the next morning," the old woman looked down at the opened photo album for a moment and then straightened up to answer the sheriff's question.

"Yes Sheriff I think he did. Yes, I know he did because his rent was due that day and I didn't see him for nearly two days after."

"Did he say anything to you when he returned?"

"No, not really. He did pay his rent though, which was always a relief because I usually had to hound him for it you know?"

Tilghman stood up and he and Charlie started for the door. "Sheriff if you and your deputy would like a cup of tea before you go I've got water on the stove."

"Thank you Bertha but I suspect Charlie and I better get on the road. We've got a lot of territory to cover today."

"I understand. Oh, Sheriff can I ask you one more question?"

"Sure."

"Have you ever been an outlaw?"

Tilghman grinned widely, taken a little by surprise by the question. "Not yet Bertha, not yet." He hesitated a second and then said, "But the day ain't over."

Bertha Selman laughed out loud.

"Oh, Bertha. I wonder if you might recognize this." Tilghman pulled the watch from his pocket.

The old woman fondled the expensive timepiece turning it over several times. "I'm not sure Sheriff but I think this is the same watch that Mike was wearing. You know I never saw him with a watch but that one time. After that, I didn't see it again. I can't be sure. Maybe that is it, maybe it's not.

The two men pulled out of Clayton and headed toward the Highway 93 junction. All the sheriff could think about was a children's playground call ... *Liar, liar, pants on fire! Liar, liar, pants on fire!* He leaned back in the seat and closed his eyes for a moment. It had been a long day and the old sheriff felt weary to the core.

"Gonna catch a wink Charlie, keep her straight and true. And slow down, will you?"

"You bet Sheriff, straight and true."

TWENTY-3   WHAT'S YOUR PROBLEM BILL?

Marshal! Marshal Earp! There's been a killin'. Sweet Dora, Dora Hand has been shot! Right in her bed early this mornin'. Come quick Marshal!"

"Now calm down Jeremiah. Tell me what happened. And what's all this crowd gathering about shoutin' and screamin' so early on this gentle mornin'?"

"That's a what I'm tryin' to tell you Marshal. That no account scoundrel Spike Kenedy has gone and shot Miss Hand in her sleep. She was in Kelly's shack out behind the Great Western Hotel and that cowboy done shot her right through the wall."

"Is she alive?"

"No Marshal she's dead, dead right away. Doc McCarty has already seen the body and he knows. That Spike has headed south out of Dodge at a quick run. Hurry up Marshal or he'll get away."

"Tilghman, get your gear and saddle up pronto. We've got a bad character to see after. Get Masterson and Marshal Bassett together. Spike is on his way to Tascosa for sure as a persimmon 'll make you pucker. He'll be headed to his daddy's ranch I'd bet a gold dollar and two shots of whiskey on it."

"We're ready Marshal Earp. Every man has his ol' Colt and his Winchester packed tight and we'll catch that hombre before he leaves and crosses into the Indian Territories or my name ain't Bill Tilghman."

"My horse is a flyin' in the clouds and lookin' down on the trail Marshal. I see that no-account, double dealin' cowpoke right there on the far side of Meade. We can head him off at the south bend."

"Tilghman, ride on up ahead and put a .50 caliber rifle round through that murderin' Spike Kenedy's shoulder. Knock him off his horse and in the dirt. We'll be right behind you for sure."

"Oh, my gun's too heavy, I can't lift it up Marshal. Come on Tilghman pull that barrel up. Can't be too heavy. Get ready, hurry up, here comes Spike a galloping like the devil."

"Where's my horse? I've got to get up on my horse before he gets to me. Where's my Winchester? Oh shit, here he comes."

"Shoot, Tilghman! Why don't you shoot that bastard? Shoot him in the shoulder Tilghman. Damn to hell, you can't be a lawman if you can't shoot the bad guys. Bat what's wrong with Tilghman? Why did we bring him on the posse? He can't do nothin'. That murderin' Spike Kenedy is gettin' away. Shoot him Bat. Show Tilghman how you do it. Shoot him in the shoulder then shoot his horse out from under that no good Texas cowboy."

"Wait Wyatt, I've got my Colt cocked and ready now. I'll do it. Wyatt give me a chance. I can do it, I can do it, I can…"

"Damn it Bat, Spike shot Bill Tilghman right in the back. He must have been runnin' away again. I don't know why you ever thought he could be a lawman in Dodge. He can't shoot a gun. It's too much for him."

"Don't know Wyatt. Some men want to be lawmen but don't have the stomach for it. Help me load his body in the wagon. We'll take him back to Dodge and put him in the ground next to Dora Hand."

"Wait! Wait! I can do it! I can do it! Give me another chance – oh! My chest hurts, my chest hurts…"

"Sheriff, Sheriff! Wake up! Your cell phone is buzzing. You're dreaming Sheriff. Wake up!"

"Wha…what is it Charlie?"

"You've been sleeping. Your cell phone is vibrating."

The sheriff reached down to his side but his phone wasn't there. "Where in the hell is the damn thing?"

"It's in your shirt pocket Sheriff."

"Damn, I thought I was having a heart attack," the sheriff started laughing as he dug in his pocket for the phone. Charlie laughed with him.

"Yeah!"

"Sheriff, where are you? You and Charlie might want to get back to the courthouse ASAP."

"Why's that Linda?"

"There's a young man here with a gun waiting for you."

"What?"

"Oh no! He's got a gun he thinks might be important in the hunter's case. He brought it to you."

"Well, well, well, what do you know about that?" Tilghman whispered to himself as he turned toward Charlie with a big grin spreading across his face.

"Linda, my chauffeur and I are about to turn north on Hwy 93. Be there as quick as a snake crosses the L.A. Freeway."

Tilghman flipped the phone closed. "Charlie put a spur to this old horse. Let's get home. There's something important brewin' in the old hoosegow."

As the Cherokee neared the curve at Buffalo Jump, Tilghman looked at Charlie for a long ten seconds before he spoke.

"Charlie was I talking in my sleep back there?"

"No but you sure was jumping around. Must have been a hell of a dream. You after the bad guys again. Or were the bad guys after you?"

Charlie looked at his boss and raised his eyebrows.

"A little bit of both I guess. You know Charlie that dream is coming a lot more frequently these days. Ever since Martha died, I have been having it about every month or so. It's always the same kind of dream. Kind of a nightmare. I'm always Bill Tilghman in Dodge City with Wyatt Earp, Charlie Bassett, and Bat Masterson. I'm always a part of a posse chasing some murdering cowboy or gambler. I suppose the conversation we had with Bertha Selman this morning triggered it."

Charlie was silent for a moment before he spoke. "You're really missing Maggie aren't you Sheriff?"

"Oh Charlie, if you only knew how much. That woman and I spent a bunch of good years together. I feel like a three-legged mule pulling a rock wagon without her. There is a big hole in my life."

"What do you miss the most about her, Sheriff?"

"What do I miss the most?" Tilghman paused. "You know what I miss the most Charlie. Every Sunday afternoon she would make cookies or a pie or something sweet. Every week there'd be something different. It didn't matter. I'd be sitting in the den listening to the banging in the kitchen. The pots, the mixer, the water running, Maggie working on those damn cookies. Then, every once in a while, the woman would just let loose with a whistle. She couldn't carry a tune in wash bucket, but she'd whistle. Usually, for about ten or fifteen seconds and that was it. Made no sense. That's what I miss Charlie."

The deputy kept quiet.

"I think that's part of what's bringing on these dreams; these damn frustration dreams."

122

"Why's that?"

"That's what they're like. You just get frustrated that you can't do something that you're supposed to do. I usually can't make my body and mind work together. One is too heavy and the other too slow. Like the one I was having, I couldn't make my arms lift up the rifle to shoot the bad guy. Wyatt kept yelling at me to shoot the bastard and I just couldn't do it. You know Charlie, I've never in all my days as a lawman had to shoot my sidearm. I've only pulled it four times in thirty years. Never pulled the trigger, thank God. Maybe that's what is causing these dreams. I don't know."

The sheriff turned his attention back to the mountains as they slowly passed by. The fresh early snows of the winter season had painted all the high ridges a soft, bright white. Tilghman liked this time of year although he dreaded the hard winter that would soon come.

"Sheriff, if it means anything, I can tell you that I don't have any doubt that, if it need be, you could do what you would have to do. You're a good lawman. Maybe that's why you haven't shot anybody in all those years. In them olden days, back when Bill Tilghman was trying to bring some kind of order and justice to the West, men just used their guns a lot more than they used their minds. It was the thing to do then. You know, shoot first ask questions later kind of thinking. Nowadays we know better. Folks expect a good lawman to use his wits more than his gun so to speak. You follow me?"

"Oh sure Charlie, I follow you. You're right about that. But you always wonder whether you're up to it or not. You wonder, that if the time came could you use deadly force; whether you could make muster. That's all."

"Sheriff, I'll trust my back to you any day. I don't care what old Wyatt Earp says about it. No sir."

Charlie Two Leaf barely slowed down as he turned off Highway 75, onto 93. They were two miles from the court house.

Custer County sheriff's report & incident log
9:55 a.m.
Tilghman was advised of a "situation" on Spruce Ave.

TWENTY-4   COMES NEWS FROM CHILLY BUTTES

THE LANKY KID HAD TO DUCK as he came through the front door of the sheriff's office. He carried a long bundle wrapped in what appeared to be a dirty Indian blanket. Linda Davenport caught sight of him as he came through the door and the sheriff's dispatcher moved to intercept the visitor.

"Whoa there partner! Stop right there! What have you got in that roll-up? We don't like packages delivered unannounced."

"I came to see the sheriff. I've got this to give him," the kid held out the bundle.

"Well, maybe you better let me see it first."

The young man backed up two steps and said with force to his voice, "No ma'am, this is for the sheriff. I need to give it to him."

"Well, the sheriff isn't here right now. Let me see what you have?"

"It's a rifle ma'am. But I want to give it to the sheriff personally. It's not loaded or nothin'. I promise."

"Okay, but lean it against this desk here and you sit down over there. I won't bother it but I'd feel a little more comfortable if there was a bit of separation. You understand?"

"Yes ma'am, I do."

"I'll get on the horn and see if I can't get the sheriff here soon. All right?"

"Yes ma'am."

"What's your name?"

"Jamie Hightower. I'm from Texas."

Okay, Jamie Hightower from Texas, put the rifle right here...That'll do, thanks."

Custer County sheriff's report & incident log
9:55 a.m.
Deputy Two Leaf responded to a suicidal person in the Challis area.

TWENTY-5   WHO ARE YOU AND WHAT IS THAT?

"I'M SHERIFF TILGHMAN SON, WHO ARE YOU and what is that?" Tilghman said as he came through the door.

Jamie was startled by the big lawman's entrance and by the deputy who followed close behind. He stood straight as a board.

"My name is Jamie Hightower, Sheriff. I would like to talk to you in private if I could."

"We can, but maybe you had better let my deputy carry the bundle and we'll go to my office. We get a little sensitive to packages like that around here. I'm sure you can understand."

"Sure Sheriff, but I brought it for you."

Jamie watched intently as the deputy picked up the blanket and the three men made their way down the hall to the sheriff's office.

"Have a seat Mr. Hightower. What's this about? Wait a minute son. I know you, don't I?"

"Yes sir, you do. I was the fellow that got a good lickin' last spring in that bar up the street."

"That you were. Looks like you recovered all right."

"I did." Jamie pointed at the blanket that Charlie held. Your deputy can unwrap the blanket and I will explain why I'm here.

127

There's a rifle in it. It's not loaded I promise. I have the cartridges in my pocket."

"That's good news. Charlie, let's take a look."

Charlie slowly peeled back the edges of the blanket, reached into the cloth and slid a hunting rifle from its cover. The composite black stock and highly polished action and barrel identified the rifle to Tilghman as something special. The deputy cradled it in his hands and easily manipulated the fluted bolt to expose an empty chamber. He drove the bolt home with some force and exercised the trigger. The rifle produced a sharp snap as the firing pin released. Charlie handed the piece to Tilghman butt end first.

"Well, would you look at this?" Tilghman could not resist repeating Charlie's action, and again the authority of a precision firearm spoke to the men in the room in a language that all understood. "Is this a present?" The sheriff smiled broadly.

The young man didn't appear to get the joke and answered "No sir. Well, yes sir, I mean no sir. I mean I stole it Sheriff and I'm bringing it to you."

Tilghman let the butt of the rifle rest against his thigh. He looked at Jamie with a quizzical glance before he handed the rifle back to Charlie and sat down behind his desk.

"You stole this rifle Jamie? Is that what you said?"

"Well in a way I did. But in another way I didn't. You see I took the gun from a couple of men up in the Big Lost range about two days back. They had wrapped it in that blanket there and buried it at the base of a big boulder. I watched them do it from up on a ridge and they never saw me."

"All right son let's back up a bit. Why were you watching those two men and what were you doing up in that country yourself? Start with the second question first."

The sheriff held up his hand for a pause. "Charlie maybe we better record this. Get that little thing-a-ma-jig recorder you've got."

128

The deputy left the room and returned with a hand-held digital recorder no bigger than a cigarette lighter. He put it on the sheriff's desk and nodded to the sheriff that he was ready.

"Alright Jamie, you can answer my questions now."

"Sheriff I work for the CAW as a night watchman..."

"Whoa again! What's the CAW and what's a night watchman?"

"*Citizen Advocates for Wildlife*, that's the CAW. CAW hired me to work with sheepherders up in the high pastures during the summer and fall helping them protect their sheep flocks from wolf attack. We're trying to find a way for the sheep and cattle ranchers to coexist with the wolves. I camp out with the flocks and at night I stay awake and monitor for wolves so that the herder can sleep and get his rest. The CAW pays me. It's kind of an experiment, so to speak."

"Where are you from son? I can tell you're not from around here, right?"

"Texas."

"I thought so; you've got a brighter twang than a banjo. I thought I recognized it. What part of Texas?"

The kid looked surprised by the question. "Near Amarillo—place called Boys Ranch. It's kind of out in the middle of nowhere—up near the Canadian River. I don't guess you've ever heard of it."

"Oh, how mistaken you are lad. I've heard of it and heard of it well. I visited the very same place about ten years ago. I went there to see the Old Tascosa town site and the Boot Hill cemetery that's just above the creek that runs by the old house site of Frenchy McCormick. Yes sir, I've been there. Is that big ol' crooked Cottonwood tree still there?"

"Yes sir, it is. That's where I grew up. I lived on Cal Farley's Boys Ranch."

The sheriff smiled at the kid. "We'll talk about that later. Now tell me about the two men you were watching. What were they doing?"

"They killed a wolf Sheriff. I don't know how they did it, they didn't shoot it, I don't think. And I can tell you that they weren't no regular hunters either. They didn't skin the carcass or tag it like they are supposed to do. I know the game rules for the wolf hunt and they weren't no hunters following the rules. When I saw them do that, I got mad. I had been up in the high country all summer trying to help make a place for the wild wolf and here were these two men just killing one. There was no sport in that..."

"What did they do then?"

"Well, what they did then was strange I'll tell you. They pinned a note to the dead wolf somehow. And they just buried that rifle and walked away in the snow."

"What did you do? I mean right after the two men left."

"Sheriff I waited for almost an hour. I was a little scared to show myself. I wasn't sure where they went. But, after a while, I figured the coast was clear so I made my way down to where they had buried the rifle. That's when I stole it, I guess."

"Did you read the note on the wolf?"

"No, I was getting too nervous to hang around. So I just took the gun and went back to our camp."

"What did the two men look like? Do you think you would recognize them if you saw them?"

"I don't think so Sheriff. They wore camouflage-hunting outfits and had sock hats pulled down pretty far around their eyes. They looked almost identical. You know kind of like twins. Sheriff, am I goin' to be in some kind of trouble for taking that rifle?"

"Well, I'm not sure about that Jamie. You know it kind of looks as if you found it up there in the woods buried in the snow. It's kind of like you found it."

Tilghman put on a show of thinking. "What do you think Charlie?"

"That's the way it looks to me too Sheriff. What kind of fool is going to stick a rifle like that in the ground anyway? I mean if he owns it proper, you know?"

"Yeah, that's kind of my thoughts too Charlie."

Sheriff Tilghman got up and moved around his desk and picked up the rifle. He fondled the piece gently and rubbed his hands along the stock. "I tell you what Jamie, I'll keep this rifle safe while I investigate your story. If we can't find the true owners, I'll give it back to you. How's that sound?"

Jamie looked at Sheriff Tilghman for a long second before he answered. "I don't want it. I know that doesn't make much sense to you and the deputy but I don't want that gun. You see, I just don't like to kill animals." Jamie looked down at the floor between his feet.

"There is nothing wrong with that Jamie. Is there Charlie?"

"No Sheriff, there sure isn't."

"Don't get me wrong, I'm not against hunting or anything. I just don't want to do it myself. But I can shoot good. I can shoot real good."

Tilghman walked to his office door and quietly pulled it shut. He returned to his desk and sat down.

"Jamie I'm about to tell you something that I probably shouldn't but I'm going to do it anyway. You see we know who this rifle belonged to. It is a part of an investigation into the death of a hunter near where your camp is. It happened a few days before you found that rifle. Since your camp is in that area, do you know anything about what happened?"

"No sir. There are a lot of hunters coming through that part this time of year. I didn't pay much attention."

"Well all right then. You see, the man's body was pretty well torn up by scavenging animals and the cause of death has so far proven to be a mystery. What I'm telling you Jamie is that in the absence of conclusive evidence as to cause of death we have to leave all doors open in our investigation; including the possibility that he was murdered. The reason I'm telling you this is because you can help us out if you want to."

Tilghman shifted a bit forward in his chair, put his hands together in front of him, and leaned on his elbows. "What do you say?"

"I guess so Sheriff. What do you think I can do?"

"Well, I've changed my mind about keeping the rifle. That gun just might be good bait for a couple of no good fish. What I would like for you to do, if you agree, is to take this rifle in its blanket and put it back where you found it. Try to make it look like it hasn't been disturbed as best you can."

Jamie sat still for a moment will no expression. Finally he said, "Okay Sheriff, I can do that. I have to get back to my camp right away and I can do that on my way."

"Jamie there is something else I want you to do. I'm going to give you a hand-held radio to take with you. It's on the frequency used by the ranger at the Challis National Forest. His station is not far from where you and your herder graze the sheep."

"I know it Sheriff and I know the ranger too. He comes by our camp now and then to check on us."

"Good. The reason for the radio is that I want you to keep an eye as best you can on that buried rifle. If those men return for the rifle, I need you to immediately get a hold of the ranger. He will give me a call. Jamie do you understand how important this is?"

"Yes sir, I think I do. You believe those men might have had something to do with the hunter's death, right?"

"Don't know. But I sure would like to find out how they came about having that special gun—that I would. Charlie, go get the radio for Jamie. One other thing, I don't expect or want you to have any contact with those men if they show up. Do you understand?"

"Yes sir."

"I mean it, absolutely no contact. Until we know for sure who they are and their business, we have to assume that they could be bad guys. I don't want you taking any chances. You're doing me a favor. That's all. Got it?"

"Yep, I got it Sheriff."

"Oh, and Jamie... Unless you think you need to do it, I wouldn't say anything to your organization. The less people who know about the rifle the better. Is this going to interfere with your duties?"

"No. The lambing and grazing season is over. I'm through for this year. I was just hanging out a little longer to enjoy the backcountry. I guess I'll be heading back to Texas soon."

"All right then. And, by the way, I've got a fund in my budget that'll let me put you on the payroll for a couple of weeks. So it's not a freebie. You won't get rich but it will keep the wolves away from the door," the sheriff broke into a wide grin at his joke.

Jamie got the joke this time and smiled.

"I've had wolves at my door all season Sheriff Tilghman. I kind of like it but the money will help too, thanks."

"Good." Tilghman picked up the rifle again and brought it to his shoulder. "Boy is this a sweet piece of work. I never was much of a hunter myself but I've always liked a well made gun and this is a well made gun." Finally, he spread the blanket back across his desk and rewrapped it.

"Here Jamie she's all yours. You're clear on everything right?"

"Yes sir."

"Okay lad, give Linda, the deputy at the radio desk out front, your name and particulars and she'll get you fixed up. As soon as you get set up on the mountain, give Ranger Clyde a call and let him know you're on duty. I'll call him this afternoon and fill him in so he'll be expecting you to call.

"And Jamie..."

"Yes Sheriff."

"When this is over we'll sit down over a beer or something and talk about Old Tascosa, would that suit you?"

"Yes sir, I'd like that."

"So would I."

3:25 p.m.
Quick investigated a traffic mishap between
a RV and a dump-truck south of Mackay.

TWENTY-6   YOUR STORY IS FULL OF
DONUT HOLES

SHERIFF TILGHMAN SAT AT HIS DESK drinking his third cup of coffee after watching Jamie Hightower and the rolled up blanket leave his jail. He was already wondering if he did the right thing with that kid. His bladder was screaming for relief so he headed down the hall. As the sheriff passed Linda at the dispatcher's chair, he paused.

"Linda, get Wishful Wicks out of his cell. I've got to release that reprobate before he starts screaming for a lawyer. Before I do, I want to talk to him one more time. Tell the Indian to bring him into my office. The three of us will have ourselves a powwow."

"Will do Sheriff."

"And Linda, get him a cup of coffee with sugar in it will you?"

"Are you serious?"

"I'm serious, coffee with a lot of sugar."

"Sure Sheriff, you're the boss."

Tilghman wasn't sure what he could get out of Wishful if anything. The man had been a fly in his ointment for nearly ten years. Every time he showed his dirty face in Custer County it had cost the taxpayers money and the sheriff aggravation.

"Come on in. Have a seat. How about a cup of coffee Wishful?"

"How about a cup of coffee Wishful! Now would you listen to that?"

The prisoner looked back at the deputy. "Isn't that a new way of treating an old and trusted friend? What's got into you my fine sheriff friend? Don't mind if I do. Did you fix it the way I like it, you know, with a lot of sweetness in it?"

"Tons of sugar, and I'll get you a donut if that would suit your fancy."

"My fancy indeed. How 'bout one with the cream fill? No, make that two, one with chocolate glaze." Wishful revealed a row of brown teeth as he grinned broadly.

Tilghman looked at his deputy. "Do we?"

The deputy grimaced as he got up from his chair and left the room.

"You know Sheriff I have always enjoyed my stays here at county with you and your crew. You people are just so thoughtful. Thoughtful, that's the word."

"Yeah thoughtful," the sheriff mimicked Wishful, "I guess that's why you keep coming back."

Charlie came back in the room and roughly pushed a donut into Wishful Wicks' chest. Wishful fingered the pastry and looked up. "That doesn't look like a creamed filled one to me deputy."

"Wicks, I want you to listen to me carefully," the Sheriff interrupted, "and I need you to come down out of the clouds for a bit and answer my questions carefully and, if possible, truthfully. You follow?"

Wishful took a big bite from the glazed sweetness and eagerly slurped at his coffee while nodding his head at the sheriff.

"Shut the door Charlie, let's get a little privacy for our talk."

Tilghman got up from his chair and walked around to where Wishful was sitting. He lifted the cup from his hands and set it behind him on the desk.

"Finish your donut Wishful. That's it, chew it all up and swallow it."

Tilghman waited. "Fine. Now, what do you know about that hunter's death up on the Elkhorn? And don't give me that crap about how you and your friends killed him. Because if you say that one more time, I'm going to book you for murder and you will be eating our donuts and drinking our coffee until the state comes to take you away to death row. You get the message?"

"Sheriff, you're so funny."

"Funny I may be but serious I am. Now let's go over the day from daylight to dark. First things first. What were you doing up there?"

"I told you Sheriff."

"Tell me again."

Wishful squirmed a bit in his chair and reached out tentatively for his coffee cup. Tilghman nodded it was all right.

"Sheriff, ever since you ran me out of Custer County last year, times have been sorely tough on old Wishful. I wandered about for a while. I even went down to Nevada but they pushed me back up north, they weren't none too gentle either. Them folks are not very nice to strangers. But Wishful can take care of himself, that he can. So I just drifted back over to the Sawtooth and settled in with the wild things. I hung out a while on the Nez Perce rez until the big chief suggested I move farther east, you know to the Southern Mountains. So I did that."

"And Wishful was glad he did. The wolves in the Big Lost are a real blessing to an old mountain man like me, that they are. The best thing ever happened to Wishful was them wolves coming back to the Rockies. Most folks just don't understand how good at killing things those creatures are. And they ain't greedy like some say. They'll share if you don't push too hard."

Tilghman looked over at Charlie and rolled his eyes but didn't divert Wishful from his tale.

"You see I'd been might hungry most of the summer until I started tracking behind that wolf pack. They'd make a kill and I'd pick up some scraps. Most times, I could carve out a prime cut or two from the carcass and the big dogs didn't even growl. I lived high on the hog, that I did. The only bad thing was those wolves liked to roam and hunt at night so they kept me a movin' around a lot. But ol' Wishful is tough, yes sir, he is. I moved right with them, that I did."

The sheriff stared at the prisoner for a moment.

"All right, let's just say I buy your tall tale about moving in with the Chilly Buttes pack, God knows you've been known to do stranger. So let's just cut to the chase. What happened on the day that the hunter's body was found on the plateau? How did you come across the scene?"

"Hunter, what hunter?" Wishful put a big grin on and glanced over at Charlie Two Leaf and winked.

"Deputy put this rag back in the cell."

"No, no, no, Sheriff! I was just kiddin'! Kiddin' I was. Truth be known, I had been watching that man for some time. Most of the time he was getting his hunting camp rigged up. The wolf pack was in that area and I had been following them when I took the high ground above him. I seen him come up the trail the afternoon before. And I watched him scratch out his little area for his blind. I figured he was a huntin' elk. I didn't know about the wolf hunt this year. I didn't think they would let folks kill wolves yet. You know, endangered species and all that stuff."

"Wishful, did you see him shoot the wolf he had hanging in his camp?"

"No, not me. I left him before the sun come up good that morning. I heard the shots though. They echoed all over the valley and across the high mountain."

"Shots?"

"What?"

"You said shots. Did you hear more than one?"

"Yes. There was one and then a little later there was another."

"About what time was that?"

"Can't say, my watch is in the shop." Wishful loved his little jokes but the sheriff was not in the mood so he dropped his grin.

"Mid-morning, I'm guessing about 9:30 or 10:00, long about then. I do know that the shots spooked the pack darn good. I saw them come a running over the ridge toward me at a good clip, yes sir, at a good clip they were running."

"Then what?"

"That's when I ran into them two brothers. The ones you talked to at the scene."

"Whoa! Stop right there. You mean to tell me that you hadn't found that man's body before you ran into the Elder brothers?"

"No Sheriff, I was heading back to the ridge above where the hunter was when I seen them two coming up the trail. We met head on we did. I stepped off the trail to let them pass. I spoke friendly like but they didn't say a word. It's like they didn't want to look at me. I'm used to that though. Lots of folks seem to want to avoid me for some reason. You know Sheriff?"

Again, Tilghman looked at Charlie, "I know Wishful, strange isn't it?" Are you saying that the two brothers were coming from the direction you were going? I mean from the direction of the hunter's camp?"

"Yep, right up that trail. I'm a guessin' again, but I think it was about a half-mile away, something like that."

"I asked the one if he had killed an elk. You know the shots and all. He just shook his head but didn't speak. I thought it might have been them that took the shot. How about another bit of that sugared coffee Sheriff, my talking apparatus is getting a tad dry." Wishful held out his cup to the deputy who took the nod from the sheriff and then reluctantly the cup from the prisoner.

"So you went back to the perch you had above the hunter's camp, right?"

"I did." Wishful glanced towards the door.

"Go on, Charlie will get your coffee. What did you see when you got back to that spot above the camp?"

"Well, the first thing I'd seen was that wolf hanging in that tree. Oh, what a sad sight to my eyes that was. That's when I knew that hunter had been setting up for a wolf kill all along. Now Sheriff, it was just at that moment I heard another shot go echoing around the mountains. It came from the direction, now you know you can't be sure about such things, but I thought it came from the direction that I had just come from. You know the direction them other hunters were traveling. Can't be sure, but I think that was it. I know that for sure because I immediately thought that maybe them brothers were after wolves too. And that was the direction that the pack was a headed. Thank you Deputy. That sure is good coffee with the sugar in it and all."

Wishful relaxed as he sipped at the hot liquid. The itinerant didn't get such luxury except when he was in jail, so Tilghman could tell he was savoring the experience.

"Okay Wishful, what then? Be careful with this part. Make sure you get it right."

"Eyes like a hawk and memory like an elephant, that's ol' Wishful Wicks, Sheriff, yes it is. Well, I kept looking around from my ridge for the hunter below, I mean the one who killed my friend. But, I couldn't see a thing. There wasn't no movement anywhere. It was a still and quiet as it can get up in that high country. You know you'd think that there would be some birds attracted to the kill site but it was just quiet." Wishful sipped at his coffee again and let out a long sigh.

"So, what did you do then?"

"Well sir, I just kept looking around for a long time. Then I thought about going down to that man's camp. You know, get a small contribution for some staples. I was a hoping I'd see him first so I could let him know I was coming. Didn't want to get shot. Don't like to surprise a man with a big gun you understand. But I waited, must have been for thirty minutes or so and still not a sign of nobody. So I decided to take a peek. I was coming down the ridge trail when I first noticed the dark spot in the snow. It was just a few feet from where the wolf carcass was a hanging in the tree."

Tilghman interrupted, "Could you tell what the dark spot was from up the trail?"

"No, I thought it was another kill, maybe an elk or another wolf. You couldn't tell much because it was down in the snow."

"All right, hold it right there. I want you to think real careful now. Think about what you saw as you approached that hunter's camp. Details are important. Because there was fresh snow on the ground when we got there, some of what you would have seen was covered up. So think a minute if you need to before you tell what you saw as you walked into the hunter's camp."

"There was a lot of tracks around, I remember that."

"Tracks, you mean animal tracks?"

"Yeah, a bunch of tracks, wolf for sure and I thought I saw bear, not sure though."

"Any others?"

"Yes, boot tracks. A lot of boot tracks around too. All over the camp there were boot tracks going in every direction."

"Would you figure they were the hunter's tracks? The one that shot the wolf I mean."

"Sure, but there were others too. I've been out in the wild country a long time Sheriff. I know my tracks. There were more than one set of boots in that camp, more than one set for sure."

"But you never saw any one else in camp before, right?"

"No, no one before I left that morning early."

"Then what?"

"That's when I saw that man in the snow. At first, I wasn't sure what it was. I thought maybe it was, you know, like I said, another animal kill. I got a little closer and then I could see the pieces of clothing wrapped around the body. That's when I knew it weren't no animal, no sir. That was a dead man. I seen many a dead thing in them mountains, that I have, but I've never seen a dead man, not like that one for sure."

"You mean scavenged?"

"Yeah, I mean scavenged real bad. I couldn't help looking at it. There weren't no face and most of both hands were gone too. And the man's chest, Holy Mother, he was pert near cleaned out. Whoa! what a sight that was, I'm here to tell you. What a sight that was."

Wishful paused and nervously took another sip of coffee. Some of the liquid spilled onto his shirt and made its place among the other stains.

"Wishful, what did you do then, exactly?"

"Sure Sheriff, I understand. Let me see. You don't have another donut do you?"

"Never mind that Wishful, what happened then?"

"I got scared, that I did, I got real scared. You know, being there with a dead body in the snow and no one else around. Man I even thought about the wolves or bears or whatever it was that tore up that guy. Then I thought about maybe it was a cougar. Yes sir, I got scared."

Tilghman got up from his chair and walked around to the front of the desk. "Wishful did you pick up anything around that site? I mean any of that hunter's belongings from the camp? Anything at all?"

Wishful took a sip of the cold coffee before he answered.

"No sir Sheriff, I didn't bother nothing, not a single thing. All I could think about then was how I was going to call for help. I didn't have no way of calling for any help from nobody. You know ol' Wishful never had one of those phones without wire things all you folks carry now days."

"So you're telling me you didn't collect anything at all lying around the camp? So then what happened?"

"Well, ol' Wishful got smart, that he did. I thought about them two fellers that I had met coming down the trail. I figured if I put a hurry to my pace I could catch up with them and tell them what I'd found. I figured they would have a way to get some help. So I struck out at a wolf's run."

"And you must have caught up with them because they are the ones who got in touch with us, right?"

"That's right. I caught up with them mighty quick too. They weren't very far away. It's like they didn't do much traveling after I saw them. I caught up with them real fast. And when I told those boys about the body they thought I was joshing them."

"What did they say?"

"They laughed at first and told me to quit trying to trick them into back tracking. I think they thought maybe I was trying to get something from them. But I showed them this piece of bloody handkerchief I had picked up next to the body and said this was proof. I said come on boys, I'll show you."

143

"Wishful, hold it. What did I just ask you?"

"Uh, you mean about did I go after them boys?"

"No, before that."

"Oh, you mean about did I pick anything up around the camp, right?"

"That's right, and what did you say?"

"Sheriff I didn't think you meant small stuff. I just picked up that handkerchief so's I had something to show them fellers when I found them. That's all I picked up, I swear, that's all."

"Alright, then what?"

"The boys came back to the camp with me. They looked at the body and the one, I think it was Henry, said he would go up on top of the ridge and see if he could, I think he said, get a signal or something like that. He said he'd try to reach a ranger. The other one and I stayed at the camp."

"What did he say or do while you waited?"

"We didn't do anything really. I do remember that he kept saying that the wolves had made a mess of that man. He kept saying how dangerous wild wolves are. How he'd shoot anyone of them he saw on sight. He said law or no law. I tried to tell him about the wolves I knew. That they weren't like that but he just said I was as crazy as a loon if I trusted wild animals like that. He said I was likely to end up someday like that feller in the snow."

"Wishful did that hunter pick up anything from around the camp while you waited? Anything at all?"

"I don't think so. We looked around a bit. He looked over the carcass hanging in the tree real close. He poked it a couple of times with a hunting knife. No, I don't think he picked anything up."

"Did you notice what kind of rifle he was carrying?"

"Oh yeah, I noticed it. A fancy thing it was. You could tell this guy had money."

"Why's that?"

"Well, anybody with a rifle like that had to have money Sheriff. He didn't buy that one at Wal-Mart, no sir, not at Wal-Mart. That gun was all business it was. Old Wishful could be a great hunter with a gun like that one, a great hunter."

"Would you recognize the gun if you saw it again?"

"You betcha I would. Some things you don't forget once you've seen them. His mate didn't have a gun like that one. No sir, his was plain ol' pawn shop. But I would remember it if I saw it again."

"One more question for you and then I'm going to reluctantly turn you back out on society. Do you think those two hunters could have been in the camp where the hunter died before you got there? Could they have been the ones who made the boot tracks all around that camp?"

Wishful shook his head no at first but then stopped.

"Well, by golly you know Sheriff that would be a possibility. Can't say for sure though. Ol' Wishful didn't see them there, no he didn't. But, it could have been by golly."

The sheriff turned to his deputy. "Charley take Wishful back to his cell. I want you to tell Linda to process him out but first go in our stash locker in the basement and see if you can find this man some descent clothes. I'm not putting him out in my county looking the way he does."

Wishful stood up and started for the door behind Charlie but stopped abruptly and turned back to Sheriff Tilghman. "That's mighty kind of you my fine Sheriff friend, mighty kind."

"Think nothing of it Wishful, but you can do me a favor. Stay out of trouble for a spell will you? There won't be any donuts the next time I put you in one of my cells. Got it?"

Again, the mountain man started for the door and again he stopped and turned back. "I'll do that. And Sheriff."

"Yeah, what is it Wishful?"

"I got something I gotta say before I go get my new clothes. I lied before. I got to tell you I lied to you. Right now I'm feeling really bad about it. I mean with you giving me that coffee with sugar in it and those donuts like you did. A man ought not to lie to people that treat him kind, but I did."

"It's all right Wishful. I'm used to it. What did you lie about?"

"You know when you asked me if I picked up anything at the camp and I said I didn't."

"Yes, you told me about the handkerchief already."

"No, it weren't the handkerchief I mean. There was something else I picked up that I lied about."

"Oh. Well maybe you had better come back and sit down and tell me about it?"

"Yes Sheriff, I better sit down to tell you about it. You're going to be kind of mad at me I suspect."

"You think, huh? Well let's hear it. Charlie come on back in, I guess Wishful's got something else he wants to tell us. Okay, go ahead."

"I buried it just up the slope from the camp under a big rock. You see I took it from the body when I found it."

"You took what and you buried what?"

"It's not like I stole it, not really. It was just lying there next to the poor man's body. I guess the wolves had torn it out of the man's pants. I don't know..."

Tilghman raised his voice for the first time since Wishful had started his account. "Wishful Wicks, you old bastard, what did you pick up?"

"The wallet, it was that man's wallet. The dead hunter's wallet."

"The wallet! Wishful you damn thief. You robbed a dead man in the wilderness? Here I was starting to feel sorry for your no-good ass. I ought to charge you with grand theft and let you rot in county for a few months. That's what I ought to do."

"But Sheriff Tilghman, Sheriff I didn't mean to. It was just right there on the ground. Right in front of ol' Wishful. Listen Sheriff I didn't take anything out of it, I swear. I just buried it." Wishful hesitated, "You know so the animals wouldn't get it. Yeah, so the animals wouldn't get it."

"And you just forgot about it until now, right?"

"Right. Until now."

"Charley get the Cherokee. We're all going to take a ride down to Elkhorn right now and find us a wallet. Wishful you better be able to find the spot you buried that wallet when we get there, you hear me?"

"I can find it Sheriff. Wishful is like a badger, he knows his holes, yes sir, he does."

"He'd better," Tilghman started for the door grabbing his heavy coat on the way out. "Charlie, grab a fire shovel and throw it in the back."

"Charlie, got the siren fixed yet?"

"Not yet Sheriff."

Custer County sheriff's report & incident log
9:55 a.m.
Stanley volunteers and deputies
responded to a fire at milepost 111 on Highway 21.

TWENTY-7   SWEET CAKE

VICTORIA WILDS LEFT THE PAVED SURFACE of Highway U.S. 95 fifty miles north of Sandpoint, Idaho and headed north by northwest on the gravel. The chunky surface soon gave way to dirt and Victoria engaged the four-wheel drive lever of her 4Runner. Most of the early season snow had melted with only graded remnants along the outside boundaries of the one-lane roadway that led into the Kaniksu National Forest.

The eight hours from Boise to northern Idaho had taken its toll and the professor hoped she would find her colleague soon; especially since the sun was beginning to wane and she didn't want to be in the wilderness after dark. It had been too many years since she had done her fieldwork and the professor knew she had gotten soft.

The road narrowed as she navigated the twists and turns through the forest. Finally, she saw an opening ahead and Wilds offered a soft prayer that it would be her destination. As the trees receded and she drove into the opening, she saw a steady rise of fire smoke coming from a black pipe chimneystack elbowed out of the side of a long camping trailer.

"That has to be Jennifer's place," she figured. As she rolled up in front of the ugly quarters, a tall, thin woman came bounding

148

out of the front door and began to wave vigorously. There was little doubt that was Jennifer Carl. The two wildlife biologists hadn't seen each other for nearly five years but Victoria could see her friend and colleague hadn't changed. Even in the rough clothes of the backwoods, Jennifer had a natural beauty that Victoria could only envy. Her long, shiny black hair was tied back in a tight ponytail that swung easily from side to side as she trotted up to the driver's side of the Toyota. For an awkward moment, the two women just stared and smiled at each other through the glass.

Finally, Victoria shut down the engine and opened the door to get out. "Well would you look what the cat drug up? Professor Victoria Wilds, I presume?"

"You presume rightfully my dear Dr. Jennifer Carl. I was beginning to wonder whether I would have to cross into Canada to find you. We're close aren't we?"

"Less than fifteen miles right over that mountain range behind you. You cannot imagine how happy I am to see you. When I got your message that you were coming north for a visit, I almost decided to bake a cake. But you know me, I soon thought better of that notion."

"That's just fine. I hate to say it but any cake you would make would be as hard as a brick or fall apart in your lap. Am I right?"

"You are definitely right about that. But, my dear professor, I do have some of your favorite snacks inside. If I remember correctly, you were a Twinkie fanatic during our graduate school days."

"I've had to back off of that habit. I know you wouldn't understand but some of us have put on a few pounds since then."

"Well Vic you come on out here for a few months and work with me and I guarantee that you'll be back in top-notch shape before you know it."

149

"Jennifer, if I only could. I am afraid the classroom is to be my fate."

"Oh, but Vic that is what they call justice. You are good in the classroom and that is a commodity hard to find. You remember all those boring ones we had don't you?"

"I do, indeed I do. How in the world have you been way out here in the backwoods? It doesn't look like you have a whole lot of friends to talk to."

"Oh! Oh how wrong you are. I have more friends out here than I ever had in the world of people and cities. Come on in and I'll brew us some tea and we'll sit by the fire and I'll fill you in. Oh, Victoria it is so exciting what is going on in this piece of wilderness. You just won't believe what is revealing itself here. But enough of that, come on in to my humble abode."

The moon was not full in the evening sky but it was still bright. Jennifer had gone outside to get a couple of fire logs and Victoria sat relaxed next to the warmth of the pot-bellied stove. She let her eyes roam around the inside of the trailer. She was surprised how big it felt even though there was something for every bit of space available. She thought how strange academicians are in their love of books. Jennifer had almost as many books in her small trailer home as Victoria had in her entire house. What books were not on shelves were stacked in every corner and on every surface. Most of those had little paper tabs sticking out of the pages of various lengths and colors.

As Jennifer came through the door, the first of the evening howls echoed distinctly from the woods. Jennifer set down the wood and smiled at Victoria. "There's one of my friends starting to sing right now. Just wait, the chorus will begin shortly."

Jennifer was right. Several different scale notes soon joined with the base line and suddenly the night came to life with the music of the wilderness. "They're making sure everyone knows the top dogs are around and that they are open for business," Jennifer said as she pushed another log among the coals.

Victoria hadn't heard that call for quite some time but, it caused a torrent of memories to flow through her consciousness. She listened and sipped her tea. "What a magnificent sound that is," she said finally. "I miss it."

"Yes, it does sort of penetrate to your soul doesn't it? I sometimes think that call on a bright night is as close to the meaning of wildness that one can find. I often think about what it must have been like for the first group of frontier people who came into this land. Two-hundred years ago there would have been two hundred thousand of those howling animals calling across the West. What a sound that must have been to the ear."

"Does it ever frighten you Jennifer? I mean being out here alone. It is such a lonely sound for humans to hear."

"No, it doesn't frighten me because the wolves don't frighten me. I know them too well. I know their ways, what makes them strong, and what makes them afraid. Besides, what would a wolf want with this scrawny body anyway?"

The howling abruptly stopped and the silence was as impressive as the wolves calls had been a moment before. Victoria got up and put her cup on the counter leading into the kitchen. She walked to the front window and stared out into the silhouetted tree line about a quarter mile up the ridge.

"What a magnificent place is your backyard Jennifer. I want to hear about your work. I can stay tomorrow with you if that's all right. I would really like to see what you are doing here in this place so close to God."

"What do you mean if it's all right? You just try to leave before I show you what I'm doing here. Wait till you see the data. Your old research juices will begin to flow like water over a fall, I promise."

"Jennifer I will, but I will definitely need another Twinkie?" Both women laughed and did a little dance.

"You know Jenn, sometimes I think that Twinkies and tobacco could have and may still destroy the whole of western civilization. What do you think?"

"Good point. You must have read the statistics on Mississippi?"

They laughed again and tore into another plastic wrapper.

"Here's to Mississippi," Victoria screamed.

Custer County sheriff's report & incident log
7:55 p.m.
A deputy responded to a report of an abandoned car near Leslie.

TWENTY-8   TREE HUGGING PREDATORS

DR. JENNIFER CARL BOUNDED ACROSS THE OPEN VALLEY like an elk. She had a notebook in one hand and binoculars tethered around her neck. Victoria Wilds looked at her colleague with a mixture of happiness and envy. No one, she thought, should be that contented at their work. If only the classroom provoked the same response. If only, she thought.

"Vic, come on. Look at this."

Victoria followed the instructions and moved to Jennifer's side.

"See this."

"Yes, wolf scat right?"

"Yes, and look here, tracks, both wolf and bear. And over here, look at these. That's elk there and right next to it are deer tracks. This place was pretty lively last night. The predators were out in force hunting in the night—it's their favorite time.

"Now I want you to look up towards the west—just where the grasslands meet the aspen on that knoll. Look at the edge of that tree stand. Do you see the first row of ten footers all around the meadow's edge? And, behind them, the stand of mature tall aspen? Now what is missing?"

Victoria knew the literature and understood what Jennifer was leading to. "The middle growth of trees."

"Exactly, and I know you know why," Jennifer let her friend take the lead.

"That missing middle-age stand reflects the absence of the wolf from this valley after they were more or less driven to extinction in this region in the 1930s."

"That's it," Jennifer became excited, "when man took one of the primary predators out of the environment the balance that nature had for thousands of years created between plants and animals was suddenly thrown awry. Oh boy is the evidence so clear. Without the wolf, the elk, over 60 years, got lazy and contented in their browsing habits. They could just stay unhurried in one place and munch on the young trees to their heart's content. No wolves, no threat, no problem.

"But then man got lazy in his persecution of *canis lupus* and the wolf drifted in from Canada and repopulated this valley about 20 years ago. And, when they came back, the old order was reestablished. Those trees show us that clearly. One-hundred-year-old trees lived with the wolf and the young 20-year-old trees again lived with the wolf."

"And the knee bone is connected to the thigh bone, right?"

"Ain't it so professor, ain't it so? I call it cascading. You take one species away from the natural order and the whole changes. You remove the top predator, in this case the wolf, and you now have a greatly reduced number of trees reaching maturity because the elk are more numerous and they can stand over a young tree and eat it to death. Now with fewer aspen and the rich habitat it provides, you have a greatly reduced number of songbirds. Take the bird numbers down and you raise the bug numbers dramatically. And the bugs munch on the trees further reducing habitat. It's an old story to us, isn't it Vic?"

"Oh yeah, too old for me. I'm getting very tired of telling it and hearing it. You would think our behavior would change in light of the evidence we have collected over the last 30 years. The only thing that keeps me sane is seeing the work like yours—work so clear and overwhelming—that our society and its political establishment are finally having to deal with it realistically if not begrudgingly. "

"Come on with me Vic, I want you to walk the transects with me. I want you to see the richness of this environment. I want you to see what all your classroom work is helping to teach your students about how the natural world really works when it is healthy and left to its own wisdom."

"Gladly."

The two women methodically and systematically covered 10 hectares of ground gathering the news from the night before. The animal news in scat, bone, hair and hide. Victoria enjoyed herself at a level she could scarcely remember.

After the morning spent in the field, they were hungry and ready for a rest. Victoria finished her tuna sandwich and sweetened her palate with a leftover Twinkie and its double dose of sugar from the night before.

"There's an old sheriff down in Custer County that needs your expertise," she began finally. "There's been a very unfortunate death near Chilly Buttes that is in a way connected to your work here."

Jennifer looked at Victoria but didn't comment. "You want another bit of tea Vic?"

"No thanks, I'm fine. The man who was found dead was a doctor from Pocatello. He was an avid hunter and had gone to Custer County to participate in the first legalized wolf hunt, as you know, in more than 50 years. Well, to make a long story short, they found him dead in the snow. He had been horribly scavenged by large and small animals alike. Probably wolves and coyotes and maybe bears, we're not sure. His body was in such bad shape that the autopsy and coroner's report was inclusive as to the cause of death.

"The sheriff, his name is Chester Tilghman, has asked me to help him with a couple of questions about wolf behavior. And here is the part that I bet you are not going to like—some are suggesting that the wolves killed the hunter."

Jennifer quickly looked up from her lunch and seemed to be stunned by Victoria's statement. She got off her stool and went rigid like a boxer ready to fight.

"You have got to be kidding me."

"No. I'm not. In fact, there was a newspaper article about a week ago reporting on the death that fanned the flames of that theory. And now there are people and groups calling again for the complete removal of the wolf from Idaho. Jennifer it is the same old song just a different verse. Some people are never going to accept the wolf under any circumstances and they are going to fight until their dying day. This is just the latest example."

"This is so sad," Jennifer sat back down. "I mean what does it take to get people to live with nature? How do we get them to understand the benefits of these animals to their own well-being?"

"Jennifer some people are not open to reason and scientific evidence. It is not the language they understand, or even if they do, want to hear. They have their ways, their interests and that's it, end of story. And you know as well as I do that there is this element of the outsider telling them what to do. By golly, they fought for and settled this land and by golly, no one from the east or west coast is going to tell them how to live on it and use it. You know that."

"I hate that attitude. It so frustrates me that people are like that. It seems that no matter what we do, what we find out, that it is never going to change that kind."

"Nope, it probably isn't. But things have changed in the last 20 years and you know that too. The whole wolf reintroduction program in our state and in Montana and Wyoming has, for the most part, been an overwhelming success. There are at least 1200 wolves in the Northern Rockies that would have not been there accept for the efforts of dedicated scientists like you. Resistance is still there, right, but so too is progress—and it is gaining momentum."

"Yeah."

"Okay, here is what I need for you to tell me. I'm sure I know what your answer is going to be but I want to hear it anyway. Sheriff Tilghman, who by the way, I believe is on our side or at least neutral, needs to hear it too."

Victoria got up from the counter and walked towards the front of the trailer. She stood between two tall stacks of books and turned again to face her friend.

"Based on your knowledge and study of the behavior of the wolf in the wild, do you believe that it is possible that wolves killed this man, this hunter?"

Jennifer hesitated.

"Vic, you of all people should know that I can't answer that the way you have phrased it in any other way but in the positive. Of course, it is possible. Wolves have killed people throughout history just as people have killed people. The wolf is a very proficient predator. If a wolf pack can bring down a 1500-pound buffalo, a wolf pack can kill a human being. The short answer is yes."

"Well you surprise me a little. I figured you would go against your brain and let your emotions answer that question. Save the wolf at any cost. I'm proud of you."

"Do you want the long answer?"

"I know it. But we can talk through it anyway. Using your work here, what would you say are the odds that wolves attacked and killed a healthy hunter in the wild?"

"Well to give you my best scientific answer, I would say slim and none,"

Jennifer smiled for the first time since this conversation began.

"The overwhelming evidence, and you know this Vic, is that in the wild, unless wolves are somehow habituated to man, they make every effort to stay away from humans. There's a case in Alaska where is it is claimed wolves attacked and killed a young man, a geologist I think, who was out walking at dusk."

"Yes, I know the case well."

"But even in that case, which was in no way conclusive that wolves killed the man, the wolves had been accustomed to feeding in a garbage dump nearby and had grown habituated to the people working in the garbage dump. They had lost their natural fear of man at least enough to challenge a lone individual in their territory."

Jennifer went on. "I think you know this story but let me refresh your memory in the Yellowstone soft release case. It's a good example of what I am suggesting. In that case, wolves were captured in Canada and brought to the Yellowstone Park to be a part of the wolf reintroduction program in the Lower 48. The soft release idea was to put them in a large fenced-in pen that would allow the wolves to have some time to acclimate to their new environment. The fear was that if they were released directly in the wild they would try to make their way back to their old territory.

"After that period was up the wildlife biologists came to the pen and opened the gate. They left it wide-open but, and you remember this, the wolves wouldn't leave the pen. They wouldn't cross that gate line where the humans had come and gone. They waited and waited off in the distance but the wolves were not going to cross the human scented line.

"Yes, I recall. If I remember correctly, they had to cut a hole in the chain-link fence before they could finally get the wolves to leave the pen, right?"

"Right. So, you see wolves are instinctively wary of humans. They do not want to have anything to do with them. Smart wolves, huh? But, and this is why, you can't be absolutely sure about a wolf attacking a human. When wolves become used to humans through some kind of regular contact, just like bears, they lose that natural aversion to man. And, when that happens the wolf, being the top predator that he is, can and will in certain cases attack humans. But that's no different than most predatory animals. Bears and cougars do the same. Hey, I read recently about a bunch of raccoons that attacked some woman in Missouri in her backyard when she tried to shoo them out of her garbage. Wild animals under certain conditions will do what wild things do. They protect themselves just like any creature that feels threatened or is hungry."

"So what do you think about our case with the hunter at Chilly Buttes? The evidence suggests that he had killed one of the Chilly Buttes pack and had skinned the kill. He was still in his camp when whatever happened to him happened. What would be your thinking, Jennifer, on this case?"

"The quick answer again is that from all that I know about predators, especially wolves, there is no way that wolves came back and attacked that hunter. My guess would be that they scattered and put distance between the pack and the source of danger that had already killed one of their numbers. To me it is pure fantasy to think they regrouped and came back to challenge that hunter."

"So there is no way they killed Dr. Cahalan?"

"No way. But Vic, that's not to say that a bear or cougar, smelling the fresh kill didn't come to have a look and then attack the man who was smelling of blood. And certainly, after the man is dead and on the ground, the whole scene would have had a very strong attraction for scavengers of all sorts. And wolves—like coyotes, eagles, magpies and most eaters of meat in the wild—will take advantage of a kill no matter who makes it."

"A dead-end."

"Excuse me."

"I said a dead-end. I mean we may have to accept that we will never know what killed that man or what happened up on the Elkhorn Creek. We can't prove the wolves didn't kill him, and those who might suspect that they did, can't make their case either. A dead-end."

"I'm afraid you're right. The sad point though is that those who want to make some political hay out of the notion that wolves are to blame will do so regardless of the ambiguity of the evidence. They're going to claim the wolf is a vicious man killer and use that sensationalism to continue to resist the reintroduction of these necessary animals into the wild. The bottom line is they are using the well-worn but always effective fear card to get what they want. And what creature on God's green earth is more feared than the wolf? After all, look what happened to Little Red Riding Hood's poor old grandmother. How can you argue with that?"

"Scares me to this day, it does," Victoria Wilds smiled and moved toward the small kitchen. "Let's have some more of that hot tea, Okay?"

"You betcha Professor. Twinkie anyone?"

"Sounds good to me."

Custer County sheriff's report & incident log
7:55 p.m.
*The Mackay ambulance and deputy responded
to a vehicle vs. person accident in Mackay.*

TWENTY-9   HEAR YEA, HEAR YEA ALL

RACHEL FORD WAS LATE FOR THE HEARING. The toll that the all-night drive from Boise, Idaho to Missoula, Montana and two hours sleep had taken was evident. The young activist hated being late for anything so she chaotically tied up her long brown hair in a ponytail. Quickly, she zipped up her make-up bag, tossed it into an oversize leather purse, and headed for the motel door. The day was going to be huge and Rachel wanted to be in the front row to hear the Federal Judge's verdict. The activist was both excited and scared. Rachel and her small staff in the regional offices of the Citizen's Advocacy for Wolves had worked as hard as the lawyers from CAW's national headquarters in Washington, D.C. All of them wanted to prevail in Federal District Court.

Rachel was relieved when she entered the courtroom in the Russell E. Smith Federal Building on East Broadway Street. It was crowded but everyone was still talking so she knew she was on time. Bill Beacon saw Rachel come in and quietly slid in on the bench next to his colleague.

"Boy am I glad you are here. A big day, no?"

Rachel flashed a smile at Bill and pushed her purse under the bench between her legs. "A big day, yes. Any word from national?"

"No, nothing new. You'll need to call them sometime today depending on what the judge says this morning. No matter the decision there will be a lot to do I'm sure."

"Yeah, me too."

"Have you seen this?" Bill handed Rachel a rolled up skinny newspaper.

"Seen what?"

"Just open it up and take a look."

Rachel opened the *Salmon River Sentinel-Record* and the headline hit her like a fast-pitch softball between the eyes.

"You've got to be kidding me. Is this what I think it is? What's this headline?"

"You can read it later but the gist of this story, now get this, is that maybe wolves killed a hunter down near Mackay at a place called Elkhorn Creek near the Chilly Buttes. I'm sure you recognize that name."

"I do. That's the home territory of the Chilly Buttes pack — the ones that have been causing a little stir down in south Custer County with the summer sheepherders. Right?"

"I'm afraid so. It seems that some hunter died up on the plateau and there wasn't enough left of the body to determine clearly the cause of death. It appears that wolves, bears, whatever had scavenged the body pretty badly. I think they have a coroner's inquest scheduled this week to present a final ruling of cause of death."

Rachel tried to skim the story but her mind was racing too fast with the implications.

"I bet this is causing quite a stir in central Idaho."

Bill looked at Rachel and let out a big sigh. "Oh you can count on it. I don't think stir is the right metaphor. More like whirlwind or maybe tsunami might work. When I called the newspaper yesterday to see if I could get hold of the reporter for some details, the secretary said he had gone to see the sheriff about something. She said the sheriff hadn't ruled out homicide in this case."

"Homicide? What's that about?"

"Don't know; that's all she said."

Rachel leaned back on the bench. "Bill you know what the anti-wolf groups are going to do with this story don't you?"

"They've already done it. The web site for the KWiI posted a call for a rally in Challis for Saturday. And get this, the banner over the notice was—you guessed it—*It's time to get the man killers out of Idaho.*"

"Oh wow, here we go. *Man killer!* Give me a break."

The clerk of the court asked all to rise and announced the court in session. The Honorable Judge Henry Barrett was presiding. He entered the courtroom and took the bench. Judge Barrett opened a file folder and leaned forward in his large leather chair.

He didn't hesitate. "First let me say that my decision today will only pertain to granting the extraordinary relief of a preliminary injunction. The Plaintiffs have challenged the U.S. Fish & Wildlife Service's decision to designate and delist the northern Rocky Mountain gray wolf distinct population segment under the Endangered Species Act.

"The Plaintiff's motion is for a preliminary injunction to stop an ongoing scheduled wolf hunt in the state of Idaho, administered by the state of Idaho and following the delisting of the wolf as an endangered species in that state. The Citizen Advocates for Wolves is claiming that if the hunt proceeds, irreparable harm will occur to the reestablished wolf population in Idaho and will again place the wolf in that region in jeopardy of extinction contrary to the provisions of the Endangered Species Act.

"Because there appears, in the judgment of this court, to be insufficient proof as presented by the Plaintiff's filings to support the claim of irreparable harm to the wolf population in Idaho, the request for an injunction to stop the scheduled state hunt is denied. The state of Idaho can proceed with the hunt in accordance with the state's plan for the management of the gray wolf."

Rachel Ford slapped her thigh noiselessly with the rolled up copy of the *Salmon River Sentinel-Record*. She could feel Bill's hand squeeze her forearm as they both rose from the bench. The wolves, she knew, had lost an important round. Bad things were coming. Suddenly she wondered why she had come all the way from Idaho to hear this. "Poor judgment," she said softly to herself as she and Bill made their way out of the Federal Building.

Custer County sheriff's report & incident log
7:55 p.m.
Deputy took a report of credit card fraud from a merchant in Stanley.

THIRTY-0   ENJOY THE HEAT

"THAT'S WHAT THEY WANT IS IT? Well, war they shall have and I hope they enjoy the heat."

Jeremy Junco was not quick to anger. That was one of the reasons the board of directors of the Citizen Advocacy for Wolves hired him. If anything, his life and training forbade irrational outbursts. Junco's arguments, along with an unfailing logic, and his behavior were dictated by reason and science. He was recalled by those who had opposed him in a courtroom as one with ice in his veins. But Junco's veins now boiled and the rational man was angry, very angry. The news that lay across his desk required it. As he stared at the notice, the ice that had long symbolized Junco's actions now heated into a flow of molten lava. The eruption was about to follow.

"Son-of-a-bitch! how can these morons do this? After all we have accomplished, how can they just shoot these magnificent animals?"

The Director of CAW picked up the document and then fiercely slammed it back onto the polished walnut surface. He tensely paced between his office door and the expansive plate glass window that overlooked the Capitol. Barnett Peters stood silent trying not to react to his boss's outburst. He had never witnessed this display before.

Junco finally calmed himself and returned to his leather chair.

"Barnett I want you to go outside and wait for five minutes and then I want you to come back in and be ready to work on a letter I am going to write to our members. Do you understand?"

"Yes sir, five minutes."

"And get in touch with Rachel Ford in our Boise office and let me know as soon as you've made the connection."

"Yes sir."

"And Barnett."

"Yes sir."

"I want you to get angry."

"Yes sir."

Custer County sheriff's report & incident log
7:55 p.m.
A vicious dog was reported near the HUB in Challis.

THIRTY-1   WE'RE LOSING

"RACHEL WE'RE LOSING THE DAMN WAR," Junco shouted in the direction of the speakerphone on the far corner of his desk.

"Our inside man at Idaho Fish and Game leaked me a memo which I have just received. It's circulating within the agency for comment. And guess what it says? No, don't guess. I'll tell you what those bastards want to do. They want to exterminate the Chilly Buttes pack. They claim the pack is responsible for an increase in livestock depredation in the Southern Mountains. As soon as they get the go-ahead from the director, they're calling out the helicopters for the round-up and the aerial extermination of the whole damn lot of them."

"What! Jeremy that can't be right. That's where we have our field tech intervention program going full bore. Jamie Hightower has been doing a great job. Something's not right."

"You're telling me. On every front the anti-wolf extremists are gaining ground and we are losing wolves in the wild and all we have worked for. If we don't turn this around soon, 40 years of work is going to be for nothing." Jeremy was pacing as he spoke across the room and to Rachel Ford 2400 miles away. "What's it feel like on your end?"

Rachel tried to collect her wits. She was tired, really tired. The disappointing trip to Missoula had taken about all the physical energy she had left. The news that Jeremy gave her added to the strain.

"It feels like, oh Jeremy, I feel lost. I thought we were making so much progress. The wolf numbers were up all across the Rockies. Our outreach programs were doing so much. The public was beginning to come around. To be honest, I don't know what to do."

The director walked over to the window and looked out at the Capitol Building less than a mile away. The connection across the country was silent. "Jeremy, are you still there?"

"Yes Rachel I'm here. I hear your tiredness all the way from Idaho. War is hell isn't it?"

"Yes it is."

"Okay. Let's air it all out, all the dirty laundry." Junco sensed he had to pump some new life into their effort; to find some new energy.

"Here's what has happened in the last few months. First, the Feds delisted the wolf from the Environmental Protection Act and turned over control of the reintroduction program to the states. Second, Montana and Idaho instituted the first legal wolf hunt in 60 years. Third, the courts have denied our petitions for injunctive relief for delisting and to stop the wolf hunts. Fourth, other states in the region to wit, Utah, have introduced legislation to legalize the destruction of any migrating wolves into their territories from packs in Yellowstone or Idaho. Fifth, Idaho is instituting an arbitrary aerial campaign to exterminate any wolves that they deem guilty of livestock depredation. Sixth, wolf numbers are declining to dangerous levels all across the original reintroduction area. Have I left anything out?"

"You mean can it get any worse?" Rachel let a short chuckle come out.

Jeremy forced a laugh as well. "Yeah, can it?"

"Well, I guess it can. Jeremy if you're standing up you might want to sit down for this one, number seven in your litany of woes."

"That bad?"

"I'll let you be the judge." Rachel Ford read the director the newspaper article detailing the death of the surgeon from Pocatello. When she finished she said, "What do you think? Bad?"

"Oh my, my! What's your take on this?"

"Well, I can tell you one thing for sure. It's lit a fire under some of the anti-wolf boys. The KWiI is putting together a rally in Challis this weekend. And to add insult to injury, the *Friend's of the Hunter* group just announced their *kill the wolf* derby competition. Can you believe it? Prizes for the most proficient group kill within the various hunting regions of the state. And get this, some very recognizable outdoor outfitter corporations sponsor the prizes. Is that enough, or do you want more?"

"I'm afraid to ask. What?"

"Such as, I think we may have the first of an organized illegal wolf killing group in operation. The ranger at Challis National Forest reported an illegal kill to the sheriff of Custer County."

"We've had those before. What's new about that?"

"Just this... This kill had a note attached that declared that the group was coming together to eliminate the wild wolf from Idaho. Jeremy if this gets any traction we could have a huge problem on our hands. With the number of wolves steadily declining, the viability of the packs is really going to be threatened. Any other pressure on their numbers is going to be catastrophic."

Jeremy let out a long sigh.

"Well, I guess we better get it in gear then hadn't we? I haven't fought this battle for all these years to raise a white flag now. I'm going to get an emergency appeal out to our members today. The first thing we've got to do is get some operating money in the till. And then, I'm going to start to rally the troops at all levels, starting here in Washington, D. C. Rachel, we've got a lot of friends in this fight. We need to let them know how deep a hole we've gotten ourselves in and ask for their help. I'll do that from Washington and you coordinate it in the West. We can't give up now. There's too much at stake."

"We won't," she answered simply.

"I'm coming to Idaho, Rachel. I want to be there at that rally. I want to see how much local support the anti-wolf groups really have. What do you think?"

"I think that would be good. You need to see for yourself. Get outside of the beltway as they say. Let me know your schedule and I'll meet you at the airport."

"I will. And keep me up to date on the hunter's death case. That's important to watch."

"Will do."

"Hang in there Rachel, we'll get through this."

Jeremy hit the intercom button on the phone. "Barnett, come on in here. We've got some work to do. And I want to hear you growl as you come through the door."

"Growl. Yes sir."

<u>Custer County sheriff's report & incident log</u>
2:55 p.m.
Dispatch was advised of a death in Moore.

THIRTY-2   I TOLD YOU SO

"CHESTER I'VE GOT A BIT OF NEWS FOR YOU that you might find interesting."

"Oh yeah, and what would that be?"

"We found an illegal wolf kill this morning on the road coming into the Challis National Forest boundaries up by the earthquake scarp. You know it, there's a little creek running through there called Willow Creek.

"Yeah, I know it."

It was a big male, probably weighed 110 pounds are better. He was wearing a radio collar. Another one of the Chilly Buttes pack is my guess."

Tilghman interrupted the ranger, "I know about it. And he was from the Chilly Buttes pack, you're right?"

"How did you know about it? We just found it."

"Had a young man come to my office. He told me about it. I think you know him—name's Jamie Hightower."

"Sure, I know him. Good kid. Works for CAW as a field tech."

"He does. And now he's working for me. He'll be calling you on a radio we gave him. We're headed up to the scene. There've been several developments in our mystery Rick. Do you have time to meet us there? I'll fill you in then."

"Sure. But you might want to hear what a note says that was attached to the wolf's carcass.

"You bet I would."

"Oh, before I forget. We called the state Fish and Game folks. They're on their way to retrieve the wolf.

"Good. So are you going to tell me what the note said?"

"Just this.

Here is one of your man killers. If you people don't want to take care of these varmints, then the good citizens of Idaho with full protection of our rights will do it for you."

"I don't suppose there was a signature?"

"Nope, that was it. The note was wrapped around the collar with a rubber band."

"How was the wolf killed?"

"I don't know for sure, just a guess. But I'm betting he was poisoned."

The sheriff exhaled slightly before he spoke. "Rick this thing is getting out of hand. I don't know whether you've been to town lately but the emotions are running pretty high around here. That damn newspaper article that Hawk wrote is not helping things a bit. People are lining up on one side or the other and some of them are spoiling for a fight. And, the best I can tell they are going to play rough."

"Chester is there anything I can do for you? I know you've got a load in your wagon."

"As a matter of fact you can. If the state boys get there before we do, ask them if they could do, what do you call it, it's like an autopsy on a dead animal."

"It's called a necropsy."

"Yeah, have them do one those on this critter. I want to know what that animal has had to eat lately. Just a hunch. Can you do that for me?"

"They'd do that anyway on this one because he was collared. He's part of their wolf management plan. Do you think he was at the hunter's banquet?"

"I don't know. Like I said, just a hunch. Charlie and I will be at Elkhorn Creek in about two hours, can you meet us there?. Oh, and we're bringing Wishful with us."

"Wishful? What's he done now?"

"Like I said, I'll fill you in when we get there. We are on our way right now."

"Okay Chester. I'll see you there."

10:25 a.m.
Fish and Game officer investigated report of injured deer at the golf course.

THIRTY-3   FOUR DOGS SNIFF A TREE

RICK CLYDE WAS RIGHT. Most of the snow had disappeared but the climb up Elkhorn Creek was still tough. When they reached the spot where Cahalan's body had been discovered, Tilghman instructed his deputy to move out to the perimeter and snoop around.

"Use your Nez Perce nose Charlie," the sheriff said.

Tilghman put Hot Sauce down and then rotated his gaze slowly around in a wide arc to take in the lay of the land. Everything looked different from the day they found the body. The monochrome of the snow-covered ground had given way to the textures and colors of the dirt and rocks and the stunted brush and trees that lined the wet-weather creek on both sides.

The sheriff could see why the hunter had picked this spot to set up his blind. The field of vision was broad and perfect. It ranged down the long slope all the way to the Big Lost River Valley below. The sheriff noted that the sticks, one leaned against another, which had been the doctor's blind, were still standing.

"Okay Wishful let's go find your badger hole and the good doctor's wallet."

Wishful Wicks appeared to hesitate. "I think it's up this way," he muttered finally.

"There's no thinking to it. Let's go, move it!"

The sheriff followed Wishful closely as they made their way to higher ground. Every few steps Wishful paused and looked back down the ridge, towards the valley below.

"This way Sheriff — I think it's this way." As the two moved higher, Tilghman could see his deputy below occasionally drop down on one knee to study something on the ground. The sheriff liked his deputy. He didn't like to tell him, but Tilghman believed that as he got older there was no way he could do this job without the Indian.

"Here's the spot Sheriff. I'm sure. This is it." Wishful fell to his knees and impatiently began to push dirt and leaves from around a big rock. Soon he rammed his arm up to his shoulder into the hole. "Got it!"

"Well damn it Wishful bring it out and let's all have a look."

"Here you go Sheriff; here you go my fine feathered friend. Didn't old Wishful tell you he knew his holes? Didn't he tell you he was like the badger?"

The wallet was damp and caked with dirt. Tilghman looked at it and at first thought he should preserve the evidence in a plastic bag. Then he said to hell with it. He didn't have any plastic bags on him anyway. He flipped it open. It was empty except for a picture of a woman behind a clear plastic window. The sheriff didn't think it was Sarah Cahalan but he wasn't sure.

Tilghman studied it for a second and then looked deliberately at Wishful. "Well, well, well. You want to tell me what hole you stuffed the contents in. The credit cards, driver's license and, oh yes, the money?"

Wishful Wicks appeared shocked. He frantically looked first away from the sheriff and then back towards the wallet in Tilghman's hand.

"Sheriff, I didn't take nothin' out. I didn't even look in it. I promise on my sweet aunt's mother's grave I didn't. I found it and I buried it. That's what Wishful did, that's what Wishful did for sure. Holy shit, Sheriff, you've got to believe ol' Wishful, you've got to believe ol' Wishful."

Tilghman could see the crazy coot was scared. He had peed in his britches and was swaying back and forth like a hula doll on the dashboard of a 57' Chevy.

"You know Wishful, you're more trouble than a new puppy. If only I could believe one thing you say, I might know what to do. But, since that's impossible..."

Tilghman turned away and started to walk towards his deputy. "Come on you ol' rustic, stay close."

"Charlie," Tilghman hollered at his deputy. "Come over here and look at this."

Charlie slow jogged over to the sheriff. "What is it? Find something?"

"Here's Cahalan's wallet. Empty as Wishful's head. Bag it up for me. You come up with anything yet?"

"Well, take a look at these."

"Well, I'll be the south end of a mule going north." Tilghman took the three shell casings from Charlie's hand.

"What caliber are they Charlie?"

".270. Looks to me like they are fancy hand loads too. These are special."

"Yeah, to fit a special gun wouldn't you think?"

"Without a doubt. If I were a betting man, I'd say they were from the victim's rifle."

"I think that would be a pretty good bet Charlie. I guess we may need to collect that rifle after all. Do you think we will be able to match those casings with it?"

"Oh sure Sheriff, see this pin mark. They're all a bit different where they strike. And those special made guns are always distinctive in one way or another. We'll match 'em."

"Looks like he must have taken several shots at that wolf or at something, wouldn't you say Charlie?"

"At least three for sure. I'll keep looking, there might be more."

"Wait up Charlie. I've got something else I want to try, just to see what happens. You know we've never come up with a cell phone for the victim. People now days don't go anywhere without a cell phone. Even if he had it turned off, my guess is he had one on his person when he was killed or died or whatever happened here. You wouldn't think that a wolf or bear would have eaten the plastic thing, would you?"

"They might have chewed it a bit Sheriff but I don't think they would have swallowed."

The sheriff nodded his agreement. "I'm guessing it is still up here somewhere just lying around waiting for us to find it. I've got an idea. You go over to the west about 50 yards and listen."

"Listen for what?"

"Listen for a phone to ring you thick headed Indian." Tilghman pulled out his cell phone and held it up for Charlie to see. "I've got Cahalan's number in my directory. Let's see if that little bugger will play us a ring-tone in the wilderness."

"Wishful make yourself useful for something besides giving me a headache. You go east about 50 yards and listen for any noise. You hear one you yell. Got it?"

Wishful jumped for joy at being temporarily out of the doghouse. "You betcha Sheriff, any noise, I yell out. I'll yell mighty loud too. Do I need to be deputized for this?"

Tilghman groaned aloud and waited for his deputy and Wishful to move off. He dialed the number. The display said *G B Cahalan* in bright blue letters, and after a second or two the connection was made.

"I've got a connection Charlie," the sheriff shouted. "Listen up you two."

Tilghman swiveled his head trying to hear. He motioned for Charlie to move around. On the third ring, the sheriff thought he heard something but wasn't sure. The fourth ring came and then the message service kicked in. When the beep came Tilghman decided to leave a message, he wasn't sure why, but he did. "Call Tilghman at this number ASAP, do you understand?" is all he said.

"Anything Charlie?"

"Nothing over here," the deputy shouted back.

"How about you Wishful?"

"Nothin' Boss."

Tilghman moved about 50 feet to the east and motioned for Charlie and Wishful to do the same. He hit redial. Again, the connection was made. Four rings and again the message service appeared in the sheriff's display.

"Anything Charlie?"

"Nope, nothing."

Again all three men moved their position and Tilghman punched redial. He nodded at Charlie and Wishful when the connection was made. He could have sworn he heard something apart from the noises of the mountains. But he wasn't sure. He closed the lid on his phone when the message display came up and walked towards Charlie and waved at Wishful to join them.

"Anything, could you hear anything at all?"

"I thought I heard something but I guess not. You going to give up?"

"Yeah, I don't think it's here. Damn it, I wanted to find that phone."

"Sheriff where is Hot Sauce?"

"He's right over...well he was right over there by where the wolf was hung up in that tree. I don't see him...Hot Sauce, come on partner, Hot Sauce, you little devil."

"Sheriff I'll go look for him. The wolves would take about one bite if they got hold of that little guy."

"More like a half bite Charlie. Let's find him before he gets into trouble."

Charlie crossed to the other side of the plateau and moved in behind an outcropping of rock. Tilghman couldn't see him but he heard Charlie shout at him. He moved towards the deputy's voice.

"Did you find him?" The sheriff moved around the rocks and could see Charlie with the squirming Chihuahua in his arms.

"I found him, and look here what else I found." Charlie held out a small black object covered with mud.

"What's that?"

"Hot Sauce dug it up. It's a cell phone."

"Well, I'll be damn. I guess it was ringing and that crime-fighting dog in your arms just went right to it. Like a catfish to a wiggly worm he did."

"I guess he did. Them big ears are for more than show ain't they?"

"Yep, that they are. Well we just might have something here with this phone.

Tilghman fondled the phone. "I wonder how the thing got buried — Charlie, you did say Hot Sauce dug it up?"

"Yep."

"Progress Charlie, we're making progress. We've got the man's wallet and his cell phone, we know where his gun is and I've got his watch in my pocket. Pieces to the puzzle, pieces to the puzzle Charlie."

Ranger Clyde and two of his rangers came up the trail. "Got you a new deputy Sheriff?" Rick nodded toward Wishful Wicks as a sarcastic grin covered his fuzzy face.

"You're a funny man Rick. Look at these. Our scene is giving up some evidence." The sheriff handed the wallet and the cell phone to Rick.

"Whoa, would you look at this."

"Yeah, and we've got some .270 shell casings too. Don't know what it all means but we've got things to chew on."

The ranger looked at Tilghman and said, "That you do my friend that you do. Now chew on this..."

"On what?"

"We've got a break, I think, for another piece of the puzzle. You're not going to believe this but some professor-type down at Boise State picked up a satellite signal for a wolf this morning, in the deep forest. It's one of the Chilly Buttes pack wolves."

"So what's special about that?"

"Just this. That wolf is the one that our victim hunter killed up on that ridge right behind us. The wolf that used to belong to the missing pelt. And guess what, that signal is not stationary, it's moving steadily. But the signal comes and goes. That's strange."

Tilghman motioned for Charlie. "Charlie get on the radio and tell Linda to tell the deputy down at Mackay get us some foul-weather gear together and get it up here pronto."

"Chester," Rick interrupted. "I don't think you want to come on this one. It's going to be a bit rough on that climb up the Borah. And, to tell you the truth, we need to get to it right now. I've got a tracker and some ATVs ready to go."

Sheriff Tilghman paused.

"Okay Rick, this old man will take that slap in the face without comment. Charlie forget the gear, we'll wait this one out in Challis. Rick I'm going to feel like a daddy waiting for his teenage daughter to get home from her first date. So as soon as you find that collar and whatever it is attached to you get back to me, got it?"

"You can rest assured daddy-o, I will do that."

"Who's your tracker?"

"Lincoln Redd, know him?"

"Yeah, I know him. He's an old friend. He'll get you there if anybody can. What do you think is moving that collar around the wilderness?"

"Not sure. Do know it's not the wolf that owned it unless he has a ghost out there. It could be being dragged around by some other critter."

"Or some other person," Tilghman added.

"Or some other person, yes sir. If that were to be the case, you might finally have a good lead on what happened that day to our unfortunate doctor from the Pocatello."

"Wouldn't that be a surprise?" Tilghman watched the rangers move off. "Alright Charlie let's head back to Challis. Where's Wishful?"

"He's right over there," Charlie turned and motioned towards a stand of fir trees, "well he was right over there Sheriff."

"Son's-of-bitches to hell, Charlie. Go find that no account, we need to get out of here."

After an hour spent looking for the escapee, Tilghman and Charlie Two Leaf, with Hot Sauce's front paws leaning against the dashboard, headed to the county seat—they left Wishful Wicks behind somewhere on the mountain.

Custer County sheriff's report & incident log
2:15 p.m.
*Tilghman tagged an abandoned vehicle on Highway 75
near Buffalo Jump.*

THIRTY-4   THE BLOOD NEVER LIES

DR. VICTORIA WILDS CARRIED HER OVERSIZE CUP of black coffee to the meeting room on the second floor of Miller's Hall. The professor had hurriedly arranged for the group of investigators to assemble and report their findings and impressions in the case of the death of Gerald B. Cahalan. She wanted as much information as she could get before she called Sheriff Tilghman. Settling into her chair at the head of the long conference table, the biology professor pulled out the preliminary coroner's report and laid it on top of a stack of papers in front of her.

The deeper she explored the facts surrounding the death the more she became intrigued by complexity of the circumstances. Professor Wilds lived to answer the unanswerable. It had been this singular urge that had brought her into the world of academia in the first place. She often thought that if she hadn't become a scientist she would have become a detective or a forensic expert or something of that sort.

There was a new energy about her the last few days as she pursued the task for the Custer County sheriff. For a reason she couldn't explain, she took a liking to the old lawman, even though his request for help was causing her to fall hopelessly behind on her duties as a teacher. But, for now, she put that aside as she sipped at her coffee and glanced through the report. Occasionally she looked up at her colleagues filing into the meeting room. After all had finally settled, Wilds began.

"First let me say welcome to the campus of Boise State," she started. "We all know each other so I will dispense with the usual formalities. I want every one of you to know how grateful I am that you have agreed to lend your particular expertise to the question before us without compensation. I am sure I can speak for Sheriff Tilghman when I say he and the taxpayers of Custer County are grateful.

"I know you haven't much time to conduct an inquiry and I will take all that you say as preliminary and subject to review and revision. I would like to begin with a synopsis of what we do know so far.

"On the fifth day of October, 2009, the body of Dr. Gerald B. Cahalan was discovered on a small plateau between the western slopes of the Big Lost River Range near the Challis National Forest and U.S. Highway 93 where it intersects Trail Creek Road. This is in the area known as Elkhorn Creek and is near the Chilly Buttes. On that morning the sheriff received a call from two hunters who said that they had been told of the body in that location by an individual known as Wishful Wicks, somewhat of an eccentric well known throughout the region.

"The sheriff, Chester A. Tilghman, and his deputy, Charlie Two Leaf, immediately drove to the location and notified the local coroner. They were joined by the ranger from the Challis National Forest, which borders the death scene. After a preliminary investigation, which was severely restricted by the amount of new snow, the cause of death of Dr. Cahalan was not evident due to the condition of his remains. The initial speculation by the hunters and Mr. Wicks upon questioning by the sheriff and the ranger was that the hunter had been killed by wolves.

"We know that Cahalan was on that ridge hunting wolves. He obviously had been successful that day because a wolf carcass already skinned was hanging in a tree. He was clothed in typical hunting gear although scavengers had torn much of his clothing away. We also know that an established group of wolves known as the Chilly Buttes pack is in the area and very active. In fact, during the preliminary investigation at the site, the wolves were heard calling in the area.

"There are some very troubling facts that also need to be addressed in our observations. As I said, the search of the scene was made very difficult by the weather conditions. The foot of new snow made a normal investigation of the crime scene almost impossible. For example, any animal tracks around the body had been either partially or completely obscured by the new powder or by human tracks at the scene. In addition, items that you would expect to find at the scene were not immediately located.

"One particularly puzzling fact was the absence of the pelt known to have been taken from the wolf killed at that location. The sheriff did find a properly documented wolf permit lying at the base of a tree. This permit and a nearby Toyota FJ Cruiser are how he made an initial identification of the body. I will save the report on the condition of the body for others although I did go to view the remains myself and have some thoughts about their condition.

"One other thing I need to say before we begin our discussion. This inquiry is unofficial. Having said that, I would like to suggest that given the nature of this death, we keep in mind that our comments are likely to be solicited in a court of law at some point in the future. All right, let me ask Dr. Rafael Moncada, our forensic anthropologist and a good friend, to make a few initial comments about the autopsy that was performed on the victim."

Moncada leaned forward in his chair and ran his fingers through his thick black hair. He pushed a small brown spiral notebook to one side.

"Thanks Victoria. I must begin by saying that you have really found yourself a mystery to solve with this. I was present at the autopsy and must restrict my comments to the evidence suggested by that. But before I comment further I would like to raise a cautionary flag. Lacking an eyewitness account, all we can say for sure beyond the facts that Victoria has outlined, is the description of the traumas suffered by the victim. To speculate on who or what caused those injuries and the sequence in which they occurred is problematic to say the least.

"With that in mind, let me also say that the evidence revealed by the autopsy indicates that there is a real probability that Dr. Cahalan died of wounds suffered due to an attack of a large predator. Now I know that the first conclusions put the wolf as the culprit but we cannot rule out the same result occurring because of an attack by a black bear or cougar or even feral dogs. I will ask Dr. Marini to use his expertise as a carnivore biologist to help us understand the differences associated with those kinds of attacks on humans in a moment.

"I want to caution that the same wounds that I am about to describe could also have occurred due to scavenging by the same animals I have just mentioned after the victim was dead. In addition, Dr. Cahalan may have died as the result of some other trauma, accidental or otherwise, death by natural causes or even murder.

"However, let me say up front that the autopsy revealed no evidence of foul play. Again, although I hate to be equivocal, there was so much damage to the body that evidence of murder could have very well been obscured or eliminated by the damage caused by post mortem scavenging. We did see one curious incision-like cut on the lower abdomen that could have been made by a sharp object like a knife. Nevertheless that evidence was inconclusive."

Moncada retrieved his notebook and studied it for a few moments.

"All of the evidence of damage to the victim's body is consistent with an animal attack," he continued. "The type of wounds and the subsequent feeding patterns are consistent with this conclusion. The hunter was likely surprised from behind by one or more predator animals and quickly brought down and killed. It appears that death was swift and we can only hope relatively painless. Having said that; if an animal was the cause of death, it is also important to note that the type of predator cannot be confirmed by the forensic evidence of the autopsy.

"Before I turn it over to Dr. Marini, I would like to make these observations about the condition of the body as it relates to which type of animal might be responsible, if indeed an animal was the culprit. We discovered several claw marks on the body around the shoulders and also around the area of the hips. This might indicate that the body was gripped and dragged about although neither the coroner's report from the scene nor the sheriff's investigative notes indicate that the body had been moved. The claw marks are not indicative of wolf-induced trauma. This is more in keeping with a bear or cougar, particularly a bear."

Professor Wilds interrupted, "Rafael, are you prepared to offer your opinion as to what killed Dr. Cahalan?"

"Well Victoria, before I answer that I would like for you to listen to Josh's comments. Go ahead Josh; tell us what you have discerned from the evidence of the body."

Dr. Josh Marini had been Victoria Wilds graduate advisor ten years before, and the two were the best of friends. As a carnivore biologist, Josh had seen about every form of animal depredation possible. He had taken human remains from crocodiles and tigers. His latest unsavory task was to retrieve the body of a child from a twenty-foot, four-hundred-pound boa constrictor in the Everglades. Victoria was anxious to hear his observations.

"I can say right from the start there are more mysteries here than answers. I observed…"

"Excuse me please," a graduate assistant stuck his head in the door, "Professor Wilds, a Sheriff Tilghman is here to see you."

Wilds gave a quick nod to the group. "That's good, would you please show him in?"

The assistant moved away from the door. "Well gentlemen I guess we will get the chance to brief the sheriff in person. I hadn't expected this but I'm happy he is here. It will save us time."

Sheriff Tilghman came into the room with his big broad-brimmed hat in hand. He seemed a bit ill at ease as he walked directly to Victoria Wilds and extended his hand.

"My apologies for this surprise. I hope I'm not imposing."

"Not at all Sheriff. We are very glad that you are here. It will save all of us a great deal of time to be able to speak to you directly about the group's findings. Please let me introduce you to the people that I have asked to help us out with this investigation."

Professor Wilds carried out the introductions without hurry and the sheriff seemed to relax as he took his seat next to Wilds.

"As I was saying," Josh Marini picked up where he had left off. "There are as many questions posed by our examination of the remains as there are answers. For example, the claw marks mentioned by Rafael are not consistent with a wolf attack. Wolves kill primarily with their teeth. Although we did find teeth imprints, both upper and lower jaw, on the victim's forearms; and there was flesh removed from that area. In addition, there were only two clearly discernible bite marks on the torso outside the area where massive amount of flesh had been removed. In both cases, there was no clear impression of pre-molars, which you would expect from a wolf attack. Again, I must be ambiguous. In many cases, it is very hard if not impossible to determine the species responsible for the depredation given that the bite marks of an adult wolf and a similar size black bear are very nearly the same.

"Victoria I will give a detailed description of my findings in report form for you and Sheriff Tilghman but I can give you my conclusions now. I must say that in the absence of an eyewitness account that it is virtually impossible to say with any degree of certainty the cause of death. Most of the soft flesh had been removed which made it impossible to determine whether an animal attack had caused the victim's demise or whether that fact merely indicated scavenging post mortem. Also, the fact that the body had not been disarticulated probably indicates that the feeding was interrupted by some disturbance. Furthermore, we are hampered by the lack of evidence from the scene. The inability to observe and document the animal and other tracks around the body provides a great gap in the evidentiary chain that might help us reconstruct the event."

Rafael Moncada interrupted. "I too share Josh's conclusions. But, let me add this speculation. If, for example, there is no evidence of human foul play involved in this man's death, then I think the case can be made for animal attack. And, if that supposition is reasonably supported by the evidence, then I for one think the likely cause of death would have to be wolves. I say this because of several factors that we do know. First, we know clearly there were wolves in the vicinity. The fact that the hunter had shot a male of the Chilly Buttes pack supports that. Second, in discussion with the managing ranger of the Challis National Forest, he assured me that there had been no cases of black bear or cougar sightings in that area all summer. And, as far as bear are concerned, they most likely had retired to their winter dens by the time the attack occurred. Josh may dispute this but I am assuming that a cougar would most likely have dragged the body to some form of isolated shelter before feeding. Although having said that, I too caution against making any definitive conclusions. We just don't have the evidence."

Wilds monitored the silence that filled the room for a few moments. "Well I suppose that's not too encouraging for you Sheriff. But before we open it up for a general give-and-take let me ask Erin Moss, our wolf biologist, who is here today. Erin is from the Idaho Fish and Game Department. He has been working on the wolf re-introduction from the beginning of the program in the 90s. Erin what do you see here?"

"A mess—a mess in more ways than one. As you might expect we are very sensitive in the agency to any claim that wolves are responsible for aggressive behavior against livestock or humans. We walk a tightrope between our duties at the agency and public opinion on this issue all the time. You see this is not just a simple case of a wolf stepping over some boundary. This is the kind of question that takes on both a biological and political significance. So whatever we conclude best be as near to right as we can make it.

"We have been studying for some time now documented cases of wolf attacks on humans. Not just here but around the world. Of the 60 odd cases I have reviewed, we have found evidence in about half of them that healthy wolves can and will become aggressive towards humans. Moreover, I will say that I also agree with Dr. Marini's conclusion that the bear or the cougar is not likely the culprit as far as the feeding on the victim's remains is concerned.

"In the case of death by bear attack, usually you see severe head trauma. In this case, even though the flesh from the face was removed, the skull was intact. Also, you might note that the feeding patterns on the body were in several areas. This too is inconsistent with a lone predator such as a bear but common among group feeding animals such as wolves. Most of the victim's stomach and intestines were consumed as were the flesh around the thighs down to the knees. The chest cavity was also cleaned out. The man's heart was gone, which is part of the body preferred by wolves. There were also a couple of bite marks on the lower legs that were made from behind. This too is consistent to wolf attack.

"But at the end of the day, I too must be cautious. There is just not enough evidence in cases of wolves attacking, killing and consuming humans to say with any scientific degree of certainty that this is the case here."

The room fell silent as everyone looked toward Professor Wilds. "Thank you gentlemen, thank you all. Sheriff, do you have any questions you would like to ask our experts?"

"Just one Professor, just one." The sheriff stood up and extended his six-foot-five frame. "Who or what caused the death of Dr. Gerald B. Cahalan up on Elkhorn Creek?" Tilghman paused for effect.

"Right now I have these possibilities. It could have been wolves, bears, or cougars. It could have been another hunter deliberately or by accident. It could have been by natural causes. Maybe the man's heart just quit on him during all the excitement of the hunt. Although no one has suggested it, I don't think I could even rule out aliens."

The sheriff displayed a big smile, but the members of Wilds' ad-hoc investigative committee didn't appear to appreciate his humor. The sheriff returned to a serious expression quickly as he felt the rush of blood to his face.

Custer County sheriff's report & incident log
8:35 p.m.
Deputy investigated a report of harassment in Challis.

THIRTY-5   A RUDE WAY TO LEAVE

THE SHERIFF FELT AN EDGY LONELINESS as he drove back to Challis. Driving in the mountains was a time he normally enjoyed. It was a time to be alone and to think. But this trip was different. The self-inflicted sting of embarrassment at the meeting in Boise was still fresh. He disliked that feeling. He hated that he had done it in front of Victoria Wilds, someone he liked.

There was a light snow falling and he put the wipers on intermittent. His hands were cold so he turned the heater up a notch. He flexed his fingers to move the blood. The Idaho winters were getting harder to take as he aged. Tilghman suddenly hated the thought of growing old alone.

He missed his wife. His rock, he always called Maggie. Whenever he couldn't seem to get something straight, she would help him think through it. Most times, he'd talk and she would listen. But the conclusion would be clearer to him after their one-way discussion. Not like now. Nothing was clear.

Tilghman reached over, plucked the sleeping Hot Sauce from the passenger's seat, and put the insignificant dog in his lap. The sheriff resisted, but his thoughts drifted back to the Cahalan case—to the meeting at Boise State that went nowhere and decided nothing.

"A man dies in the snow," he said aloud as he stroked his Chihuahua behind his oversized ears. The sheriff let his thoughts roam as he drove northeast.

A man dies alone and cold in a desolate and bleak place. His body torn in bloody bits by creatures in an intolerant wildness. I want to know what happened. How it happened.

"Not for my sake," he spoke again, "but for his." Hot Sauce squirmed in the sheriff's lap.

The man was born, he worked and planned and schemed to shape some pre-conceived end. Then, in spite of it all, he came to a gruesome and unthinkable end, an end he could never have imagined, not in his wildest dreams.

Where in the hell is the justice in that? Forget justice, where is the damn purpose? Is God's hand in this mix? Could He have anything to do with such a tragedy? God or otherwise, what does it matter if your flesh is consumed by some wild and terrible beast or merely by a bunch of worms? It's all the same. It's all there is. Maybe it's all there should be.

Tilghman watched the mountains pass by for a time.

But I want to know. This case may be my last. I don't want it to be the one that goes unsolved – to be what they remember me for—the one that I have to wake up at night and wonder if I had followed this lead or that might have come to a resolution. I have enough nightmares as it is.

Maggie would have wanted to know too. Even if it were my last one, she would have wanted to know what happened to Cahalan. She believed in justice. The human kind.

She hated to hear of the human cruelty I witnessed. It made her angry. I'd kid her that I was glad I was the sheriff and carried the gun and not her. She'd laugh and shake her head when I'd suggest she'd be like those Wild West lawmen: the ones that shot first and asked questions later, the ones that called their actions justice. She would have too. She hated the long drawn out legal process that afforded every right to those that were villains.

If Cahalan had been killed and left to the ways of the forest and its creatures by some fellow human, I want to know. Find the culprit in the woods and confront him with the facts of his evil. Invite him to run. No, to attack. A chance to bring a western justice to his final moments. That's what Maggie would want me to do.

Hot Sauce stirred a little in Tilghman's lap and licked at the sheriff's hand.

Sheriff Tilghman swallowed hard. The old lawman wiped the moisture from his eyes and turned the heater down. It was getting hot.

Custer County sheriff's report & incident log
10:15 p.m.
Deputy Wilman took a report of property damage in
Mackay.

THIRTY-6   WINNEMUCCA BOUND

"WELCOME HOME SHERIFF," Linda greeted the sheriff as he came in through the back entrance to the jail past the row of three cells with their stacked bunks and complement of prisoners. "How'd it go at Boise State?"

The sheriff hesitated before he responded to the question.

"Another dead-end, and I'm not tryin' to be funny. The fact is I'm 'bout ready to give this case over to the state boys. Any word from Ranger Clyde about the collar?"

"The what?"

"The radio-collar of that damn dead wolf Linda. Wake up!"

"Oh, sorry." Linda was surprised by the sheriff's display of anger.

"Yeah. He called. Another one of your dead-ends. He said the signal just quit. They had to turn around and come back.

"CJ Fry called too. He wondered if you were going to the gathering in Winnemucca this weekend — said he could use a ride." The dispatcher followed the sheriff into his office past the counter that separated the dispatcher's station from the lobby.

Tilghman looked down at the pile of paperwork that covered the fake oak desk.

"To hell with this. Tell him yes to both questions. I've got to get away from this damn place for a while if I'm going to keep my sanity. Call him for me, will you?"

"Sure Sheriff. And Sheriff," Linda turned back as she reached the door. "I think it's a good idea."

"What's that?"

"I'm glad you're going down to be with all those no account cowboys for a couple of days. It will do you some good."

"You're such a mother hen.

"Tell CJ to meet me here at the courthouse early Friday morning and we'll head out before the sun gets above the eastern mountains. And you tell that old worthless range rat that if he ain't here on time for once I'm leaving him in the street. You tell him that for me. And use those exact words."

"That I will Sheriff. Range rat, gotcha."

Tilghman felt better. He liked the gatherings. He liked CJ Fry. He peered at the wall and at his picture on the stage from last year. He thought his big Stetson hat and blue wool vest looked mighty handsome for an old guy. He liked seeing himself in something other than a badge and gun. He liked the gentleness of the image. He studied his picture and then the one of his great-great grandfather next to it. Tilghman laughed aloud as he thought about that famous lawman getting on a dance hall stage in Dodge City and reciting a stanza of cowboy verse.

Maggie returned to his thoughts as he stared at the picture. He couldn't get her out of his mind. She liked that picture, he knew she did. She had wanted Chester to get involved with the cowboy poets. She chided him to do something besides chasing bad people around Custer County. She said she just wanted to talk about something besides all the troubles he brought home from the courthouse. She was tired and wanted a bit of sunshine, she chided, to go with all the dark clouds.

The truth be known, the sheriff figured his wife wanted him to quit being Sheriff altogether. When things were tough he did too. Tough like now. But, he didn't know anything else and he damn sure wasn't ready to retire. Not just yet. He promised Maggie just one more election and that was it. She agreed if, if he started writing cowboy poetry and performing at gatherings. As she put it, "before this world we have known all of our lives is gone forever."

Her comment had gotten his attention. He never knew Maggie paid notice to such things. Tilghman had long suspected that America's Great West was moving to something he didn't recognize or understand—but he didn't know Maggie did too. He hated the vision he conjured of the future. Everything was different by the day. The rules, the people, the values, everything was changing from the way it was to the way it would be. And, everything that he and Maggie saw about the way it would be, they didn't understand or like. But they could do nothing but watch and get ready. To get ready for the worst and hope for the best.

Custer County sheriff's report & incident log
5:15 a.m.
*Challis fire and ambulance volunteers responded to
vehicle rollover on Highway 75.*

THIRTY-7 TILTED CROSSES

THE TRAVELING COWBOYS HAD JUST MADE A PIT STOP in Elko, Nevada and pulled back up to speed on Interstate 80, headed west to Winnemucca. The two had been on the road for over eight hours and both had sore butts. CJ Fry was eating again. This time he was chewing on a breakfast burrito and loudly slurping a fountain root beer.

Tilghman was driving. He had the whole way. He was anxious to get to Winnemucca. He wanted to relax and practice his poetry before the Saturday morning performance.

"CJ are you going to sing those same old songs you always do?" Tilghman knew the answer but prodded a little conversation to pass the time.

"Yep. They're the only ones I know and I'm too damn old to learn new ones. Besides, most folks like 'em anyway. What about you Chester? You got anything new?"

"Yeah, as a matter of fact you ol' reprobate I've got a new poem I kind of like. I think I'll try it out on this bunch."

"Try it out on me, why don't you?"

"Kind of hoping you would ask. I could use the practice."

"Well then just go about your practicin'. Don't mind me."

Tilghman cleared his throat and tried to get the first line to step forward. He had never been much at performing in front of people. It got easier the more he made himself do it, but he always

197

got nervous at the prospect of making a mistake. He cleared his throat one more time and began. "It's called *Tilted Crosses*."

> *What makes these drovers think their friend is of a different kind?*
> > *This pale and lifeless kid cowboy waitin' for a box of pine,*
> > > *I'll tell you somethin' for sure, they're all the same to me,*
> > > > *Strip away the boots and leggings and big hog-legs, and all I see is misery.*
> > > *But still they make believe there is something different about the way he died,*
> > *Bloody clothes and bullet holes and revenge on their minds.*
> *What an undertaker knows for sure not many will admit,*
> > > *These rough and tumble trailing boys should never take time to lament.*
> *For just as we say grace for one, another comes along,*
> > > *To take his place on the coolin' slab to hear the buryin' song.*
> > *So beat the drum slowly and play the fife lowly is how the tune does go,*
> > > *And bear your friend up the ol' Boot Hill and sing him the buryin' song.*
> > *Scratch him a hole in the soft sand and take account of your losses,*
> > > *And as you turn to walk away, look back at all the tilted crosses.*

After Tilghman had finished CJ remained silent and gnawed on his third breakfast burrito.

Finally Tilghman said, "Okay, aren't you going to tell me what you think?"

"Just hold on. I'm thinking. I'm thinking I might like it. Chester you're not a bad poet. No sir, you ain't."

"Thank you. Too damn bad I have to drag it out of you."

Silence returned as they burned highway miles toward Winnemucca. Hot Sauce had gotten comfortable in CJ's lap and was asleep. CJ took another loud slurp.

Tilghman unconsciously pushed the gas pedal down and kicked the Jeep up about ten miles an hour.

<u>Custer County sheriff's report & incident log</u>
6:15 p.m.
Constance Quick investigated a complaint
of a wild pack of dogs near Leslie.

THIRTY-8   TWO MEANS DON'T MAKE A RIGHT

"CJ WHAT DO YOU THINK MAKES A MAN MEAN?" The pair had made another 100 miles but still had a ways to go.

CJ continued to look out the passenger window as they sped along Interstate 80, toward Winnemucca, Nevada. He had known Chester long enough to know that his old friend was occasionally taken with the philosophical. Usually CJ just let the sheriff talk himself through it without much comment. This time he decided to play along. He was as bored with the long drive as Chester and wanted to be there. Maybe a little philosophy would shorten the journey.

"You know...I mean, where does that meanness come from?" Tilghman continued. "Why is it in some and not all? What gives rise to it or is it just in some by some kind of birthright?"

"You want to give me a notion of the kind of meanness you have in mind?" CJ offered.

"Oh CJ, I could give you dozens of them. You don't do the kind of work I do without having to deal with the meanness of people on a regular basis. But, you know what? You never really get used to it, let alone understand it. If you could, maybe it would make it a bit more tolerable. Does that make any sense?"

"So what you want me to tell you is, why are some folks mean to other folks, is that it?"

"Yep, that puts it in a sack all right. Where does all this meanness that we are swimmin' in come from?"

CJ had to think before he jumped in. Nervously he picked up Hot Sauce and held him to his chest. The little dog didn't protest.

"Well let me see Chester. Maybe it comes from many places. You know, comes from circumstance. Let me think on it."

Another five miles went by before CJ finally spoke up.

"What about revenge? Like, say revenge against somebody that you think has done you wrong. That's it, the eye-for-an-eye thing. Even as old as you are, you can still remember when you were a kid and some other kid was mean to you, right? You know, made fun of you or hit you or stole your bike or anything like that. What did you do? Well I know what I did. I was damn well mean right back. I got even I did. So there, there is one reason for meanness, ain't it?"

"I suppose. But that's kid stuff. That's being mean on a small scale. That's more spite than mean. You never really did any permanent damage. Just kid stuff."

Chester hit the passing gear to move around a line of trucks, and the two men waited until the speedometer had crept back to five over the limit.

"When you were a kid, too, you really didn't know for sure what to do. The turn-the-other-cheek kind of thinking hadn't taken hold yet. So you took a blow and gave a blow without a whole lot of consideration. The kind of meanness I think I'm talking about is the kind of meanness in grownups. The kind that is reasoned and calculated — the kind that is planned and then carried out. It's the kind of meanness that scares a good person. Scares them because they can't understand it. The kind that is hard to anticipate, to prepare for. The kind that comes out of the blue and knocks you down in the dirt. You know? That kind of meanness."

"Well, Chester, maybe then the kind you're talking about is nothing more than meanness for a purpose, like power or gain, you think?"

"You mean like meanness is just a tool to get to something else you want?"

"Yeah, why not? I think that's what I meant. It's kind of like all the meanness down in Mexico right now. You know, with all the drug war stuff and men cutting off other men's heads over a bunch of white powder. Now that's what I call mean. They do those horrible things to one another to get something... power, money, things like that. Meanness is just another tool in their bag. Like bribery say, or kidnapping. Like that."

Chester let the point settle for a second.

"Just a means to an end then. Do you think those kind of men choose not to do the right thing. I mean do you think they know better but still make the choice to go ahead and be mean to their fellow man? Or are they truly ignorant of the right thing to do?"

"No, they damn sure know what they're doing. All that stuff they do to one another can't be put down as being stupid. Ain't most of those Mexicans raised in the Catholic Church? They may have a path to forgiveness but they still know Jesus' teachings. I don't think Jesus would let them get away with cutting heads off, do you?"

"Well CJ maybe that's it. Maybe the fall of man can explain it. If everyone was goody two-shoes then the Bible wouldn't be very credible, now would it? All that stuff about Adam eating the apple and falling out of Grace. God needs meanness to prove a point maybe. Maybe God makes man mean."

"I wouldn't let Reverend Conner hear you say that Chester."

"Oh, the good Reverend gave up on me years back. Besides, the meanness of man keeps the preacher in business too. If everybody was good they wouldn't have much of a message to make every Sunday would they? As far as that goes, I suppose I'd be out of work myself."

"Nope, I guess not. It's kind of sad though in a way, ain't it? I mean all the pain folks inflict on one another. Kind of sad."

"Yeah, kind of sad CJ, to say the least. I read something the other day about a study some of them university types did somewhere. They looked at kids, young kids around three years old and the like. They followed a group of them into adulthood. What they discovered was that youngsters who didn't respond to the normal threats of pain did things without worrying about the consequences. These kids were much more likely to grow up and become criminals. It's like they just didn't care what happened to them. Now that's a scary idea."

CJ thought on Chester's point for a moment. "I know. I remember kids that would get spanked almost every day and it didn't faze them, not one bit. They'd go right back to doing what got them licked in the first place. Boy not me. My pap put the belt to me and I said that's enough of that. I didn't want no more of that stuff. No sir-ree-bob."

"So maybe CJ, in the end it's just genetic like they say. Some folks are just wired to be mean. I've gotten where I can pretty much tell by looking at someone if they're bad guys or not. I do it all the time. A stranger comes through Challis and I put the meanness label on him right away. Some of them I don't hardly let out of sight when they're in town. Others I don't pay a second look to. The scary thing is that I'm right far more often than I am wrong. It's like I've got this meanness instinct that takes over my sense of justice and fairness and everything else. I kind of throw out the idea of the innocent until proven guilty thing. Certain ones are just as guilty as sin from the get-go. They don't have to do a thing. If I had my way, I'd just lock the sons-of-bitches up right then and there. Save all the trouble."

"Chester, do you ever think it might be time to retire the badge?"

"Do I ever. Do I ever. I reckon I just don't know what I would do with myself. You know, without the badge and the gun. I've toted them around for so long it's like they're tattooed to my skin."

"What's really eatin' you Chester?"

Tilghman didn't answer his friend. He looked out the driver's side window pretending that he didn't hear the question.

"Chester."

"I heard you CJ. You want to hear another cowboy poem?"

"No, not right now."

Custer County sheriff's report & incident log
6:15 p.m.
Tilghman advised that a vehicle had
suffered hit and run damage on Main Street.

THIRTY-9   WOLVES: SMOKE A PACK A DAY

THE FIRST BUSLOAD ARRIVED JUST AFTER SUNUP. The dingy yellow school bus parked between the Challis Lodge and Lounge and the Yankee Fork historical marker and unloaded its passengers. Most of the adults raised hand painted signs as they stepped off the bus. Some of the kids had their faces painted in colorful patterns.

The mood was festive. By 9 a.m., the wide Main Street in Challis was lined on both sides with parked cars and buses. Several cars from Wyoming and Montana interspersed with the locals. The crowd began to swell in the west end park across from the National Forest Regional Field Office on Highway 93. A half-dozen men went to work erecting a makeshift speaker's stand just below the large area map displayed between two large square posts. The morning was chilly, but the early sun warmed the skin, and the cold air kept the first to arrive active. There was little wind coming off the mountains so the weather was perfect for the planned activities.

"Sheriff Tilghman," Linda stuck her head into the sheriff's office and looked back over her shoulder to the back of the courthouse; "you'd better come take a look at this."

"At what Linda? I'm kind of occupied at the moment."

Just as Tilghman spoke, he began to hear the shouts coming through the walls. "What's that?"

"That's what I'm talking about. You'd better come see for yourself."

Tilghman pushed back his chair and walked out of the office and to the front door of the sheriff's doublewide trailer. "Holy shit," he muttered under his breath, "it looks like the million man march right down Main Street. What is this all about?" as he turned back to his dispatcher.

Linda answered, a bit sarcastically, that the sheriff should read the signs. *"Kill the wolf before the wolf kills you,"* Tilghman read aloud.

"My, my, my, the power of the press, it never ceases to amaze me. I told Hawk he was going to stir the pot to a boil with that story. Well he got it done. Linda, call Charlie and tell him to come back home, we may need him before this is over."

"Sheriff, don't you remember? Charlie's on vacation. He's heading back to the rez this afternoon."

"I know that Linda and I don't care. Call him. Tell him to find me on the street. I'm going out to mingle and see where our little protest movement is likely to head."

"Will do. And Sheriff, you might want to take your *I Love Wolves* lapel pin off before you go mix in with this crowd," Linda smiled.

"Very funny Chief Dispatcher. Just get in touch with Charlie."

"Right."

The protest wasn't really a surprise; Lioncamp had forewarned the sheriff of the KWil's plans in advance. What did surprise him was the numbers that were coming to his town, especially on a Monday. The sheriff knew everyone in Custer County, but Challis was filled with strangers from all over the state. He was feeling a bit uneasy. The tone on the signs bothered him. *Kill the wolf before the wolf kills you* was one that was a little raw by his standards. *Trap, poison and shoot the creatures, just kill them* he didn't particularly appreciate either.

As the sheriff neared the park, he saw a table on the north side occupied by several men that were members of the KWiI. A large sign read *Sign our petition to the Governor*. Tilghman headed for it.

"Good morning boys, nice day for a protest isn't it?"

A man that Tilghman didn't know stepped forward and extended his hand.

"A nice day indeed Sheriff, I'm Billy Hagerstaff. What do you think of our gathering?"

"Kind of impressive Mr. Hagerstaff. Looks like you fellows are stirring up the natives pretty good on this wolf question. What's the petition about?"

"It's one I bet you're going to want to sign yourself Sheriff. We're trying to get enough signatures to get a state-wide referendum passed. We're demanding that the state legislature get a little backbone for a change and deal with these killers that the feds and those eastern greenies have imposed on the good folks in Idaho. We're sick and tired of outsiders telling us how to run our state and our lives. And now, by golly, I think we've got things going our way."

Tilghman picked up a clipboard with a petition sheet attached and looked over some of the names. "How's that?" he asked without looking up.

"Oh, the killing of that poor hunter up at Chilly Buttes did the trick. People are scared. If those varmints can kill a hunter then it's just a matter of time before they get one of our kids stepping off a school bus. Mr. Jackson up at Salmon…"

"Whoa! You're jumping a bit ahead of the horse. There's no evidence that wolves killed that man. None that I know of."

"Heck with your evidence Sheriff, we don't need no evidence. We know the truth and we're going to act on it. Just look around you. The good folks of Idaho are finally stirred up. We've got a runaway train going and, I'll tell you we're going to get some action out of the state capital or we'll clean them out come election time too."

Sheriff Tilghman just nodded. "Where's Hector Lioncamp? I'd like to talk with him."

"He should be over on the other side of the park. He's going to lead the march through town at noon."

"Thanks, I'll see if I can find him."

"Oh, Sheriff. You forgot to sign the petition."

"Maybe later Mr. Hagerstaff, maybe later."

As Tilghman stepped away from the petition table, a hand caught him by the left arm. The sheriff turned quickly and faced a man dressed in *L.L. Bean*.

"Excuse me, I'm assuming you're the sheriff here in Challis, correct?" The man was about three-fourths Tilghman's height and looked up through thick smoke gray sunglasses. He smiled broadly and had a young woman close at his side.

He turned to her, "This is Rachel Ford. She and I have come from Boise to visit with you."

"Well, you're right about the first point. I am the sheriff of Custer County but I'm afraid you've got me at a disadvantage..."

"Oh, I'm sorry. My name is Jeremy Junco. I'm visiting from Washington, D.C. Miss Ford and I represent *Citizen Advocacy for the Wolf*. I'm sure you know about us and our work here in Idaho, right?"

Tilghman paused and gave a long look at Rachel Ford. Finally, he turned back to Junco. "I do that. But I have to admit I'm a bit surprised to see you here in Challis, especially on a day like we have here. You're a tad far from your perch aren't you?"

"Indeed Sheriff. Unfortunately, I do know what you mean. And that may be part of the reason we've got this gathering today in your town. And quite a gathering it is, wouldn't you agree?"

"I would Mr. Junco. Can I do something for you?"

"Well, for starters, you can tell me how to counter the attitude that this protest represents. As you are aware, we at CAW believe the wolf is a rightful resident of this state. And part of our job is to educate the people to the important role the wolf plays in the overall ecosystem. Obviously, we're not doing a very good job with the locals."

"That's a fact. But that's your business and it's a business I can't help you with. Now, if you'll excuse me…"

"Wait Sheriff, Tilghman isn't it?"

"It is."

"I've got something else to ask you. It's about that unfortunate incident with the hunter. You know the one that was found dead up near Chilly Buttes on the Elkhorn Creek."

"Oh."

"Well you see … well you see, we might be able to help you with that case."

The sheriff straightened, "How do you mean?"

"To tell you the truth, I'm not sure myself. You see we have a field technician up in that range. He's been working with the herders up on BLM land all summer. We have a program that attempts to minimize the impact of the wolf on the flocks that graze on government land in the summer. Tries to do it without killing the wolves. The young man knows the Chilly Buttes wolf pack very well."

The sheriff interrupted. "His name is Jamie Hightower, right?"

"Well yes, do you know of him?"

"I met the young man on more than one occasion this year. Good kid. Says he grew up on Boys Ranch near Amarillo, Texas. I've been there myself years ago. We talked about it some."

Junco shot a quick glance toward Rachel before he responded. "Sheriff, there is something you should know about Jamie."

"What's that?"

"He didn't grow up on Boys Ranch."

"No?"

"No, he's the son of Canada and Metilda Hightower. Metilda is my sister. You see Canada, Jamie's father, was a very successful rancher in the Panhandle just outside Amarillo. He's the one that grew up on Boys Ranch. He used to take Jamie with him every year at rodeo time to visit Boys Ranch. But Canada died tragically in a roping accident on his ranch when Jamie was ten. The boy never really got over losing his dad. He tells everyone he was an orphan, thus the Boys Ranch story.

"So he lied to me about that?"

"I'm afraid he did. Sheriff, my nephew is a very sensitive kid. That's why we brought him to this country for the summer. My sister and I thought that the remoteness and the adventure of it would do him good. And, as far as we could tell, it worked. Jamie loved the outdoors work and he especially took to the wolves. He proved to be one of the best night watchmen we've ever had."

"I see. Are you aware that your nephew was the victim of a pretty brutal assault here in Challis last summer?"

"No, I wasn't," Junco turned to glance at Rachel then turned back to the sheriff. "What happened?"

"One of our good citizens, a sheep rancher, took exception to the work he was doing with the wolves and beat the boy severely. We arrested the man, but Jamie wouldn't file charges so we let him go. And then there is the matter of the rifle."

"The rifle—what rifle?"

"The rifle that belonged to the hunter that was found dead. Jamie brought it to us. Said he found it."

"Sheriff Tilghman, that lends a bit of urgency to what I was going to ask you. You see we haven't heard from Jamie since the end of the season. He's through with his regular duties and we were expecting him to head back to Texas, but his mother hasn't heard from him. We're getting a little concerned."

"He's working for me."

"For you? Sheriff you are certainly full of surprises. How is he working for you?"

"It's complicated. But it seems we both think Jamie can help us solve the question of the dead hunter. Walk with me through the crowd and I'll fill you in."

"All right, but before you do I think there is something else about Jamie I want to tell you. You see, the boy really knows how to use the kind of rifle he brought to you."

Tilghman stopped and turned back to face Junco. "What do you mean?"

"Just that. Jamie is an expert marksman. He could take a horsefly off the end of your nose at three hundred yards and all you would feel would be a little heat. And I'm not making a joke. This kid is good. His father gave him a Winchester, model 70, I think, for his fourteenth birthday. From then on, all through high school, Jamie lived and ate marksman practice. He won the state championship for his school two years running before he graduated. You put a rifle in his hands and something came over him. It got as calm as the eye of a hurricane. Nothing bothered him. He could focus on a target like no one else I've ever seen. Hell, the Marines even tried to recruit him right out of high school for sniper training. He would have gone too but his mother wanted him to take the summer off and come up here. She couldn't take the thought of her son becoming an assassin. That's part of why he's here in the mountains."

Junco paused for a moment and motioned for Rachel to rejoin the two men. "I'm glad he gave you the rifle back."

"I gave it right back to him," the sheriff said.

Junco looked surprised, "Why?"

"Like I said, let's head back to my office and I'll tell you the whole of it.

<u>Custer County sheriff's report & incident log</u>
6:15 p.m.
Deputy was advised of some stolen fruits and
vegetables from a road-side stand in Moore.

FORTY-0   I CAN FX THAT

"MY NAME IS BOSCO FX." The little man with a belly that protruded over his belt nodded toward Linda as the dispatcher left the sheriff's office. He held up his hand toward the sheriff.

"Please before you make a joke, I've heard them all. The name is a bit strange I know. I'm here because I think I can help you with a case you have. The Cahalan death, I believe it is."

The sheriff stood up from his desk and towered over the little dump of a man like a statue does over a pigeon. "You must be from Hollywood Mr. Fx." The sheriff grinned broadly, "Pardon me I couldn't resist."

"No pardon needed Sheriff, I'm used to it, believe me. No actually, I'm from Oregon. I'm what some call an animal forensic specialist."

"Well, how 'bout that," the sheriff answered. "And what would that be Mr. Fx?"

"Let me explain. I read about your case in the Portland newspaper. I think they picked it up from an AP feed that got it from your local rag. Some wolves ate a hunter up pretty bad, right?"

"Yes sir, that's the way some would like to tell it."

"Sheriff I travel the country offering my services for any criminal case that involves animals. My headquarters is in that RV out front." Bosco leaned towards the window and pointed.

Tilghman did likewise and looked out at a long silver RV with *Fx Services* stenciled in ornate letters covering most of the side.

"Believe me, I can tell you might near anything you want to know about animals. Especially animals that are involved in a criminal matter."

The sheriff again glanced out the window and then at Mr. Fx. "Can you tell me whether or not wolves killed a man, Mr. Fx?"

"That's why I'm at your doorstep sir. I might just be able to do just that, if you'll permit me to help."

"If you could answer that one question for me, I'd buy your breakfast. That's about all I could afford to pay you." Tilghman moved to his desk. "You might find more fertile ground in a big city Mr. Fx than in Challis, Idaho."

"No doubt I could Sheriff. But you see, believe it if you will, I'm not a man chasing money. I've got all of that I'll ever need. No sir, I'm what you might call a techno nut. Made my fortune in technology and now I'm out for a little fun. And fun for me is solving a mystery."

Tilghman sat down heavily in his chair. The sheriff didn't know how to take the man from Portland. So, as he usually did when something or someone puzzled him, he kept his mouth shut and just stared.

"Sheriff, do you know much about forensics?"

"You mean that crime lab stuff on TV?"

"Sort of. Specifically, it is the application of science to the law, in this case, the criminal law."

"Mr. Fx we're a back-water jurisdiction here in central Idaho. We don't have budgets for all the fancy technology. I'm lucky to keep a couple of deputies on the payroll."

"I figured as much Sheriff. That's part of the reason I'm here. Like I said, I don't do this work for the money. I do it for the thrill it gives me. You know, doing good for my fellow animal and all that."

Bosco approached the window. "That trailer," he again pointed toward the parking lot, "is full of the state-of-the-art scientific crime fighting technology. If you'll trust me with the evidence in the Cahalan case, I might be able to help you come to some conclusion. What do you say?"

Tilghman didn't immediately respond. Finally, he looked directly at Fx. "Can I trust you Mr. Fx?"

Bosco Fx seemed a bit surprised by the sheriff's question but answered. "You can, Sheriff."

"You know I'm going to do a little checking on your background."

"Yes, I figured you would. That's fine. I've got a reference or two if you want to start there."

"All right. You come back to this office tomorrow afternoon and we'll talk."

"That's good with me. I'm parked just out of town at the *Moose Crossing RV Park*. If you need me before then, my cell phone number is on my card."

"That's good. Why don't you head over here about 2 p.m.?"

"Oh Sheriff, just one more thing."

"What's that?"

"There's a truth in my profession called the *Jocard's Law*. It states that any contact leaves a trace. If there was any foul play up at Elkhorn Creek, the evidence is there. And, you may already have it at hand."

"We'll see Mr. Fx."

The plump man nodded and moved briskly out of Tilghman's office. The sheriff watched through the window as Fx climbed awkwardly into his fancy RV and slowly pulled out of the parking lot. He turned and faced his office door.

"Charlie, he shouted. "Charlie Two Leaf, come in here."

As Charlie came through the door, "Did you overhear any of that?"

"Most of it."

"Well, what do you think about Mr. Bosco Fx from Portland, Oregon?"

The deputy stared out the window. "Sheriff, it seems to me from where I'm standing that you've got nothing to lose. Your pretty much dead-ended on this case. If this guy is for real, why not?"

"You've got that right. I want you to be here for the meeting with Mr. Fx tomorrow."

Tilghman looked past Charlie and shouted out the door. "Linda, call Professor Wilds at Boise State for me.

Custer County sheriff's report & incident log
9:55 a.m.
*Tilghman investigated a report of black smoke
near the intersection of Highways 75 and 93.*

FORTY-1   CRIME WITH A TWIST

"HELLO SHERIFF. IT'S A PLEASURE TO HEAR FROM YOU." Tilghman smiled as he heard her voice. "Kind of thought we disappointed you the other day, and I was afraid we wouldn't hear from you again."

"Professor I'm a realist. I knew this case was of a special kind and, to tell you truth, I expected what I heard from your committee. Got another question for you though. Ever heard of a Bosco Fx?"

"The Bosco Fx from Portland, Oregon?"

"Well, well, well. The same."

"I have. Indeed, I have."

"That's good. What can you tell me about him?" Tilghman leaned back in his chair and propped his boots up on his desk.

"To start with, the man is as eccentric as they come but he is also a forensic genius. He is a specialist in criminal matters involving animals. He's a piece of work, that's for sure. Most wildlife biologists know of Mr. Fx. How did you run across him?"

"He's at my doorstep offering to help out with the Cahalan case. What do you think about that?"

"As you say; well, well, well. I can tell you this, if Mr. Fx shows up, it means he believes you have a singularly important case on your hands. He has a knack for attaching his name to cases that are ground breaking. The little fat man takes to publicity like a California governor. The other thing I can tell you is that he is the best at what he does. If there's any evidence out there, he will find it and probably give you more information about it than you need or can understand. In a nutshell Sheriff, use his expertise if he offers it. From what I know of him he works cheap too."

"That's what he says. I appreciate the info. The next time I get to Boise and if you will allow this old worn out sheriff, I will buy you dinner."

"You've got a date Chester. Just call. And make it soon, will you? I could use a little company that's not of the academic kind, if you know what I mean."

"That I will Victoria. You can count on it."

Tilghman swung his boots off the desk and jumped to his feet like a man twenty years younger. Finally, he felt like he had a chance to get some answers in the Cahalan death. The sheriff stuck his head out of the office and hollered at Linda to get Charlie for him. When he walked into the sheriff's office, Tilghman looked up and grinned.

"Hop in the Cherokee and go get ol' Bosco and bring him back right away. I've changed my mind. I'm going to turn that guy loose on this case before the sun sets on the Big Lost.

Custer County sheriff's report & incident log
6:15 p.m.
Charlie Two Leaf called to a report of domestic abuse in Mackay.

FORTY-2   PUT A SOCK IN IT

MIKE'S KISS WAS ROUGH AND HARD. More lust than passion. Sarah whimpered under his weight but didn't protest. She hated Mike but loved the feeling. She had for a long time. It was a feeling she could never tell Jerry about. It was her secret. Mike penetrated Sarah like he kissed her. She groaned at the pain but absorbed his aggression. Then abruptly he withdrew and rolled over and off the side of the bed. He stood there, erect and waited. Sarah knew Mike's mind and his habits and obliged him.

The phone on the nightstand began to ring loudly. Sarah kept at her duty and tried to ignore the sound but couldn't help wondering who the caller might be. To her horror, Mike, without moving his body from the pleasure, reached down and picked up the receiver. Sarah skidded across the bed and silently shook her head no. Mike ignored her plea and said hello. He listened for a moment and then reached out the phone to Sarah. She was stunned but took it.

Meekly she answered, "Hello."

The voice on the other end, when she recognized it, nearly took her breath away.

"Mrs. Cahalan, this is Sheriff Tilghman from Custer County. Are you all right?"

At first, Sarah didn't how to answer and remained silent for an awkward moment.

219

"Mrs. Cahalan, are you in any trouble?" the sheriff repeated.

Sarah found her voice, scooted off the bed, and tucked the phone between her shoulder and cheek. She reached out for the robe that draped across the end of the footboard.

"Yes Sheriff, I'm fine." She walked out of the bedroom and left Mike standing by the bed. He was still aroused and brashly grinned at Sarah as she moved out of the room and down the hall.

"I'm sorry to bother you. Was that your brother-in-law that answered the phone Mrs. Cahalan?"

Sarah's mind raced, trying to calculate an answer. "Well yes, yes it was. He's here picking up some things of Jerry's that I said he could have," she volunteered. "He's just leaving."

"I see. I really am sorry to have to call you but I have a bit of news that I think I need to share if that will be all right."

Tilghman wanted to continue with the purpose of his call but couldn't shake the notion of Mike being at Sarah Cahalan's house, especially after what she had told him about their relationship. At that moment, he hated he was so far away.

"Mrs. Cahalan, I can call and officer in your area if you need any assistance."

"No! No Sheriff. I'm all right I promise. My sister is here with me too. This is difficult but Mike will be gone soon. I can handle it."

"Okay. Well what I called you about is not very pleasant. Again, I hoped I wouldn't have to tell you this but it's important. You see...well, we found something of your husband's. It was his wedding ring."

Sarah interrupted. "Wedding ring, did you say wedding ring?"

"Yes. And what I am about to say is why it is so difficult for me to tell you this. You see, they found the ring when they performed what they call a necropsy on a wolf that was illegally shot near where your husband died. Mrs. Cahalan the ring was in the intestines of the animal."

Sarah didn't respond.

"We know it was your husband's because it had his initials on the inside of the band. It doesn't help us understand exactly how Dr. Cahalan died but it does confirm the wolves' involvement. Sarah," the sheriff softened his tone, "I'm so sorry for this."

"It's all right. I've worked through most of it. In a way, as unpleasant as it is, I want to know as much about Jerry's death as we can find out. Do you understand?"

"Yes I do. I do completely."

"But, there is something you need to know about the ring," Sarah said but then hesitated.

"Yes, what is that?"

"Well, you see, Jerry hadn't worn that ring in years. The fact is he thought he had lost it shortly after we were married. I can't imagine how it could show up as it did."

Tilghman didn't know how to respond to the information. It made no sense. "Are you sure he didn't have it with him when he went on the hunt? I mean, could he have found it and not told you?"

"I guess it's possible but I don't think Jerry would have kept something like that from me. You see, he was hurt deeply when he lost the ring. He apologized to me over and over."

"If you don't mind, how did he lose it?"

"We were not sure. It disappeared about the same time several other things did from the house. It was strange. You know one of those things that are hard to explain."

"Were the items stolen?"

"We didn't think so at the time. There was no break-in or anything like that. We didn't know."

The sheriff hesitated but then asked Sarah, "Was Mike around about the same time?"

Sarah hesitated. "Well yes, yes Mike was around a lot in the early part of our marriage. That was before the hard feelings over money began." Sarah looked over her shoulder down the hall.

"Okay. I'll let you go now. Are you sure you don't need anything?"

"I'm fine Sheriff, thank you."

"All right, if you do, anything at all, just call."

"I will."

Sarah put the phone down on the kitchen counter and headed to the bathroom. She needed a shower. She felt dirty.

Mike appeared at the other end of the hall and blocked her path.

"What was that all about? That was Sheriff Tilghman wasn't it?"

"Yes. He said they found Jerry's wedding band. And in of all places inside of one of the wolves that got to him that day. I told the sheriff that was strange because Jerry had lost it long ago. I don't see how..."

Mike spun around and raised his hands to his face. "Shit Sarah, you dumb bitch why did you do that?"

"Do what Mike. I don't understand. Why are you upset?"

"Because you told him about the ring, that's why. You're going to get us caught yet. Damn it, keep your fucking mouth shut will you! Especially to that hick sheriff. Do you understand?"

Sarah just shook her head. "Mike, I don't..."

"Do you understand?" Mike glared at her hard. Sarah began to shake slightly.

"Yes. I just don't see..."

"I put that ring on Jerry's finger after he died up there in the mountains."

"You had Jerry's ring? How did…"

"I took it years ago. Along with some other stuff I sold to get some cash. I just couldn't bring myself to sell the ring. I've had it since then." Mike reached in the bathroom, grabbed a towel, and wrapped it around his waist.

"Did Jerry know?"

"Yes, I think so. He never said anything to me."

Mike reached out for Sarah but she backed away.

"Why did you put the ring back on Jerry's finger?"

Mike leaned against the wall and looked away. "I don't know. When I saw him fall something went off in my brain. You know, what we'd planned to do and all that just backfired on me. When I got to him it didn't even look like Jerry. His face was contorted and screwed around. I stared at him for a long time. I guess I suddenly realized he was my brother. I don't know why, I put the ring on his finger. That's all, who knows."

Sarah looked for a moment at Mike. She almost felt sorry for him. Then she turned and walked to the couch and sat down on the edge.

"Maybe we should tell Sheriff Tilghman what happened. Mike, we haven't done anything wrong. I know what we planned but that didn't happen. No one will know."

"Are you crazy or something? How are we going to explain why I was there and didn't come forward when they found Jerry's body? Huh? Think about that Sarah. You think they're going to believe me now?"

Sarah looked down at the floor and muttered. "That sheriff is going to find out what happened, Mike. I just know it."

"That sheriff couldn't find a dump-truck in a two car garage. We just have to keep our act together and your mouth shut. As soon as the final inquest ruling is done, the insurance company will be sending you a fat check. Then my little whore it's off to the races."

"What about those men from Nevada? What about them?"

Mike leaned his heft against the couch and let out a long sigh of exasperation.

"Sarah, sometimes I swear, you haven't got the sense that God gave a screwdriver. That's what I mean. When we get that insurance money, I will be out from under those guys once and for all. All they want is the cash. That's all those kind care about. So don't fuck it all up now. We're almost home."

Sarah didn't appear to hear Mike's rant.

Mike looked long at Sarah. He could tell the good time was over for now so he started for the bedroom to retrieve his clothes. He stopped at the door and turned back.

"I'm going home to Clayton and back to work. It would be just like that John Wayne sheriff to rush down here to save the fair damsel in distress, so I'd better get back to looking normal. You know, fry a few fajitas. You be a good little girl while I'm gone. Okay? You hear me, right Sarah?"

Sarah stood up too and, as she headed toward the kitchen, she murmured an inaudible yes.

Custer County sheriff's report & incident log
6:15 p.m.
*The Blaine County sheriff's office notified dispatch of
an abandoned vehicle near the Chilly Buttes cutoff.*

FORTY-3   AN OLD DEBT

"LINK REDD, HOW THE HELL ARE YOU?"

The rancher was astride his horse, Bucky, up in the mountains looking for strays when his cell phone played *Giddy-up Little Doggie*. He thought he recognized the voice but wasn't sure.

Chester, Chester Tilghman, is that you?" Link's dog Leroy looked up at the rider, confused by the sudden one-way conversation that didn't seem to be directed at him.

"Of course it's me you ol' thick brain cowboy. Who'd you think it was, your mother?" The sheriff hadn't talked to Lincoln Redd in a couple of years and now, at the sound of his voice, he wondered why it had been so long. Tilghman liked the man and envied his life. He always thought if he couldn't be a sheriff he would want to be and rancher and a cowboy. The kind that was Link. The kind of the old school, of the old values.

"How's Melissa and the family Link?"

"Fine. Better than me. What brings you to call Chester? If you want to borrow money, I ain't got none."

"Well that's two of us. No, I've got to admit this is not a social call. I need your help with something down in your neck of the woods. I've got a someone missing down near Mackay, might be in the mountains above your ranch. Rick said you helped him do some tracking last week for that radio collar thing. I was hoping you might help me out and ride around the territory a bit; see what you can come up with."

"Who is it, one of your girlfriends?"

"Nope, don't have any of those. No, it's a kid, about nineteen years old. He's been working in the mountains all summer with those wolf advocate people. I'm sure you know about them."

"I do."

"He's working, or at least I thought until yesterday, for me. You know on that dead hunter case."

"Yep, that's all anyone down in this part of the county can talk about. Figured out how the man died yet?"

"Nope. That's kind of why I need to locate the kid, his name is Jamie Hightower. He's a Texas boy."

Link leaned back in the saddle and threw one leg over the horn. "Is he lost or hiding?"

"Not sure. I hope he's lost but I doubt that. And you need to know this. He might have a high-powered rifle with him and from what I have learned, he really knows how to use it. And from what I can figure out, he's learned the mountains pretty well and seems to be comfortable up in the high country."

"What's he got to do with the dead hunter?"

"I'm not sure about that one either but I don't think he's dangerous or anything like that."

Link scooted back in the saddle, "You're not sure about much of anything are you Chester?"

"Seems that way, doesn't it. No, the pieces of this mystery are still scattered all over the countryside. It's worse than a jigsaw puzzle with the center pieces and the corners all missing. But, I'm working on it. What do you think? Got time to give me a hand?"

"Tell me where to start lookin'."

Tilghman took his boots off his desk and sat up straight. He had the map of the *Salmon-Challis National Forest* spread out in front of him.

"Well Link there's two places I want you to check out. Both are just up from your place. If you go east up Elkhorn Creek, where the hunter was found, look for any sign as far up in the mountains as you think any sane person would go. If there's nothing up that way, try up the Burma Road on the way to Copper Basin."

"Hell Chester, I'm sitting on my horse right now at the base of that road, near Leavitt Spring. You think he might be in Copper Basin?"

"Don't know. I've just got a feeling. You know Link, if I was going to get lost, that might be a good direction to head. With all those BLM roads and trails in that area, you'd have a hard time putting someone in a corner."

"Chester, it sounds like your chasing a suspect to me."

"No, I don't think so but like I said, I'm not sure. It may just be a missing person. His uncle is here from back east and he's worried. See what you can do, will you? I'll owe you."

"Well, nothin' unusual about that. You're still in arrears for that rodeo wager you made about five years ago you ol' cheat."

"Thought you might have forgotten that one. Guess I was wrong."

"Yep, you were. I'll spend some time today and tomorrow snooping around. Give you a call one way or the other."

"Thanks friend. Why don't you take a little time and come to Challis? I'll buy your breakfast and settle up that other matter."

"That's a deal Chester. Getting blood out of a turnip was always something I'd drive thirty miles to do. Get back to you."

Link flipped the phone shut and looked down at his companion. "You want to go with me or head back to the ranch?"

The rider and dog started moving up higher in the foothills along the Burma Road. Link figured he'd start with Copper Basin. He knew the couple that manned the guard station in the flats. If there were any strangers around they'd know of them. Anyway, the day was as nice as the cowboy had seen for quite some time. He'd just as soon stay on his horse as be back at the ranch doing paperwork. As he headed to higher elevations, Link was glad he'd heard from Chester. He missed the old lawman.

Custer County sheriff's report & incident log
9:15 a.m.
The sheriff's dispatcher received a walk-in accident report.

FORTY-4   ON THE TRAIL

IF THERE WERE A MORE BEAUTIFUL MORNING, Bosco Fx had slept through it. He had just finished filling his tank at the Phillips 66, across from the Salmon-Challis Ranger District Office when the sun began to paint the ridges over the eastern range. As Bosco pulled out onto Highway 93, and pointed south, he felt a sudden rush. He was excited. His plump round face flushed as he rolled down the driver's side window and sucked in the Idaho mountain air. It was crisp and burned his lungs slightly. He felt like a man that could fly.

The evening before Sheriff Tilghman and Charlie Two Leaf had worked with the forensics expert until nearly midnight. They went over every piece of physical evidence in the Cahalan case that the sheriff had. The trio speculated on what significance each item might have.

They had gone back in the sheriff's jail and spread all the items out on the two bunks of an empty cell. On the top bunk, they put the collected belongings of the dead hunter. Charlie arranged the items across the rough weave blanket in a single row. The deputy placed the watch, the cell phone, the empty wallet, the wedding ring and a note that read *.270 hunting rifle* in an orderly fashion. On the bottom bunk, he laid out the shell casings and a bag of white powder he had collected at the scene. In addition, he put down a note that read *radio collar (missing)*, alongside an evidence bag with several snips of wolf hair from the carcass that had hung in the tree. The sheriff had also collected a remnant of what was thought to be Cahalan's hunting cap. Charlie gave it a place on the bottom bunk.

The two lawmen explained as much as they knew about each item and about how they had collected the remnants surrounding the body. Tilghman tried to think of something he'd missed, to explain how the watch turned up in a pawn shop and how his Chihuahua dog had sniffed out the cell phone at the scene. He noted that they had never come up with any of the missing items from Cahalan's wallet after Wishful Wicks had dug it out of the hole. The fact that the wedding ring had been retrieved from the intestines of a wolf was particularly intriguing to the investigator, more so after Tilghman recounted his conversation with Sarah Cahalan. Bosco asked the sheriff if he knew what the bag of white powder was. Tilghman said he knew it wasn't drugs but didn't know what it could be. He did say he had persuaded his deputy to taste it. Charlie said it tasted real sweet.

As for the rifle, represented by the note, the sheriff admitted that he'd probably made a mistake letting Jamie Hightower take it back into the mountains. He told Bosco he'd taken steps to try to retrieve it.

He also explained that the radio collar was still missing, thus the note on paper. The puzzling thing, he said, was that it sporadically barked; but the signal never remained active long enough to pinpoint where it was coming from. Tilghman said the one thing for sure was that someone or something was moving it around in the mountains. Why, he didn't have a clue.

Bosco had all the items in the back of his mobile laboratory, and he let the conversation of the night before pass through his thoughts as he sped by the Moose Crossing RV Park at the Highway 75 junction. As the highway stretched out of town, he increased his speed to 65 and glanced at the odometer. Charlie had told him that the Elkhorn Creek turnoff was about twenty-five miles south, *just after you pass the Trail Creek Road on your right heading south*, he had said. Charlie said he would meet Bosco there about 7 a.m.

Bosco was finding it hard to keep his concentration centered on the investigation and the evidence as he watched the early sun distribute rich colors all across the Salmon River Valley. The fact was that he was having a hard time containing his enthusiasm. This was the first case the forensic dilettante had worked involving a human death, and maybe a murder. Bosco didn't tell Sheriff Tilghman that. He wanted this case too badly to let the sheriff entertain any doubts. He figured that the two million dollars worth of forensic equipment in his mobile lab and an offer of free service would be enough for a rural county sheriff, so Bosco kept his resume of animal abuse investigations to himself.

The most serious investigation Bosco had participated in before now was a case involving a dog-fighting ring in northern California. He was proud that the evidence he had developed was the primary reason that group was busted and convicted. The DNA analysis had done the trick. It had conclusively put the two men at the scene of a particularly gruesome dogfight. The event, held in a dilapidated barn, had left three dogs dead and two others so mangled that they had to be euthanized on site. The bad guys were now in a California prison and Bosco was happy about that.

Bosco reached the peak of the Willow Creek summit quicker than he had anticipated and pulled off the highway onto a cutout to read the marker. The little man had two compulsive behaviors. One was eating and the other was roadside historical and informational markers. He was about to indulge the second in spite of being late for his meeting with the deputy.

Bosco slid out of the driver's seat, shuffled through the loose gravel, and stood for a moment in front of the marker. Before he read the sign, he took a second to admire the Big Lost River Valley. At six-thousand feet, and in the clear mountain air, he could see forever. The deep blue sky contrasted with the shades of gray running freely up and down and across the mountains and the dry arid browns of the valley floor.

The marker let him know that he was in big elk country. He was standing in the middle of their winter range. The words admonished the users of off-road vehicles to not venture into the elk's grazing range in the winter months. In these hard months, their food was scarce and the disturbance of off-roaders would put dangerous stress on the animals.

Bosco thought about that and let his eyes pan the high country peaks. He was a city boy and he hoped he would see something wild. He didn't care what, just something that was not constrained by fence or cage. Nothing broke the stillness of his surroundings however, except for the breeze that climbed the mountainside and flowed over the peak and gently across his cheeks. At that moment, Bosco didn't want to move. The first day of creation with all its promise couldn't have been any better than this, he thought.

A big semi suddenly interrupted that thought and sent a thin coat of dust rolling over Bosco and his RV. The sudden jolt to his senses moved him quickly back toward the driver's side of his mobile lab. But again he paused as he climbed back in the cab. He tried to register the scene solidly into his memory. He stared at Borah Peak as he started the engine.

By the odometer reading, he figured he was only five miles from Elkhorn Creek. As Bosco began his descent toward the valley below, he could see the Chilly Buttes just ahead. Just beyond the buttes he could also make out Trail Creek Road as it intersected with Highway 93. He wondered what, if anything, he would find at the scene of Dr. Cahalan's demise. Bosco could feel the blood rush to his fat face again as he thought about the prospects.

"Damn, this stuff is fun," he said aloud.

Custer County sheriff's report & incident log
10:15 p.m.
Deputies were called to a fight on Capital Street in Mackay.

FORTY-5   TWO TAKES ON TRUTH

SENSIBLE ELDER AND HIS SON HENRY WAITED patiently for the sheriff to finish his lunch. They sat in the unadorned hardback chairs that faced the dispatcher's counter. Sensible altered his gaze at regular intervals, first to the clock and then to the front door of the sheriff's office. Henry kept his eyes glued to his boots; his hands clasped between his legs. Finally, Sensible got up from his chair and walked tentatively to the counter.

"Excuse me, when did you say the sheriff would be back?" he glanced again at the clock for emphasis.

Linda looked up at the large wall timepiece too before she answered. The clock displayed a bear eating berries and an advertisement for Salmon River Propane stenciled on its face.

"He should be back any moment now, "the dispatcher answered. "Can I get you a cup of coffee while you wait?"

Sensible just shook his head no and returned to his chair.

"You all right Henry?" he asked his son as he sat down.

Henry didn't look up or respond to his father.

Sheriff Tilghman walked through the door and looked over at Linda. The dispatcher nodded at the two men. He turned and approached his visitors.

"Hello, I'm Sheriff Tilghman. What can I do for you men?"

Before Sensible could answer, the sheriff spoke to the boy.

"Well hello Henry. You are Henry Elder, aren't you? Or are you Harry?"

For the first time Henry raised his face as he met the sheriff's gaze.

"Yes sir. I'm Henry," the boy said softly.

The sheriff returned his gaze to the older man.

"And you would be?"

"Sheriff, I'm Henry's father, Sensible Elder. We live down at Arco."

"Yes, I know where you live Mr. Elder. Where's your son Harry? I didn't think your boys ever split up; two peas in a pod and that kind of stuff."

Before Sensible could respond the sheriff turned and started walking. "Why don't we go to my office?" he asked. He led the two men down the short hall and through the door of his cramped space.

"Have a seat. Did Linda offer you coffee?"

"Yes sir, we're fine."

Sensible sat down and waited for the sheriff to do likewise.

"Sheriff it's my other son, Harry, that I'm here to talk to you about. You see, I'm worried about him."

The sheriff rearranged a stack of documents on his desk before he responded.

"How's that Mr. Elder?" He leaned back in his chair and folded his hands across his stomach. He let his eyes go to Henry for a second. The boy again was looking down at his boots. The sheriff turned his attention back to Sensible.

"I don't know how to put this. It's hard to explain to you, Sheriff, because I don't know myself. You see, ever since that terrible thing happened to that hunter up on Elkhorn Creek my boys have been acting—well they've been acting strange. Henry here," Sensible looked at his son for a moment and then back to the sheriff.

"Henry and his brother have had some kind of falling out. And that ain't natural for these two boys. Ever since they could walk on their own they have been like your left and right hand, they go together. But since that day, you can hardly get them to be in the same room. There ain't no words between them either, just silence. And besides, Harry is gone all the time. We hardly see him at all."

Tilghman let his chair come forward. He rubbed his bushy mustache with his forefinger. "Mr. Elder I'm going to put this to you directly. Do you think it has something to do with what happened that day?"

The father hesitated.

"I don't know but I suspect it does," he said finally. "Neither one of the boys will tell me what happened up in those mountains the day the hunter was found. I mean, they won't say anything other than what I think they told you."

"What do you think they told me Mr. Elder? I'd like to hear it from you." Tilghman again looked at Henry, but Henry continued to stare at the floor.

Sensible glanced at his son before he continued.

"Well, you know. About that old mountain man and how he led them to the body and how the wolves or other critters had torn it all up."

"That's all?"

"Yes sir, that's about it."

"Where's Harry spending his time lately?"

With that question Henry finally looked up from his shoelaces and met the sheriff's gaze. His expression seemed strained to Tilghman, as if he was dreading his father's answer to that question.

"Harry has been with his uncle a lot lately, up in the mountains. You know, hunting and such."

The sheriff sat quiet for a moment. Finally, he said, "You mean with Rave Elder?"

The question seemed to take both men sitting across the desk by surprise.

"Why, yes. Rave's my older brother. How'd you know?"

The sheriff ignored the question, stood up, and walked to the front of his desk. His stance suggested authority as he looked down on the pair.

"Mr. Elder I would like to speak to Henry alone for a moment."

Sensible nodded and started to get up but the sheriff put his hand on his shoulder.

"No, that's all right Mr. Elder. I want to show him something. You stay here and we'll be back in a few minutes. Henry I'd like you to follow me?"

Henry Elder didn't move and stared at his father. Sensible nodded toward his boy, and Henry slowly got out of his chair, and he and the sheriff started out of the office. Tilghman led the boy past the dispatcher's counter and into another narrow hallway. The sheriff stopped for a moment, unholstered his Kimber .45 pistol, and put it in the first of a row of five metal boxes with keys sticking out of the locks. He stuck the key in his shirt pocket and continued into the jailer's office. Henry dutifully followed.

As the two men stepped down into the jail area, the prisoners in the first two cells rose up off their bunks and stared. The sheriff ignored them and moved down the row of three cells into a larger room with only one cell, cell number four. The cell was empty and the bunks, one above the other, were neatly ordered. There was a small no-lid toilet bowl in the far corner.

"Henry come here. Look into this cell for a moment. What do you see?"

Henry cautiously did as the sheriff asked and looked through the bars. He gave the sheriff a puzzled look.

"What do you mean Sheriff?"

"Just what I said. What do you see?"

"Well, I don't know. It's a jail cell. Kind of small I guess. I've never been inside one. Is that what you mean?"

"Sort of. Come on. Follow me."

The sheriff led Henry through a short passageway and unlocked a heavy metal door. As he pushed it open, the sunlight of the day spilled through the opening and sent a shock of bright light down the passageway and into the jail.

The two men stepped outside, and the sheriff closed the door and locked it from the outside. He stood still for a moment and let Henry look around at the scene. The inmates exercise yard was all hardness. A concrete pad was about twenty-five feet square, and the fifteen-foot heavy chain link fence was topped with two rows of cruel razor wire. A basketball backboard was positioned at one end. The hoop did not have a net.

The sheriff motioned for Henry to follow; the two walked to the far end of the enclosure, and the sheriff asked the young man to sit down on a metal bench. Tilghman sat down next to him.

They sat quietly for a time before the sheriff spoke.

"Those mountains are sure pretty, aren't they? he said."

Henry first looked at the sheriff and then at the Big Lost Mountain Range in the distance. He just nodded.

"Henry, you really like those mountains, don't you? I mean, the hunting and the freedom they give you and your brother." The sheriff paused for a moment to let Henry answer, but the young man did not say anything. He continued to look toward the far-off mountains.

"It would be hard to give them up, wouldn't it son?"

Finally, Henry spoke. "Yes sir."

"I mean especially for some place like this."

"Yes sir."

The sheriff slowly stood up, faced the chain link fence, and grabbed the heavy patterned mesh with both hands. He gently pulled at the cold metal webbing that gave only slightly to his effort.

"Son, have you got something you need to tell me about that day on Elkhorn Creek?" Tilghman turned around slowly and faced Henry. He looked down at the boy and remained silent, waiting for his answer.

"Yes sir."

Tilghman sat down again. "I suspected you two boys might have left something out that day. Did you?"

"Yes sir, we did."

"Well, why don't you tell what it was?"

"Am I going to jail?"

The sheriff looked at the scared young man. He softened his look with a slight smile.

"Henry, I've been in law enforcement for many years, and there is one thing that I've learned about the lady called justice. She doesn't always require a pound of flesh to balance her scales. But what she does require is the truth. Why don't we start with that and we'll see where it leads us?"

Tilghman stood up and motioned for Henry to do the same.

"Let's go back into my office. I suspect your dad might like to hear this part."

"Yes sir."

Custer County sheriff's report & incident log
11:15 a.m.
*Two Leaf was called to investigate hitch-hikers
said to be panhandling along Highway 93.*

FORTY-6   BITTERSWEET IS THE TASTE
OF DEATH

RAVE ELDER AND HIS NEPHEW HARRY had been at it for almost a week. The weather had cooperated and the morning was crisp and clear. The terrain in the higher elevations on the west side of the Lost Mountain Range had proved almost more than Rave's old ATV could handle, but the pair ignored the danger and kept at their work. To Rave it was important to get this done.

The two men had begun across Highway 93, from the Mackay Reservoir on the Upper Cedar Creek and moved from southeast to northwest. They took each drainage creek as they came to it. They had worked their way through Jones Creek, Cedar Creek, and the Sawmill Gulch all the way up to Leatherman's Pass. At each watering hole, Rave filled a small metal tin with the white powder of Xylitol out of a two-pound cotton sack he carried in the box behind the driver's side. Their routine was always the same. As he partially hid the tin under brush or sage, Harry would bring his uncle the rolled up wolf's pelt and Rave would lightly scrape the fur across the ground and foliage to leave a scent. With any luck he knew that the smell would attract the wolves of the Chilly Buttes pack to the bait.

Before they left for the next bait site, Rave always gave a long and sustained howl. The sound would run up the foothills into the mountains and echo back off the high ridges. There hadn't been answers this morning, but Rave told Harry sooner or later the mangy carnivores as he called them would come to the bait.

Their supplies were running low so Rave told his nephew that as soon as they finished with Elkhorn Creek and the West Fork of the Pahsimeroi River, they'd pack it in and head back to their truck parked down by the Chilly Slough and resupply. As they rode along the high ridge near Pass Lake, Rave could see down the Elkhorn Creek drainage. He spotted what appeared to be a sheriff's Cherokee and some kind of fancy van parked in the turnout next to the highway.

Rave decided to skip Elkhorn Creek for the time being and avoid whatever was happening below. He sure didn't want to revisit that scene with the deputy around. He was about to turn back and head for the truck when Harry nudged his elbow and called his attention to a horseman coming towards them on the high stretches of the Elkhorn Creek trail. At first, Rave backed off the throttle; but then, looking at his nephew, he mouthed wordlessly that it didn't matter.

Rave figured it was only a local rancher looking for strays. Most likely he wouldn't pay them much attention since they were in the middle of hunting season. Rave did decide that he would rather not have the rider see the wolf pelt in the small open box in the back though, and reached behind him and pushed it deeper down into the box. He lifted his rifle from behind him and put it between him and Harry. Harry gave a glance at his uncle and then back at the approaching rider.

As the two drew closer, both men on the ATV recognized the rider. They knew who he was though they figured he wouldn't know them. The cowboy was the first to speak.

"Mornin'."

Rave just nodded cautiously but didn't respond to the greeting.

The rider's horse shied a little and pranced around the front of the noisy four-wheeler. The man in the saddle pulled him in and when he calmed, he stepped down off his horse. He held the reigns in his left hand and stuck out his right to the driver.

"Don't believe I know you fellows. I'm Link Redd. I own that ranch you see down there in the Big Lost River Valley."

Again, he got no response to his friendliness so he withdrew his offer of a friendly greeting. Link was the kind to respond quickly to an insult.

"I guess you don't realize that you're not supposed to be driving off-road vehicles up on these trails," Link said with a tone that was now all business. He figured that if these fellows were not going to be sociable he would push them a little.

"I see you've got a wolf pelt in the back there. Where did you get him?" Link reached out and handled the fur, partially pulling the pelt out of the box.

Rave revved the engine on the ATV. The noise again spooked Link's horse, and the gelding spun nervously around him in an arc at the end of his tether. Link backed away from the four-wheeler and spoke to his horse to calm him. He looked hard back at Rave. Harry squirmed in his seat and tried not to meet Link's stare.

"Damn it mister, that's another thing you don't seem to know. You're supposed to turn that engine off when a rider comes up the trail. Can't you see this horse is about to bolt?"

Rave finally spoke.

"You're plenty nosy. Why don't you mind your own business? Now get your horse out of my way or I'll push you both off this trail." Again, Rave revved the engine to emphasize his demand.

"Well, tie it in a sack and beat it on a tree." Link muttered to himself.

He pulled the reins of Bucky closer before he spoke.

"Mister, you know, besides being an asshole of the first magnitude on such a pretty morning, you're displaying an amazing amount of stupidity as well. Like I told you, my ranch is right down below you. What happens in these mountains, I'm telling you right now, is my business. And, especially when people like you come up here and ignore not only the law but common courtesy that's due every man, especially strangers. So, if you'll step down off that loud piece of junk you're ridin' and tell the boy here to hold my horse, I'll see if I can change your manner of thinking and maybe a bit of your behavior.

Before Link could react, Rave came at him with the ATV at full throttle. The front wheels left the ground and the front rock rail brushed Bucky. The horse reared violently; the cowboy lost control of the reins, and the dun headed down the trail at a full gallop, kicking out his back legs as he went. Link lost his balance and stumbled backward. Rave spun around quickly and Link had to dodge him again. This time he fell backwards off the steep side of the trail and tumbled head first down through the sage and rocks. He was fifty feet down before he came to rest against a boulder. The lights went out and the noise of the ATV faded.

Custer County sheriff's report & incident log
11:15 a.m.
The Mackay deputy was called to a
report of petty theft at the Borah Peak grocery store.

FORTY-7   A BUMPY RIDE

"LINK! LINCOLN REDD! Are you all right? Link!"

Link took his time to look around before he answered. "Charlie? ...Charlie what are you doin' in my house?"

"Link, I'm not in your house. We're on the side of the mountain. What happened to you? Did you get pitched off your horse?"

"Bucky? Where's Bucky?"

"He's right over there tied to that tree. He's why we found you. What happened?"

Link rose up with Charlie Two Leaf's help and tried to stand.

"Whoa there cowboy! Give it a minute. You've got a bump on your head bigger than a baseball and just as hard. Take a deep breath and get your bearings."

"What happened Charlie?"

"That was my question. When your horse came running down the Elkhorn Creek trail we figured you must be up here somewhere so we started looking. Sure enough...do you remember what happened?"

Link struggled to his feet with the deputy's help and looked around. He looked back up at the trail above where the two men stood for a moment.

"Give me a minute. Got any water?"

"Yeah. Over by the horse. Come on, let's move over there; get a little shade on you. Do I need to get on the radio and get the medivac folks up here?"

"No. Just give me a minute to get the cobwebs cleared."

"Okay. Take a drink of this."

"Charlie, did you see anybody else up here?"

"No but I did see some dust coming off the trail about a half mile north along the ridgeline. Why?"

"I had a run-in with a couple of fellows on an ATV...at least I think I did."

Charlie took the water bottle from Link and walked around his horse.

"Ol' Bucky seems to be all right. Link, did you have a rifle with you?"

Link looked puzzled. "A rifle? I don't think I did. No, I know I didn't. What kind of rifle?"

"It's a Winchester, model 70. It was lying about fifty-feet from you, down the side of the creek trail. We found it as we came up the trail. I thought it might have been yours."

"No, I don't own a Winchester. I'm a Remington man."

"Could it have been the fellows that you had the run-in with?"

"No, I don't think so. They had a rifle but I'm pretty sure it wasn't a Winchester."

Charlie moved in front of Link and looked into his eyes. "There looking a little less glassy. Feeling better?"

"Yeah. Sort of."

"Let's get your horse and go back down to the Jeep. I'm going to get on the horn and see if we've got anybody to see if they can find those guys on that ATV. They're not supposed to have one of them up on that trail anyway. Maybe we can find out what happened to you."

"Guess they got the best of me. It's hell to get old Charlie."

"Link, I would like you to meet Mr. Bosco Fx. Mr. Fx, this is Lincoln Redd. His friends call him Link. He's a local rancher."

The two men shook hands and Charlie held out the rifle to Bosco.

"Got a prize for you. We found this up the creek a ways. It was up higher than we went when the sheriff and I came to the scene to investigate. You think it might be a part of what we're doing here?"

Bosco took the rifle by the barrel. "Mr. Redd, are you all right? That's kind of a nasty bump on your head."

Link massaged the swollen roundness with the tips of his fingers and shook his head yes. Bosco turned his attention back to the rifle.

"Could be Charlie. It might just go with another piece of evidence I discovered while you were on your rescue mission. Come take a look at this."

Bosco led the deputy about twenty yards down from where Cahalan's body was discovered.

"Look at this tree Charlie. See anything?"

"You mean besides that hole in the trunk?"

"Exactly. Look what I dug out of that hole. You think this round might fit this Winchester, model 70?"

"If I was a betting man, I'd say it just might."

"It just might, indeed," Bosco responded. "This type rifle is a favorite with target people and marksmen. It's also standard army issue for sniper gear; has been for many years. This little baby did a lot of mighty ugly work in Viet Nam and probably still does in Iraq and Afghanistan."

"How's it fit?"

Bosco thought for a moment. "Don't know, but it could be another piece in the puzzle."

Link walked up to the pair. "Charlie now that my head is clearing out a bit, I think there is something about those two men on the ATV you ought to know."

"What's that?"

"They had a wolf pelt in the gear box. It was rolled up and tied with cord. I picked it up and the driver, an old guy, got pretty testy after that. Something else. There was a cloth bag under it and there was white powder all over the back of the ATV."

"Did you say white powder? Bosco asked."

"Yeah, Mr. Fx, white powder. Looked like sugar but not as coarse."

Bosco glanced at Charlie and displayed a wry smile.

"Well, I think that solves the powder mystery at the scene. I'll have to run some tests but I'm pretty sure I know what's going on with the white stuff."

"Yeah. You want to fill us in?" Charlie asked.

"Let's get back to my van so I can be sure and then I'll explain."

Custer County sheriff's report & incident log
1:45 a.m.
Fish and Game officers were advised of a bear in Clayton
near the Hoo Doo Saloon. No word on what the beast was
doing.

FORTY-8   STUPID'S MASCOT

SARAH CAHALAN WALKED AROUND BEHIND Mrs. Selman's house
and down the weed-covered path to the small cabin in the back. She
stepped over a wood planter box full of dead flowers and stood in
front of the dingy white door. She stood there for almost a minute.
She was trembling faintly. Finally, she shyly knocked twice in
between the strips of peeling paint; the red metal mailbox without a
lid loosely hanging by one screw, rattled next to the door. She could
hear loud music coming from inside. Sarah waited. At last, the
volume on the music diminished and she heard movement inside.

The man that opened the door wide was naked to the waist
and barefoot. It looked to Sarah like he just got out of bed.

"Well, would you look at this," Mike said. "If it ain't my
sweet little sister-in-law."

Mike moved to one side. "Come on in little lady. You know, I
was just thinking about you. Yes, indeed, I was. Come on in."

Sarah stepped into the one-room apartment. Everything
about the inside was as disheveled as the outside. Mike shoved

sections of a newspaper off the end of the bed and invited Sarah to sit down.

She ignored his offer. "Mike, I've got to talk to you. I'm on my way to Mackay. I want to see where Jerry died."

"Hold on there. We've got time to talk about that later. Come over here and sit next to me. You're looking mighty inviting right now. It's been a while. Come on, let's play? Then we'll see what it is you've got on your mind."

Sarah felt herself about to lose control. She was abruptly sick to her stomach. All she could think about was her mistake. How could she have ever have let this man touch her?

"Mike, listen to me," she said, trying but failing to put force into her voice.

"Well, if you won't come to me, I'll come to you."

Mike got up and quickly moved to Sarah. Before she could react, he had her pulled against him. Sarah screamed.

"Wow!" Mike jumped back at the suddenness of Sarah's protest. "Easy there missy. What's got into to you?"

Sarah was shaking and walking in circles. Finally, she stopped.

"I cannot stand it any longer," she said in a high pitched squeal. "The guilt is killing me Mike."

Sarah was talking rapidly. All she wanted was to get it all out quickly and leave this man to his squalor.

"I'm going to Mackay and see where Jerry died," she repeated, "and then I'm going to Challis and talk to Sheriff Tilghman. I'm going to tell him everything about our plans. We didn't do anything, we just talked about it. Maybe nothing will happen. I've got to get it off my conscience. I do Mike—Jerry's haunting me."

Mike moved back to the bed and sat down. He started pulling on his shoes over his sockless feet.

"You know Sarah; if stupid had a mascot you'd certainly be at the end of the leash." Mike stood up and went to the small refrigerator in the far corner of his room. He reached in and got a beer.

"Want one?" he sarcastically held up the can to Sarah. "Guess not."

"Mike, I..."

"Shut up Sarah! Just shut the fuck up! There's something you might need to know before you go running off to spill your guts to Tilghman. Something that just might make you think over your sudden urge to cleanse your guilt, as they say."

Mike took a long drink from the can and then walked to the corner and retrieved a folding lawn chair. "Here, sit down." He unfolded the chair and Sarah reluctantly obliged. She waited.

"You remember when I told you that Jerry was dead when I got to him that morning?" Mike didn't wait for Sarah's response. "I lied Mrs. Cahalan. Your husband wasn't dead. Oh, he was in real bad shape alright, I guess his bad ticker finally caught up with him. He most likely was on his way to his reward, but he wasn't there yet."

Mike paused for a moment. He took another swig and looked long at Sarah.

"Just before Jerry fell over, there was a gun shot. It was close by. At first, I thought Jerry had been shot by some other hunter. I couldn't believe it. After all we had planned, some real accident happens. That's when I left my hiding spot and went to him. He was laying face down in the snow so I turned him over. But he wasn't shot. There was no sign of blood or any wound. That's when I also realized he wasn't dead. He opened his eyes and looked at me with those baby blues. He was trying to speak."

Sarah stood up and moved toward the front door. "Is that when he died Mike?"

"No." Mike took another long drink and then loudly crushed the can between his fingers.

"No my little lover, it's not. But it is when I killed him," Mike spoke softly. "I smothered my own brother with this hand—just like you wanted." He held up the hand with the crushed can in it.

"It wasn't hard either, not like I thought it would be. He was too weak to resist. It just took about a minute. I smothered him right there in the snow and then I put the ring on his finger. And, this is the part you're really going to like. I took his money and credit cards out of his wallet. I robbed him and then I left him. My own brother. Cain slays Abel. It's an old story."

Mike pitched the can in the sink and opened the refrigerator.

"So you see Sarah, you might just want to think again about playing true confession. They call it murder. People get the death penalty in this state for such behavior. And Sarah, don't make a mistake, you killed Jerry as much as I did. You run out on me now, before that insurance money comes through, and I promise you one thing, you'll roast right alongside me. So, go on. Go to that sheriff and spill your sniveling guts."

Mike sat his beer can on top of the refrigerator and walked toward Sarah. "Before you do, why don't you give me one of those specials you're so good at? What do you say?"

Sarah didn't turn around to look back at Mike as she stood up and reached the door. She felt sick again as she ran out, tripping over the flower box. As she came down the weed covered sidewalk, Sarah thought she saw the blinds in the big house close. There was no sound behind her but she was afraid to turn around and look. Sarah got into her BMW and drove out of Clayton. She tried to focus on the map display on the dash but the moisture in her eyes blurred the screen. Sarah took the first turnout off the narrow highway and dried her eyes. Again, she looked at the map and found the town of Mackay on the display. She punched in the address for the Bear Bottom Inn and pulled back out onto Highway 75.

Custer County sheriff's report & incident log
1:15 a.m.
*Stanley Fire and Search and Rescue volunteers
responded to a vehicle rollover in the Seafoam area.*

FORTY-9   SEEING DOUBLE

"WHAT DO YOU THINK OF HIS STORY MR. ELDER?"

Sensible Elder looked a long time at his son before he answered the sheriff.

"I believe him Sheriff. Henry is a good boy. We taught him to know right from wrong; his mother made sure he learned that. What their uncle had these boys do was as wrong as wrong gets. I'm ashamed to call that man my brother."

"Mr. Elder, Hector Lioncamp warned me about Rave a couple of weeks back. It seems his suspicions were well founded."

Linda stuck her head into the sheriff's office. "Excuse me Sheriff, Charlie and Mr. Fx are back from the Elkhorn and they've got a friend of yours with them. You need to come take a look."

Tilghman stood up and asked Sensible and Henry to wait a minute.

"What in the hell happened to you? That wild horse of yours finally kick some sense into you?"

Link grinned and stuck out his hand to the sheriff. "I wish it was that simple Chester. I got dry gulched up in the mountains doing your work for you."

"By who?"

"I'm not sure. Two fellows on an ATV."

Charlie spoke up, "Sheriff they had a wolf pelt with them, all rolled and tied up tight. And we've got us another rifle from the Cahalan scene too."

Tilghman looked over at Bosco Fx who was standing just inside the door. Bosco nodded his confirmation.

"Hold on a minute Charlie, this day is coming a little too fast for this old sheriff. You got anybody looking for the men that waylaid Link?"

"Yeah, I called the ranger. Rick and Deputy Gulliver are up there now riding the back trails. He'll call if he turns up anything."

"Link, you need any medical..."

"No Chester, just a bump. Nothin' unusual in that."

"You have any luck with finding the kid Jamie Hightower?"

"Yeah, a little. I found a camp above Copper Basin on the old Burma Road that I'm betting is his."

"Good, I need to finish up something in my office and then we'll talk."

Before the sheriff could turn back to the hallway, Sensible and his son came out of the sheriff's office. Link reacted like a man stuck with a cattle prod and pointed at the boy.

"Chester, that's one of them. That boy there, he was one of the two that bushwhacked me. How'd he get here?"

Link started toward Harry.

"Hold on Link that boy couldn't be one of them; he's been here all morning. Him and his dad."

"Chester, I'm sure of it. That's one of the men on that ridgeline."

"I know your sure Link. But that boy is not one of them. It's his twin brother."

The sheriff motioned to Sensible to come to him. "Mr. Elder, this man says two fellows attacked him up near the Elkhorn this morning. He says one of them looks just like Henry there. What do you think that means?"

"Well Sheriff, I think it means we know where Rave and Harry are. I suspected as much. I think I know, too, what they've been up to. They're baiting wolves; that'd be my guess."

Tilghman looked at Henry. "Is that what they're doing in the mountains son?"

Henry reluctantly nodded.

"Henry, we recently found a dead wolf with a note attached to its carcass. Is that the work of your uncle?"

Henry nodded again.

"You know Mr. Elder," the sheriff spoke softly, "it appears that your brother is damn determined to become an outlaw."

"Yeah Sheriff, it sure seems to be the case. Those wolves have driven that man wild. But I'm pleading with you not to let him take Harry with him."

Sheriff Tilghman glanced at Henry and then back at Sensible. "I'll do what I can."

Linda spoke up. "Sheriff, I've got a Bertha Selman on the line. She says she would like to talk to you."

"Get her number. Tell her I'll call her back as soon as we get on the road."

The sheriff turned to Charlie Two Leaf. "Charlie let's go join the hunt. Call Rick on the radio and find out where he is. Bosco, I need you to wrap up your work ASAP. I'll want to go over what you have, especially the meaning of that Winchester, when we get back."

"I think I might have a surprise or two for you. Before you leave sheriff, I'd like to rub some of the sticky tape on Mr. Redd's clothing."

The sheriff looked at Link. "What's that about?"

"Just a hunch Sheriff."

"That okay with you Link?" the sheriff asked.

"Sure, why not."

"Okay Bosco, get it done. I want Link to go with us if he's feeling all right." The sheriff glanced at the rancher who shook his head.

"Saddle up the truck Charlie, I'll take the Cherokee. Let's head out. I've got a hell of a story to tell you, but it will have to wait until we get back. Link you ride with Charlie."

Tilghman turned to Sensible. "Mr. Elder, I'd like for you and Henry to stay in town until I get back. Do I have your word on that?"

"Yes Sheriff, we'll stay close."

"Let's go hunting Hot Sauce." Tilghman's little dog flew into the crook of the sheriff's left arm and the sheriff walked briskly to the Cherokee.

He looked back at his deputy and shouted, "Charlie, did you get the siren fixed?"

"Not yet Sheriff," Charlie responded without looking directly at his boss. The two vehicle posse pulled out onto Main Street and headed for Highway 93.

Custer County sheriff's report & incident log
4:45 p.m.
*Deputy called to the scene of an accidental shooting in
Clayton.*

FIFTY-0   BLUETOOTH BLUES

THE SHERIFF LOVED HIS NEW HANDS-FREE CELL PHONE connection in
the Cherokee. He didn't understand how it worked but he loved it.
The geeks at the Radio Shack had convinced him he needed it. They
argued, appearing serious, that he could shoot out the window at
the bad guys while going 90 miles an hour and still talk on the
phone. They said it would revolutionize his law enforcement
capabilities—bring him into the twenty-first century. The sheriff had
just shrugged but had them install the thing anyway.

"Is that you Mrs. Selman?"

"Yes, yes it is. Is this Sheriff Tilghman?"

"Yes ma'am it is. Linda said you called. Can I do something
for you?"

Hot Sauce hadn't gotten used to the new device and jumped
from the front seat into the back fretfully trying to find the source of
the strange voice.

"Hold on for a minute Mrs. Selman. I'm about to go through
the gap at Grand View Canyon on Highway 93; we'll lose our
connection for about a minute. Don't go away, just hang on the line.
I'll be right back."

Tilghman was trying to stay up with Charlie Two Leaf in the
truck but was having a hard time of it. His deputy always drove,
the sheriff liked to say, like a wild Indian chasing Custer. Charlie

always ignored the sheriff's weak attempt at humor and did as he pleased; which usually meant he drove a little faster.

The sheriff completed the slow S-curve through the gap and listened for the signal beep. When he heard it he said, "Bertha, I'm back. Can you hear me all right?"

"Yes Sheriff, just fine. And I'm glad you called me Bertha. That means we're friends, right?"

"Well of course we are Bertha. Now what's on your mind?" Hot Sauce jumped back into the front seat.

"The reason I called...well, the reason is that I'm a bit worried about my boarder."

"You mean Mike Cahalan?" the sheriff asked.

"Yes. You see, yesterday a young woman came to the house looking for him. She had a fancy car, one of those German things I think. You could tell she was a lady of some means just by the way she talked. She asked if Mike was at home and I showed her how to get to his little room out back."

The sheriff interrupted. "Did she tell you her name?"

"No, she just thanked me and went to see Mike. You know me Sheriff; I'm a curious old woman, so I watched as best I could through the blinds to see what I could see. Well, about a half an hour later this lady came out of his room and you didn't need binoculars to know that she was very upset. And I do mean very. I think she was crying on the way to her car. And, there was no sign of Mike."

"What happened then?"

"She got into her nice red car and left."

"Is that it?"

"No Sheriff, there's more. A few minutes after the lady left, Mike went across the street to the Hoo Doo Saloon. He did that sometimes—usually when he was upset about one thing or another. Well, here is the part that worries me. It wasn't but about an hour later that two men showed up looking for him. You remember me mentioning those men don't you?"

"I do. You said they were kind of tough looking fellows, if I recall."

"That's the ones. They weren't unpleasant with their questions mind you but they scared me anyway. I probably shouldn't have, but I told them where Mike was." Bertha paused.

"And?"

"They took him away with them Sheriff. I saw them come out of that bar and take him to their car. And Sheriff, I don't think Mike wanted to go with those men. I can't say for sure, but I don't think he did. He was talking a mile-a-minute and waving his arms like a wild man. I could see, I just couldn't hear."

"Mrs...Bertha, did you notice what kind of car they were driving?"

"I did. It was one of those big square box looking things. Ugly as a mud fence. It had all the windows blacked so as you can't see inside. You know Sheriff, the kind that army fellows drive."

"You mean like a Humvee?"

Bertha thought for a second. "Did you say humming bee?"

"Never mind Bertha, what color was it?"

"Black, black like the windows."

"Did you see which way they headed?"

"Sheriff, that's easy. Like you know, there's only one way in and one way out of this little burg. They headed back toward you, back toward Challis. Sheriff I'm..."

"I know Bertha, we'll look into it. I'll get my deputy on it right away. Now, if Mike comes back you let me know, will you? Call me on my cell phone. You have my number; I left it with you last time on the card."

"Oh my yes Sheriff, as soon as I see him I will call. And Sheriff..."

"Yes."

"Are you still an honest lawman? I mean you haven't crossed over have you?"

"Like I said before Bertha, not yet."

FIFTY-1   THICK GRAVY

TILGHMAN COULD SEE CHARLIE TWO LEAF'S TRUCK pull off the highway at the Chilly Slough turnout. As he got closer, he also saw a Forest Service truck parked next to the historical marker. It was pulled alongside a well-worn pickup and there was a man in hunter's garb sitting on the tailgate. The sheriff noticed Ranger Rick Clyde standing next to him. The ranger waved as Tilghman pulled in and drove up next to the ranger's truck. As he got out of the Cherokee, the sheriff could see that the man in hunter's clothes was Harry Elder.

The ranger started toward him but before he could speak, Tilghman motioned for Charlie Two Leaf to come to him.

"Hello Rick. Hold on just a minute. Got something I need to talk to my deputy about."

Rick Clyde waved his acknowledgement and returned to the Elder boy.

Tilghman took Charlie by the arm and headed him back toward his truck.

"Charlie, I'll tell you; when things start poppin' they make like a string of cheap Chinese firecrackers. I just talked to Bertha Selman up at Clayton. She says a couple of tough looking hombres came and escorted Mike Cahalan away. My bet it's those gambling types out of Reno. She said they're driving a big black boxy looking vehicle; I'm guessing it's a Hummer by her description. They pulled out of Clayton headed toward Challis."

Charlie looked over at the Elder boy. "What about him and his uncle?"

"He'll tell us where his uncle is. I'll take care of that. Rick and Link can help find him. I need you to backtrack towards Clayton and see if you can spot that Hummer. If you do, don't try to stop it, just keep it under surveillance. From all I've heard today, we need to get Mike Cahalan in custody."

"He's the key isn't he? I mean to what happened to his brother."

"I think so Charlie. We need to get our hands on him. The boys that have him now, if I know anything at all about those collection types, are not taking him for a vacation. We don't get him before he leaves our county, we likely don't get him ever. You got it?"

"I got it. I'm on my way."

"Oh, and Charlie; one other thing: Mrs. Selman said there was a lady of some refinement that came to see Mike just before the Reno thugs got him. Got any guesses who that might have been?" The sheriff raised his eyebrows and looked obliquely at the deputy.

"My, oh my. When the gravy thickens it does it fast, no?"

"Yes it does at that. Keep your eye out for Sarah Cahalan's car too. I'm betting it's a red Mercedes or BMW. It will be a stranger to these parts for sure. Okay Charlie, get on your horse. Let me know if something turns up."

Tilghman turned away and headed for Rick Clyde and Harry Elder. He stopped and spun back towards his deputy just as Charlie was climbing in the truck. The sheriff hollered.

"Charlie! Charlie!"

The deputy turned. "Charlie, remember what I said, and this is an order straight from the High Sheriff. Don't try to stop the Hummer if you run across it. Got me?"

"Yeah, I got it."

Custer County sheriff's report & incident log
1:45 a.m.
*A caller complained that his neighbor's music
was blaring and that he couldn't sleep.*

FIFTY-2 THE SECOND TELLING

"WHAT HAVE WE HERE RICK? Hello Harry. How are you son?"

"Hello Sheriff. I've been better. I guess you want to talk to me."

"That I do. I've already had a chat with your father and with your brother. Henry tells a pretty good tale. They're back in Challis waiting on word about you. Did you know that? I also spoke with that man you see over there. That's Link Redd standing by my car. I suspect you recognize him, right?"

"I figured that would happen. What did Henry tell you Sheriff?"

"Enough. It seems you boys forgot a few details when we first visited back on Elkhorn Creek."

"Yeah, I guess we did. Henry tell you about it?"

"He told me his version. Harry, I need three things from you. First, I want your version of what happened to Gerald Cahalan. And, second, I want you tell me where your uncle Rave is. And third, and this is the most important of the three, I want the truth. Think you can do that?"

"Yes sir. I wish I'd done it before now. I feel awful bad about how it's all turned out. Am I in a lot of trouble Sheriff?"

"We'll see about that after you tell me your side of everything. Okay?"

"Yes sir."

"First, how did you end up here with this pickup? Is this your uncle's truck?"

"Yes. He's kind of mad at me right now. After he hurt that cowboy over there, I told him I was through with what we were doing. He got real mad. He told me I was like all the rest. A wimp he called me. He brought me back here to the truck on the ATV and told me to wait for him. He was going to finish what he started. Then he headed back up the Big Lost valley. He was going up the Burma Road over the White Knob to Copper Basin—put out more wolf bait."

The sheriff sat down on the tailgate next to Harry. "Rick will you let me talk to Harry alone for a minute?"

"Sure Chester." Rick took a couple of steps backward and then turned and headed over toward Link.

"All right Harry. Let's go back to the morning you found the hunter. Let's hear the real story this time."

"Sheriff, this is none of Henry's doing. I don't want him to get into trouble."

"Don't worry about that right now, just tell me the truth about that morning."

"Okay. Everything we told you that day was the truth. You know, about that crazy guy coming to get us and taking us to that hunter's body. That was right. What we left out was the part about our uncle. You see, Rave was with us. We always hunted with him. He taught us how since we were just kids. Our dad didn't like to hunt so our uncle taught us." Harry scooted forward on the tailgate until his left foot touched the ground.

"When we got to the dead man he was lying face up and he looked real creepy. His eyes were wide open. And, there was frozen spit around his mouth. Real scary looking. He was the first dead man I'd ever seen."

Tilghman turned slightly more toward Harry. "Could you tell what caused his death?"

"No sir, he looked like he just fell over. There weren't no blood or nothing."

"You mean he hadn't been scavenged by animals or didn't have any visible wounds?"

"That's right. He just was there, dead in the snow."

"What time was it?"

"Real early Sheriff, 'bout 9:00 or 9:30."

"Okay Harry, here is the tough question. If I've got it right, there was you and your brother and your uncle and Wishful Wicks at the scene. Anyone else?"

"No sir."

"So, it's obvious then that you, in fact, all of you, that morning made no effort to contact the authorities about your discovery. Why not?"

"That's what I mean. Henry wanted to go back down to the highway and get help; he started to do just that."

"So, why didn't he? The sheriff interrupted.

"My uncle stopped him, that's why. He said to leave it. He had an idea. That's what he said."

"And, what was his idea?"

"Well, he told me to take the dead man's rifle and for all of us to head back to camp. He said he would take care of the body. That strange fellow didn't want to leave; but Rave can be kind of scary when he wants to, and that fellow got the message and went with Henry and me."

"You just left, that's it?"

"Yes sir. But then, just as we got out of seeing range we began to hear the howls, the wolf calls. Henry and I knew right away that it was Rave doing it; we knew his call. He was real good at wolf calling. If you didn't know better, you'd think them wolves was coming back."

"What did Wicks do?"

"Strange. He started to call back at uncle Rave. Crazy like. The two of them sounded just like the real thing, I mean it sent chills up your back. And, did Henry tell you this part? The Chilly Butte pack started to answer. Henry and I made it double time back to camp."

"What happened to Wicks?"

"Don't know. He disappeared. We didn't see him again until the next day when he came back to get us. That's when we went back to the spot where the hunter was. And then you and the deputy and the ranger showed up."

"You didn't call us? You mean to tell me that you waited in camp until the next day and you never thought to call someone?"

"No, Sheriff. Henry and I were scared like I said. We waited for our uncle to come back to camp and tell us what to do but he never showed up. I don't know who called you unless it was Rave. He never told me if he did. When that Wicks guy came back to get us, he acted like he had never seen us before. He was real strange, real strange I tell you."

"Did you still have the hunter's rifle?"

"Yes, I had it. But after we talked to you, Henry and I got scared you'd find out so we buried it."

Tilghman stood up and faced Harry. "Anything else?"

Harry stood up as well and stood straight. "No, I guess that's about it. I feel better even if I am in trouble. What do I do now Sheriff?"

"You say your uncle was headed for Copper Basin?"

"Yes, that's what he said. He knows where the Chilly Butte pack hangs out over there so that's where he was going to do some baiting."

"Okay, I'm sending you back to Challis with the ranger. I want you to join up with your father and brother and stay in town until I get back. Got it?"

"Yes sir."

The two men began walking toward the ranger and Link. The sheriff put his arm around Harry's shoulders as they walked.

"I think we can figure this thing out Harry. I don't want you to do too much worrying. Okay?"

"Okay." Harry looked up at Tilghman and nodded.

Link and Tilghman watched the ranger's truck pull out on Highway 93 and head north toward Challis.

"Link, I'm going to take you home before I head out to look for Elder."

"Let me go with you Chester. I've got a stake in this."

"Yeah, no doubt, but you need to see to that bumpy head first. I'll let you know when I've got him and you can come look at the bad guy through the bars. That ought to make you feel better."

"What would make me feel better is a little payback. You sure you can handle this alone? That guys no namby-pamby. He's a dangerous character."

"Link, you must have forgotten. I've got my wonder-dog with me." Hot Sauce jumped up on the dash and shook all over. He knew the sheriff was taking about him.

Link got into the passenger side and reached out to pet the Chihuahua. "Yeah, I guess that changes everything."

Custer County sheriff's report & incident log
2:45 a.m.
Deputies responded to two separate fire alarms in downtown Challis.

FIFTY-3   I SPY

THE MAN WAS OVER THREE HUNDRED YARDS down the side of the mountain but he appeared as a big as a video game in the *Monarch Gold* riflescope. The sharpshooter had watched him for nearly a half-hour as he filled the tin with white powder and prepared a place to hide the bait. Several times, Jamie thought about stopping the bad character at his work but he didn't.

He knew what he was doing and he knew who he was. They had met once before, in Challis. Jamie would never forget that meeting either. He still had a scar over his left ear as a reminder. He could also see the white powder in his scope and he knew what that was too. He knew what it could do to any wolf that tasted its sweetness.

Jamie had only been in the mountains a couple of weeks when he was told about Xylitol. The shepherds told him. They said that three grams of the artificial sweetener, benign as it is to humans, can kill a 65-pound dog in a matter of minutes. The stuff, they told Jamie, is easily purchased at any health food store and is widely used in baking and low calorie chewing gum. In all canines, the sweetener causes a sudden and dangerous surge in insulin. And it happens quickly. As the blood sugar levels drop, the sheepherder explained, the animal becomes weak and lethargic. Within 30 minutes, without medical help, it would suffer brain trauma and die. The man at work below Jamie knew all of this too. He was counting on it. It made Jamie very angry.

Jamie hoped that Rave Elder would finish and move along. He'd collect the white death after he left and no harm would be done. Then, as Jamie adjusted the optics on the scope, Rave pulled the pelt from the travel box on the ATV and scraped it on the ground around the bait station. Jamie's face flushed and his finger moved over and lightly touched the trigger. The shot would be easy. He had made ones that were more difficult many times before. He increased slightly the pressure on the curved metal piece and felt the tension on the inside of his finger. It would be a simple thing to do.

Rave heard the noise before Jamie did, but Jamie could tell that someone or something was coming by the way the man hurriedly scampered back to the ATV and returned the pelt to the box. He watched Rave quickly gather his materials and attempt to start the ATV. As Jamie looked away from the scope, he could see the sheriff's Jeep top the ridge and come quickly down the Burma Road. Jamie looked again through the scope at Rave. He could tell he was having trouble getting the ATV to crank. Jamie was happy about that. The bad character would have to confront the sheriff. He would have to explain what he was doing; and the sheriff would take care of that. Jamie squirmed down in his prone position and waited for the drama to play out. He nestled his eyes deep in the scope rubber and watched the two men come together.

Custer County sheriff's report & incident log
5:25 p.m.
A call that an officer was down came in to dispatch.

FIFTY-4   MEXICAN STANDOFF

THE JEEP RAISED A THICK CLOUD OF DUST as it approached the man sitting nervously on the ATV. Tilghman had no doubt who the rider was. The thought of what he had done to Gerald Cahalan and what he had done to his friend, Link Redd, made the sheriff press down on the accelerator harder. He wanted this guy. He wanted to see him in a cell in the Custer County jail.

The sheriff could tell that Elder was trying to get his ATV started and had a plan to cut him off if he did. But that didn't happen and the sheriff pulled up to within twenty-five feet of the suspect. He exited the Cherokee quickly and unsnapped the restraining strap on his holster as he did. Hot Sauce made an excited leap to the ground right behind the sheriff.

"Rave Elder, I'm Sheriff Tilghman" he exclaimed loudly, "and I want you to sit real still on your ride and keep your hands where I can see them."

The sheriff had almost reached Rave when the ATV suddenly came to life and the rider gunned the engine. Rave spun it in place and the spinning wheels threw dust and small stones up into the sheriff's face.

Tilghman was momentarily blinded by the debris and his nose and mouth felt the bitter taste of clay. He could hear Hot Sauce barking and he put his hand blindly to his sidearm. Suddenly he heard the engine sputter and die and a man cuss. The sheriff blinked over and over. When his eyes cleared enough to see, what

271

he saw was Rave standing in front of him with an old Smith and Wesson .38 revolver pointed at his chest. The sheriff squeezed his sidearm in his holster and knew that the day had finally come. He deliberately pulled his .45 from the holster and raised it toward Rave. He blinked again and rubbed his hand quickly across his eyes.

"You're in enough trouble without this Rave. Put that pistol down and let's get this thing settled."

The sheriff expected to hear the explosion of Rave's gun. He thought about shooting first but then realized the bad habit he had gotten into over the years now came into play as well. The chamber in his semi-automatic was empty. He hadn't chambered a round when he put the gun on that morning. His sidearm was *cocked, locked and ready to rock* as the saying goes. He hadn't done that for a long time. Tilghman had gotten careless over the years, or maybe it was lazy. Now his bad habit had put him into a no-win situation. It would take two hands to chamber a round. If he did that, Tilghman figured that Rave would probably kill him before he finished the task. He held his ground.

"Rave, you know you will have to face justice sooner or later so put your weapon on the ground and let's go back to Challis. You're in enough trouble as it is; killing a law officer will get you the death penalty for sure."

"Justice! Did you say justice, Sheriff?" Rave finally spoke. He was calm and he held the revolver without shaking. "There's your justice, that white powder on the ground over there. That bait will rid my land of those varmints that prey on my livelihood. It will do what most people in Idaho want. That's my kind of justice, peoples' justice."

Tilghman sensed that if he could get Rave to talk he had a chance. The sheriff holstered his sidearm but didn't snap the restraining strap.

"OK. Lower your gun Rave. Let's talk. You don't want to shoot me. Lower your pistol." The sheriff waited as Rave held firm for a moment but then slowly let the revolver come down to his side.

"Rave, I've been sheriff in these parts for over 30 years. This badge on my chest stands for something that I believe in strongly. It stands for the rule of law. It stands for settling our differences according to that law. Law not made by each and every one of us but law made by all of us, together. It's that idea that makes the land you live in every day worth living in. When you stepped over that boundary, then you violated the basic idea we live by in our country; you sent us back to a time when it was every man for himself. When you couldn't raise a family or your stock without a gun on your hip and another propped inside your cabin door. When you got up every morning afraid and you went to bed every night the same way. That's why I'm here to take you back with me to Challis, Rave. I can't let you do what you're doing."

Sheriff Tilghman took a step forward. "So, come on. Give me your pistol and let's go to the car."

Rave looked confused for a second. Then he raised the revolver again and pointed it at the sheriff about chest level. "No! No, you've got it all wrong. This damn law you're talking about ain't our doing. We didn't make this law. The damn easterners and the fuckin' feds made this law. It weren't the people in Idaho that made it. They're the ones that put the mangy, no account wolves in our land. And, I'll be damned if I'm going to stand by and watch these foreigners take what's mine. Take what I've worked all my life to build. Hell with you Sheriff and your damn law! Hell with you!"

Rave took a step back and turned to get on the ATV. Tilghman whispered *shit* under his breath and once again reached for his sidearm. This time as he cleared the leather he simultaneously exercised the slide and chambered a round.

273

"Rave, stop right there! This thing is over. Put down your weapon!"

Rave Elder, without a word, spun, raised his gun and fired.

Jamie Hightower flinched as he watched the sheriff fall to the ground. He put his eye deep into the scope rubber and watched as the shooter approached Sheriff Tilghman. There was no time to think, only time to act.

Custer County sheriff's report & incident log
5:45 p.m.
A medical evacuation helicopter was called to the White Knob mountains somewhere on the Burma Road.

FIFTY-5   FASTER THAN A SPEEDING BULLET

THE COPPER COATED, SOFT LEAD ROUND passed through Rave's upper torso with a velocity of 3000 feet per second. The man's beating red heart muscle was instantly turned into viscous mush. There was no time for his life to flash before his eyes—the bullet and God merely flipped the switch and the body hit the ground before the brain recognized the death of the body. What had been good or bad about Rave Elder was rendered irrelevant by the custom 150 grain-Swift A-Frame bullet from the fine custom rifle with the initials GBC and the date engraved into the barrel.

Jamie held his position for a moment and then returned the scope covers to their protective position and stood up. He smiled slightly, he couldn't help himself. He was relieved that he hadn't missed his target a second time. There was something about the feel of a fine firearm that gave him cheer and comfort.

Jamie looked down on the two men sprawled out on the ground; unloaded the clip and ejected the spent shell casing from the chamber. As he slammed the bolt back into position, he started down the steep slope toward the Copper Basin. He thought he saw the sheriff move but he wasn't sure. He hoped the old lawman was alive—he needed to finally get the hunter thing off his mind and out of his conscience. Jamie knew he would be ready to let justice make account of his actions. The killing of two men in his young life was

275

more than enough for him. He thought about Canada. He wondered what his father would make of all of it.

As he walked by the body of Rave Elder he approached the sheriff and bent down. "Sheriff, do you remember me?"

Sheriff Tilghman looked up through his clouded vision at the young man that stood over him. He gripped the flesh just under his left shoulder tightly, trying to stem the flow of blood.

With some tremolo in his husky voice he answered. "Yes, I remember you Jamie. Kind of been wondering where you and that rifle got off to son. Now I know."

"You hurt bad Sheriff?"

"Bad enough I suspect. You'd better get some help to us quick. I don't know how much blood this old body can spare. There's a radio in that Cherokee, or wait, you can try my cell phone. It's in my shirt pocket here. It may have a little blood on it."

"Who do I call?"

"Just hit the 5 key. That'll get the deputy down in Mackay. Tell her, her name is Constance Quick, where we are and that if she doesn't get the medics here pronto, she's going to be working for Charlie Two Leaf. Tell her to get on the radio and get word to that Indian too."

The sheriff forced himself to stand and he looked around. "Where's my dog?" He tried to call out but his voice was shaky.

Jamie handed the phone back to the sheriff. "What can I do Sheriff?"

"Find that damn dog of mine, will you?"

Jamie started to do as the sheriff asked but then he paused. "Sheriff, am I in trouble for shooting that man? I had to do it. He was going…"

"He was going to kill me Jamie. Son, you saved this old sheriff's life. What do you think?"

"Sure, thank you. Oh, and Sheriff, I need to tell you something else I've done."

"Save it Jamie, just go find my dog, will you? You remember don't you? You're still working for me."

"Right. I'll do that right now. What's the dog's name?"

"Hot Sauce. When you find him, don't let that tiger get the best of you. He can be a load."

"Yes sir."

6:45 p.m.
*Coroner was called to a shooting and the death of one man
on the Burma Road.*

FIFTY-6   OUCH!

THE BLACK IMPOSING VEHICLE MOVED SLOWLY down Capitol
Avenue, past the Mackay Historical Museum and the adjoining
library and turned left on Spruce Street. The driver pulled across
two parking spaces in the lot in front of the Bear Bottom Inn and
killed the engine.

A voice from the back seat practically shouted, "See, I told
you she would be in Mackay. That's her red BMW right there. I told
you, didn't I?" The man sitting next to Mike told him to shut up.

A short, squat man in a heavy turtleneck sweater and blue
blazer stepped out of the driver's side and walked down the short
sidewalk and up on the wood porch between two carved animal
totems that held up the overhang. He tried to open the front door
before he noticed the closed sign in the window. He squinted
through the divided panes of glass. The man turned back in the
direction of the Hummer and shook his head no. As he was about to
leave he caught sight of another note stuck to one side of the door. It
read: *Mrs. Cahalan, your key is stuck in the lock of room #3. We'll see you
in the morning. Enjoy your stay.* It was signed Helen Krantz, Mgr.

Sarah Cahalan had just closed her cell phone when the
knock came. She figured it was the motel manager so she went to
the door and opened it. The man was about as wide as the door and
he looked harsh; she took a deep, quick breath. "Yes," she said.

"Sarah Cahalan, my name is Rubin. I'm from Nevada," he
continued. "I've got someone with me that would like to talk with

278

you." He turned toward the parking lot and pointed towards the black Hummer parked next to Sarah's BMW. "Would you mind walking out to the car with me?"

Sarah hesitated, took a step back and pushed the door slightly closed.

"Who is it?" she said.

The man sort of smiled. "Mrs. Cahalan, believe me, you're in no danger. I don't want you to be frightened. We just need to get a clarification of a story the man in the car has told us. I think you know him. It's Mike Cahalan. Now, will you please come with me?"

Sarah realized who the man was and she moved slightly behind the opened door.

"Please, Mrs. Cahalan." He lowered his voice and moved slightly forward. "Sarah, we are going to do this one way or the other. I think it is in your best interest to stay calm and come to the car with me. Please." Rubin emphasized his request by moving his foot inside the door jam.

Sarah hesitated but then opened the door wide and took a step out of the room. The pair walked off the wooden porch and Rubin followed just behind Sarah to the car. He walked around to the passenger's side, opened the door, and nodded.

"Please, get in." Sarah balked.

"We're not leaving this parking lot, don't worry. I just want this conversation to be private. Please, get in."

As Sarah climbed in the Hummer, she saw Mike sitting in the back seat next to a man that looked almost identical to the driver. The two were dressed exactly the same. She could tell that Mike was nervous. He started to speak but the man sitting next to him nudged him forcefully.

Rubin turned toward the passenger's side. "Okay Sarah, I'm going to lay it on the line. You can count on what I say and I expect the same from you. Agreed?"

Sarah tried to look over her shoulder at Mike but the driver shook his head no and repeated his question. "Agreed, Sarah?"

"Yes," she said quietly.

"Okay, this is what we need. You see, Mike is one of those kind of men that doesn't have a lot of self-control. You know the type, I'm sure. Those that just think first of their passions before they engage their reason. They live for today, the instant pleasure. Let the tomorrow be damned they say. That kind. I suspect you know that about Mike better than I do. Yes?"

Sarah didn't answer. She sensed that he didn't expect one.

"Well, the problem is that there are few things in life that give you pleasure that don't come with a price tag attached. And, you see Sarah, Mike has enjoyed his pleasure for quite some time at our expense. Unfortunately for him, the day to pay up has arrived. And, guess what? He tells us he doesn't have the funds to settle his debt."

Rubin reached down and started the engine. Sarah looked at him as he turned on the heater.

"Don't worry; I just thought you might be getting a little chilled." The driver adjusted the controls and then turned back to face Sarah.

"Let me get to the point. Mike owes my employer in Nevada a sizeable amount of money but, unfortunately, he tells us that he will have to wait for awhile longer before he can settle up. Well, the reality is that my boss has waited as long as he is going to wait. In other words, the day of reckoning has come for Mike and that is the reason we are here in Idaho. Now, Mike has told us that you have agreed to help him settle his arrears. He says there is money coming to you for an insurance settlement, I believe. That's his story."

Rubin paused as he reached out and turned down the heater fan. "Is that the case Sarah?"

Sarah was silent for almost a minute. Rubin didn't disturb her.

Abruptly, Mike called out from the back seat. "For Christ sake Sarah, tell him!"

"Shut up Mike!" Rubin said without turning.

"There is no insurance money," Sarah began softly. "My husband didn't have any life insurance. He had a fatal heart condition that wouldn't allow an underwriter to approve his life insurance applications. We tried but didn't have any success."

"That's a fuckin' lie!" Mike shouted.

Rubin turned quickly. "Carl shut him up. If you have to, stick a rag in his mouth. Okay, Sarah, go on."

"That's it. I can't pay you what Mike owes. I'm sorry. Mike will have to pay his debts. I can't help him."

Sarah folded her hands in her lap and tensely waited.

"I see...I see," Rubin finally responded. "All right then, if that's the way it is, you can go back to your room. That's all we need from you. Oh, and Sarah. I am very sorry about your recent loss. I know how that must hurt. Thank you for your cooperation."

Rubin quickly opened the driver's door, came around, and opened Sarah's door. As she slid off the high seat and her feet touched the gravel, Rubin stopped her.

"One more question," he said.

"Yes," she answered apprehensively.

"Well, it's kind of a strange question. You see, my partner and I are history buffs and I was wondering...there's supposed to be an old settlers' cemetery around here, close to Mackay somewhere. You wouldn't know where it is would you?"

Sarah was puzzled by the question. "No, no I don't. I'm not from here. Maybe someone in town could tell you."

Rubin just shook his head and shut the door.

"Oh, one other thing Sarah. You might want to forget about our little meeting." Rubin smiled and turned away.

Sarah didn't look back at the Hummer as she walked up on the porch and pushed the door open to her room. She checked her cell phone for messages as soon as she had closed the door.

When she parted the curtains and looked out over the window air-conditioner, she could see the big black Hummer pulling slowly back out. She watched it as it went by the city park. She said a wordless prayer that the men would leave and not come back.

She sat down on the rustic wood double bed and pulled a stuffed bear to her chest. She thought that it was a nice touch for the Bear Bottom Inn. The soft animal felt good.

Someone knocked on her door and she jumped and then froze in place. She decided she wouldn't answer. The knock came again and someone called out.

She thought she heard the word *sheriff*, so she pitched the bear onto the other double bed and scooted off the mattress. She stood up to look toward the front windows. The knock came again, this time louder.

Sarah opened the door slightly.

"Hello Mrs. Cahalan." Sarah eyes locked onto the large silver and gold badge on the man's chest. "Do you remember me? I'm Chief Deputy Charlie Two Leaf—Sheriff Tilghman's chief deputy."

Sarah imperceptibly let out a sigh and said, "Of course Deputy, I remember you."

"Would it be all right if I have a word with you Mrs. Cahalan?"

"Well, of course Deputy. Is Sheriff Tilghman with you?"

"No ma'am. The sheriff has been hurt apprehending a suspect and is in the clinic in Challis."

"Come in Deputy. Is it serious? I hope he is all right," Sarah led Charlie Two Leaf back to the small table in the corner and offered him a chair.

"He'll be fine. It's just a flesh wound. Lots of blood but not serious. I'll tell you, that old sheriff is tough. He'll be fine."

Charlie declined the offer to sit down and instead asked Sarah if they could go back outside on the porch. She agreed and grabbed her coat off the rack near the door.

"Mrs. Cahalan I need to ask you about that black Hummer I saw you get out of a few minutes ago. I assume you know those men and I need to know who they are."

Sarah felt a little faint and sat down. Charlie Two Leaf sat down next to her.

Custer County sheriff's report & incident log
6:45 p.m.
*The owner of some cows was advised that his bovines
were wandering onto the highway near Iron Creek.*

FIFTY-7   FEELIN' LUCKY

BOSCO FX HESITANTLY STUCK HIS HEAD IN THE DOOR of room number 5. The first thing that caught his eye was a pair of tall boots at the foot of the second bed in the room. The bed was mostly behind a screen so Bosco couldn't see who was in it. The one nearest the door was empty so he stepped in and called out.

"Sheriff, Sheriff Tilghman, are you in here?"

A voice from behind the screen called out vigorously. "Hell yes I'm in here. Is that you Mr. Fx? If it is come on in, if it's a doctor stay the hell out."

"It's me Sheriff, Bosco." Bosco walked around the end of the screen and faced the sheriff who was propped up in the bed on about four pillows. There were two western paperback novels next to him. One had a drawing of two riders chasing a stampeding herd over a ridge.

"They said it was all right to come in and talk with you."

"Oh, I'm fine Mr. Fx. It's just a flesh wound. There was blood everywhere but not a whole lot of damage. I'd already be out of here except they won't release me until morning. You know that observation thing these people like to do to run up the bill."

The sheriff straightened up and swung his feet off the bed. "Get those two chairs out of the hallway and let's visit. I am assuming you've got something to tell me."

"I do Sheriff, indeed I do."

The sheriff pulled the curtains almost closed and the two men settled in their chairs.

"You like my outfit Mr. Fx? It's a dandy ain't it?"

"Yes Sheriff, it's quite becoming."

"So what've you got? Linda told you the Elder brothers' side of what happened, didn't she?"

"Yes she did. That's quite a tale. But the evidence I have supports their story."

"Well, I guess we finally know one thing for sure Bosco—we know that the wolves didn't kill Cahalan. But we still don't know how the man died on that cold morning, although I do have a confession of sorts. I'll tell you about it shortly. Now what about the brothers' story. What do you think of that?"

"Makes sense. I did a DNA analysis on those wolf hairs I got off Lincoln Redd's clothes. We assumed that they came from his handling of the wolf pelt that Rave Elder was using to mark his bait traps, right?"

The sheriff nodded his agreement.

"They match up perfectly with the samples of the wolf that Dr. Cahalan killed. Simply stated, that means Rave probably took it the morning of the hunter's death. Of course, now we can do a follow up on the pelt itself and confirm that finding. And, when I get a chance to look at the rifle that Jamie Hightower had, maybe we can find a fingerprint of one of the Elder clan on it. That would support the brothers' claim that they handled the rifle that morning."

Tilghman leaned back and crossed his legs. "You know Bosco, I really don't doubt the Elder boys' story but it's nice to have the proof. What about that second rifle we turned up? That Winchester?"

"Well, it had been fired fairly recently. There was one round missing from the clip. And, a bullet from that round I found embedded in a tree; it matched up with the rifle. It was a full metal jacket round; the kind marksmen use. It's impossible to say whether or not it had anything to do with our case but it is a coincidence."

"Oh, it's more than that Bosco," the sheriff interrupted. "It seems the young man that saved my life yesterday believes he killed Dr. Cahalan on that morning. He claims he only meant to fire a round close enough to the hunter to scare him. You see, Jamie Hightower had worked with that wolf pack, the Chilly Buttes pack, all summer in the mountains trying to keep them away from the sheepherders. He'd grown attached to those wild beasts he told me. When our doctor shot one of them that morning, Jamie was watching through the scope on his Winchester rifle. He told me it really hurt him to see that wolf killed. He said he was afraid the hunter would get another so he wanted to scare him off the mountain. That's why he shot. He meant just to shoot close enough to frighten the man, he claims. But, then he watched as Cahalan fell over. The boy assumed he had missed his target and killed the man. He said he'd lined up his sight on a nearby tree just beyond the hunter and just to his left. What do you think about that Bosco?"

Bosco took a few seconds to think on the story before he answered. Finally, he responded, "I don't think he missed his target Sheriff. If that Winchester model 70, is his rifle, then he hit his target. Of course, the question is, did that bullet pass through Cahalan's body before it embedded in that tree. I think I can answer that one too. You see, I did an analysis of the bullet. There was no trace of human DNA on the round. Like I said Sheriff, I think Jamie hit his target. So where does that leave us?"

The sheriff grinned. He was glad the little round man's evidence seemed to clear Jamie. "Right back where we started, he said. What else you got?"

"What have I got?" Bosco Fx smiled broadly. "Something I believe you might like. Remember the cell phone?"

"Of course."

"They're great little gadgets those cell phones. This one, Dr. Cahalan's, had a couple of telling pictures locked in its memory. I'd like to show you one in particular."

Bosco reached down under the table between his legs and opened a canvas bag. He extracted a manila folder which he flipped through. Tilghman leaned forward obligingly.

"It seems our good doctor recorded the scene following his hunting triumph. There were images of his wolf kill. He had one with his rifle lying across the carcass. He even had a self photo showing a broad smile. But the one that was the most interesting for us is this one." Bosco spun it around. "I refined the image as best I could and took it up to an 8x10 print size. Take a look Sheriff and tell me what you see."

Tilghman studied the image. After a few moments he looked up at Bosco and then back at the image. "Is that what I think it is? Those dark outlines in that tree line."

"Yep, it is."

"You mean Gerald Cahalan had company that morning up at his hunting blind?"

"Yep, he did." Bosco grinned.

"Well hell Bosco, stop fooling around, tell me what you think about that."

"What do I think? I think it was kind of crowded up on Elkhorn Creek the morning that Dr. Cahalan died. The hunter was not alone and that's for sure. You know he took those pictures in a way that makes me believe he thought he was the only person on that mountain."

"Any way to tell who those two shadows belonged to? Or if they were aware of each other?"

"Not really. They were pretty far apart so it's possible that the one didn't know the other was there. We can't say. There's not enough detail to identify them either."

The sheriff stood up and opened the curtains. He stood in front of the window for a long minute and then turned back to face Bosco.

"If I were a betting man, I'd bet that one of those two shadows is Wishful Wicks. He told me that he had been watching that hunter. The other one; I don't know. It could have been Rave Elder. Or, it could have been..." the Sheriff hesitated.

"Or, it could have been? Bosco asked.

"Nothing, just thinking out loud. Got anything else?"

Oh, just the wallet. I looked at it. There were fingerprints all over it. The victim's were certainly there, and, as you might expect, there were prints of Mr. Wicks. I even found one from you. You know you should be more careful with evidence sheriff."

"Yeah, yeah, I know. What else?"

"There was another print, a partial that was unknown. Could be anybody." Bosco began to gather his photos and retrieved his canvas bag. "That's about it for my show and tell Sheriff."

"Okay Mr. Fx. Before you go, I have a two-part question for you. How did Dr. Cahalan die? And did someone murder him?"

Bosco looked out the window. "Don't know Sheriff. Like you said, we know the wolves didn't kill him. At least the four-legged kind."

"Yeah, it's the other wolves I'm worried about. If that man didn't die of a heart attack, which I must admit is highly probable, then I don't want the other kind getting by with his death. How in the hell are we going to ever solve this puzzle Mr. Fx?"

Bosco got up to leave. Before he started for the door, he put the canvas bag strap over his shoulder. "Well Sheriff, we'll either get a confession or just have to get awful lucky."

"Yeah, lucky. Maybe one of those shadows in your photo will bring me the answer. I bet one of the other knows what happened to our hunter up on Elkhorn Creek."

Bosco turned at the door. "I'd take that bet myself. Hey, get out of that bed soon Sheriff. These hospitals will kill you."

"Don't I know it. Thanks Bosco. Come by the office tomorrow and I'll buy you lunch."

"Will do."

Custer County sheriff's report & incident log
9:25 p.m.
Two cars came together unexpectedly on Main Street in Challis.

FIFTY-8   WHITE WOLF

SARAH HAD SEEN THE SIGN when she came down Highway 93 the day before on her way to Mackay. She remembered it was somewhere just after she had passed Trail Creek Road heading south. Now, as she drove north, she slowed her BMW down looking for the Forest Service sign again. It identified the turnout at Elkhorn Creek. As she climbed to the top of a grade she saw it and slowed down. Cautiously she turned into the rough gravel entrance just off the highway behind a barb-wire fence with no gate. As her car left the hard road surface, the tires snapped and popped as they crossed the rough irregular gravel. Sarah drove up next to the sign and turned off the engine. She sat quietly for a while just looking around through the rolled up windows. It was quiet at the base of the Lost Mountain Range. The scenery was dramatic.

Jerry had told her about this place. How untouched it was. She could see what he meant as she looked in all directions. To the east, the ground rose rapidly to the tallest peaks in Idaho. Her husband had said the mountains were still rising. Sarah didn't understand the geology he talked about but now, in the morning light, the mountains appeared stark, painted in multi-shades of gray. The jagged tops were beautifully back-lit by the new sun but the detail was hidden by the black shadows at the highest elevations.

Sarah opened the car door and stepped out onto the trail that was visible as it climbed into the foothills and disappeared into a line of tree cover. The day was clean and the skies were brilliant with only a few wispy clouds over the White Knob low mountains to the west. Sarah looked back over her shoulder down into the Big Lost River valley below; down to where a few ranches clung to the sides of the river which meandered north and south through stately cottonwoods and low willows. She opened the back door and put on a heavy short-waisted jacket. The day was not particularly cold, but the air chilled Sarah's body as she began to climb the trail. There was a light dusting of snow on the ground which made it feel colder than the ambient temperature.

As she reached into the pocket of her jacket her hand found the small camera. Sarah had forgotten about it. She couldn't remember the last time she had used it since Jerry had given the compact device to her for Christmas. She took it out and opened its side panel. She pointed the lens toward the car and pressed the record button. Sarah panned the scene in a full 360 degree arc. She looked down at the display and replayed the recording. The batteries were fine and Sarah decided to keep the camera out and use it as she went.

Sarah Cahalan was winded. She had climbed up the trail several hundred feet in elevation. She sat down on a large boulder that seemed to be made just for such a purpose and looked around as she breathed heavily. Her car and the road appeared far away from where she sat and she couldn't believe she had covered so much ground.

Suddenly Sarah felt a wave of sadness. Her body shivered inside the heavy coat. She looked around and wondered where her husband had died. It had to be here, somewhere near. She shook her head and wondered why she had come to this place. What made her do it? What made her do all of it? Suddenly her thoughts rediscovered her lover. She felt apprehensive as she thought about Mike and those men from Nevada. They were serious men, she knew it. Her lie had probably put Mike in danger; she knew that too. But, she had done it anyway. She just wanted him out of her life. Those men made it happen.

How did it all get so complicated? She thought, as her breathing returned to normal. Sarah wished she could just go back. Start over. Make different choices. Maybe it would just all go away when she got her money. She would leave Idaho. Get away from the past. Get away from all the complications. Sarah suddenly missed Jerry.

Sarah reacted involuntarily and took in a deep, quick breath. Her eyes focused for the first time on the wolf. It appeared to be frozen in place just a few feet from where she sat. She wondered how long it had been there. At first, the large white animal, didn't appear to be real. Sarah's mind told her it must be a joke someone was playing. The wolf didn't move, but a faint cloud of vapor extended from it nostrils at rhythmic intervals. Sarah was afraid to move. She couldn't think. She was alone. Defenseless.

"She won't hurt you," the voice behind Sarah startled her again and she jumped off the rock. She wanted to turn toward the voice but couldn't make herself look away from the animal that fixed on her with intense yellow eyes.

"That one is my friend, she won't hurt you, I promise. Ain't she pretty."

The dirty man, his face covered in a dark mass of hair and a long ponytail walked into Sarah's line of sight; between her and the wolf.

"It's all right. Is that a camera you've got there? Why don't you take our picture? Me and my friend over there. We would like that."

Sarah sat back down on the rock. Without knowing why, she raised the small silver box and did as the strange dirty man had asked. She forced a smile and lowered the camera.

"You really scared me," she said finally. "You and that...your friend there. Is that a real wolf?" For some reason, Sarah felt like the question was silly.

The man came closer. "Can I see? Can ol' Wishful see his picture?" He stuck his face close to Sarah; she couldn't help herself, she reacted to the smell. Sarah held out the opened panel toward the man and pressed the play button.

"That's Wishful all right. Right there. You're pretty lady. What's your name? My name is Wishful Wicks. I live here. That one right there; she's one of my friends. There is ten more of her kind right over there in those trees. There used to be two more but they got killed. You're pretty, what's your name?"

Sarah Cahalan had never felt as alone as she felt now. She glanced down the Elkhorn Creek trail again toward her red BMW. It seemed a million miles away.

"My name is Sarah," she said nervously as she turned back to face the man. I need to go now. I'll..."

"Oh no! Stay for just a little while. Wishful doesn't get to talk to people much. Just to my friends. You can stay a little while, can't you? Can't you Miss Sarah? Just a little while with Wishful and his friends?"

Custer County sheriff's report & incident log
2:40 p.m.
Deputies responded to a roll over off Highway 75 near the Bay Ridge turnout.

FIFTY-9   BE CAREFUL WHAT YOU WISH FOR

"WELL LOOK WHO'S BACK FROM DEATH'S VERY DOOR." Linda smiled broadly as the sheriff walked up to the counter.

"Boy! Are we glad to see you."

Tilghman couldn't help himself, he returned the smile. "Kind of missed me, did ya? I was just gone three days."

"Yeah, we did. Crime has been rampant around Challis since you went and got yourself shot. But now, law and order will again be the order of the day, thank Heavens."

"Linda, you're so funny; the light of my life you are Chief Dispatcher."

"Well that's the way it ought to be. And Sheriff, you'll be glad to know that there's another big fan of yours sitting in your office waiting to just make your day."

"Is that right? Who might that be?" The sheriff looked over his shoulder at his office door and then back to the dispatcher quizzically.

"Well, I ought to have you sit down before I tell you, given your injured state. His initials are WW."

"No! You've got to be kidding me; I hope you don't mean Wishful. Do you?"

"Noooo! I'm not and yes, I do. And, are you ready for what's behind door number three? He says he is here to give you his confession."

"Confession? His confession for what for Christ sake? Has he killed someone else? That's all I need right now is another confession. I really thought that mountain rat was dead and turned to dust by now."

Tilghman rubbed the bandage inside his shirt and grimaced. "Where's my chief deputy?"

"He's on his way back from Mackay. Said he talked with Sarah Cahalan and has some news about that black Hummer. You'll never believe what the Nevada plates on that one reads."

"What?"

"HumThis. Can you believe that?"

"Yeah, I can believe it. Tell Charlie to come to my office as soon as he gets here. I'll go talk with our desperado numero uno. Is there any mud left in the pot?"

"Sure. I made a fresh pot about two days ago. Should be just the way you like it."

"Better bring two—our favorite jail bird expects the amenities when he's in town."

"Of course, got to keep them bums happy these days. Don't want a lawsuit now do we? Oh, I almost forgot. We received the coroner's inquest report on Gerald Cahalan yesterday. You'll be glad to know they don't know any more than you do. They ruled cause of death unknown and classified it as a hunting accident. You got to love it."

"Yeah, you do. We'll keep our file active for a while longer anyway. Coffee?"

"Okay, coming right up."

The sheriff stopped suddenly. "Oh, Linda. Any word on my dog?"

"Not yet. He was in pretty bad shape when Jamie brought him in. Constance took him to Doc Bennett. That wolf bait liked to have done that little crime-fighter in. The vet still has him."

The sheriff nodded and took a deep breath as he walked down the hall to his office. When he came through the door, Wishful jumped up out of his chair.

"Sheriff, I need to be put in jail," he said.

"Well, hello to you too Wishful," the sheriff walked behind his desk and sat down heavily. "What for this time? Murder?"

Wishful paused for a moment. "Yeah, but how did you know?"

The sheriff shook his head. "That's easy, it's your favorite thing to confess to it seems. Who'd you kill this time? The Pope?"

Linda walked in with two cups of coffee. She put the sheriff's on his desk and reached out the other to Wishful. The dirty man took it and sat back down. He looked at the cup and then at Linda.

"Would you have any donuts?"

Linda looked toward the sheriff and frowned and then brusquely turned and walked out of the room.

"Well, who is it you killed Wishful? Let's hear the story; I've got work to do."

"A lady. Can I have cell 4, Sheriff. I like cell 4. It's more private than the others."

"Sure Wishful, cell 4 it is. Now who?"

"I killed that hunter's wife. That's the one. But you see Sheriff, I didn't mean to. I thought I would just make her quiet but she didn't move for a long time. I guess I killed her."

"Whoa, whoa there hombre! The hunter's wife? What hunter? Who do you mean?"

"You know Sheriff, that hunter that I said I killed before, you know up on Elkhorn Creek. His wife, that's the one, that hunter's wife she is...or was. That's the one I killed. I didn't mean to. I didn't really kill the hunter before though. I know I said I did but I lied about that before. But I know who did, I do, I know who did kill him up on Elkhorn Creek."

Charlie Two Leaf came through the door, and when he saw Wishful he turned abruptly to leave.

"Hold on Charlie," the sheriff shouted. "Come on back in here. You've got to hear this. Wishful has dived head first into the loony bin."

The sheriff got up out of his chair and walked to the front of the desk next to where Wishful was sitting. "Okay you old reprobate, repeat what you just said to the deputy. Go on."

Wishful took another sip of coffee and smiled at Charlie. "I killed the hunter's wife; is that what you mean?"

"Yeah, that's it. Continue."

"Deputy, like I told the sheriff, I didn't mean to. She wouldn't stop screaming and hollering. I wasn't going to hurt her none. I just wanted her to keep me company in the mountains for a while. That's all. So I made her quiet. She was scaring my friends."

Charlie showed no reaction to Wishful's claim. "Where? Where did you do this Wishful?" he asked.

"The same place where the hunter was killed. You know on Elkhorn Creek. Right there in the same spot it was. We were just talking about that day. We were just talking but she wouldn't stay."

"What was the lady's name?"

Wishful squirmed around in his chair and rubbed his coffee cup. "I don't know. She was the hunter's wife, that's all I know. She was real pretty. Yes she was, real pretty."

"How did you know she was the hunter's wife?"

"She told me she was. She told me she was when I showed her where the hunter died."

Charlie looked at the sheriff and shook his head.

"I just talked to Sarah Cahalan day before yesterday. She was in Mackay at the Bear Bottom Inn and, get this, so was the Hummer. I don't see how Wishful here could have met her."

Tilghman studied the suspect for a few seconds and then leaned forward, putting his face close to Wishful's grimy forehead.

"Why were you on Elkhorn Creek?"

"I never left there Sheriff. You know, from the day we did the investigation, the day you made me a deputy. I stayed right there in those mountains and, like before, me and the wolves got by. I know who killed the hunter too. I know. I knew who did it all this time."

Tilghman rose back up. "Who?"

"That man. That man in the trees did it. I seen him there. He did it."

"For Christ sake Wishful, what man. Who was he?"

"I don't know his name. He never even seen me. Ol' Wishful is as sly as the fox; as sly as the fox he is. But I saw him." Wishful slurped his cold coffee and smiled broadly.

"Wishful Wicks, have you ever told the truth in your whole life about anything?" The sheriff turned to head to the door. He stopped. "Charlie, put him in cell number 4 until we sort this out."

Wishful stood up to follow Charlie but then stopped. "Sheriff, I've told the truth many a time. This is one of them too. I can prove it, I can prove it."

"Yeah, you can I'm sure. Charlie."

"No, I can Sheriff Tilghman. I've got it in my pocket, right here. Look, I'll show you."

Wishful fished down in his baggy pants and brought out something silver. "See, look!" He extended his arm and held out the small object to the sheriff.

"Where did you get this camera? Charlie, look at this. It's one of those new video cameras. Where did you get this Wishful?"

"I took it. You know, like the wallet. It was hers. The one I made quiet."

Tilghman fingered the compact camera. He recognized and flipped open the small side panel and squinted at the small control panel. He pressed a play button and stood there for about 30 seconds and then the sheriff flipped the panel closed.

"Put him in the cell Charlie and then let's get on the road."

"Where to?"

"Elkhorn Creek."

"Can I go with you like last time?" Wishful asked.

"Hell no! You're not going anywhere. I ain't losing you again until I check out this crazy tale of yours. Get him in the cell Charlie."

Custer County sheriff's report & incident log
5:40 p.m.
Deputy Quick spoke to a Mackay individual about livestock not being cared for properly.

SIXTY-0   ELKHORN

"CHARLIE, TURN OFF THAT DAMN SIREN. There's nobody on the road but us for Mary's sake."

Charlie flipped the switch and the piercing scream fell quiet. "First, you bitch because it's not fixed and then you bitch when it is," the deputy said in a soft voice not turning in the sheriff's direction.

"And, what about Sarah Cahalan? What did she tell you at the Bear Bottom Inn?"

Charlie Two Leaf pushed down on the accelerator a little and the Jeep Cherokee jumped up to over 80 m.p.h.

"Slow down Charlie, you're going to get us both killed."

"That white woman's a liar."

Tilghman waited. "Okay, Charlie, what do you mean?"

"She told me she didn't know the men in the black Hummer. She said they were just tourists looking for some historical sites. But she didn't want to tell me why she got into their car. She was nervous and she was lying."

"What did you find out when you ran a license plate check? Do we know who they are? Could you see if Mike Cahalan was with them?"

"Nevada records indicated some company name for those personalized plates. No names for these guys were listed. The only one I got a look at was the one that got out of the car and went to Mrs. Cahalan's door; she was staying in number 3. He was a bowling ball kind of man—about as wide as he was tall. I was parked under some trees across the street along the far side of the city park. I couldn't see anything inside the Hummer because of the dark, tinted windows. I had followed the vehicle into Mackay. Picked them up when they turned off 75 onto 93."

"Why didn't you follow them out when they left town?"

"I thought about it Sheriff. Decided to talk to Mrs. Cahalan instead. I figured we wouldn't have any trouble finding that Hummer again if those guys hung around. Thought she might tell us who they were and what they were up to. After all, I didn't really have any reason to stop them and you did tell me not to, remember?"

"Yeah. So who do you think they are?"

"You know who they are Sheriff. We've seen that kind before out of Nevada. They're collectors of one sort or another."

"Yeah, and if they've got Mike, he'll pay up for sure."

"For sure."

As the Jeep turned into the Elkhorn Creek turnout, Tilghman saw the red BMW and further up the creek trail he recognized a Forest Service truck.

"That's her car isn't it Charlie?"

"That's it."

"Damn Charlie, do you think that crazy man back in our jail could be telling us the truth for once?"

"We'll soon find out I bet. Rick knows something, he's waving us to come up the trail."

"Drive as far as you can, I'm not sure how steady these old legs are yet."

As Tilghman and Charlie got out of the Jeep, Rick came up to them and handed the sheriff a piece of what looked like a winter lined jacket.

"Chester, I've seen a lot in my life, especially out in this wild country but I'm here to tell this takes the prize. I think we've got another body. Am I going crazy or have we done this before? Right here on the Elkhorn?"

"You don't know the half of it Rick. Wait till you hear this tale. What brought you up here?"

"Look up there," the ranger pointed up to the sky. More than thirty buzzards were riding the thermals up the side of the mountain.

"One of our rangers saw them this morning and came up to see what was down. We haven't found much, but we did find this piece of clothing. There may be more just up the trail on Forest Service land but I'm not sure. Damn it Chester, I think we've got another mystery on our hands."

The ranger pointed back toward the road. "We ran a license check on that BMW, and you will not believe who it belongs to."

"Sarah Cahalan is who it belongs to Rick. And this piece you have might belong to her. Got any flesh yet?"

"Not yet. Just this. Chester the animals in these mountains, if they get a hold of some easy protein, they're not like humans—they don't leave many scraps. We got lucky, so to speak, with the hunter."

"Well, let's find something. At least enough to do a DNA comparison. Rick, this one will solve itself if we can confirm we have a body. I've got a confession sitting back in cell #4, in my jail. And, the guy has given me some pretty convincing evidence to back up his story."

"Who confessed?"

Sheriff Tilghman hesitated. He looked at Charlie Two Leaf and then finally back at the Forest Service ranger.

"Wishful Wicks says he killed Sarah Cahalan; or as he calls her, the hunter's wife."

"And you believe him Chester? Why would he do such a thing?"

"This time I believe him, this time I think I do. As for the why. With a man like Wishful, there really doesn't have to be a why—just a circumstance and an opportunity."

Tilghman took a couple of steps up the trail and then stopped. He turned back and met the ranger's eye.

"You know Rick, there's something mighty strange about what we've found today on Elkhorn Creek, that's for sure. I'm just wondering if there's more justice behind this random tragedy than we will ever discover. Could be. I've reached the point in my life where I'm willing just to trust that there's justice to what we see around us. Whether I recognize it or not. I have to believe that's true in this crazy world of ours."

Tilghman turned and moved up the trail again. Charlie Two Leaf and the ranger fell in behind the old sheriff. The ranger picked up his pace and came along side Tilghman.

"What about the wolves Chester? What if they've scavenged again?"

"I don't know," the sheriff responded without breaking stride. "They're just doing what wild creatures do. I'm convinced that the wolves of the Chilly Buttes didn't kill Gerald Cahalan and they didn't kill the hunter's wife either. But, I'll bet you, those poor devils will damn sure pay the price just the same. What do you want to bet?"

"Is that the justice you expect Chester?"

"It ain't justice, but it's so."

Custer County sheriff's report & incident log
11:40 a.m.
Mackay volunteer Search and Rescue were called to assist in a search for a missing woman near Elkhorn Creek.

SIXTY-1   I LIKE YOU TOO

THE LOUNGE WAS ITS CUSTOMARY TOO DARK TO SEE as Tilghman came in off Main Street. He was looking for a woman who had told Linda on the phone she desperately needed to see him. The woman didn't give her name or tell the dispatcher her business only that she needed to speak with the sheriff and only him.

David Thomas, the manager of the Yankee Fork Restaurant and Lounge, stood by the bar so Tilghman walked over to him.

"Hello David. How's it going?"

"Real good Sheriff, and yourself?"

"Better than I have been for awhile." Tilghman looked around the room.

"How's the arm?"

"Better."

"Looking for someone Chester?"

"As a matter of fact, I am. Linda got a call from a woman who said she needed to talk to me. Said she would be here. Any ideas?"

"Yep, I do. I think the one you're looking for is sitting in that back booth. Came in about 30 minutes ago. Pretty lady too. What in the world would she want with you?"

"No idea."

The sheriff thanked David and started down the line of booths along the far wall of the restaurant. They had high backs so you couldn't see from one to the next. As he reached the last in the line, he could see a woman's hand with rings on two fingers; both with heavy turquoise stones. She had two leather string bands around her wrist. As he came along side the booth, the woman turned to greet him.

She smiled broadly. "Sheriff, came to buy you a drink. How 'bout it?"

"Well, would you look at this... You're about the last person in the world I expected to see."

"Disappointed?"

"About like a ten-year-old at Christmas. What in the world brings you to Challis Victoria?"

"Simple, since I couldn't get you to Boise I came to Challis. I think you owe me a dinner. I'm here to collect."

"Well, I guess you got me there. I'll get some menus."

Tilghman got up and headed back to the front. The old lawman suddenly felt as good as a man can feel.

"Find her?"

"I think so David, I think so. Can I get a couple of menus?"

"Sure Sheriff. What else?"

"Just a little time, thanks David."

Custer County sheriff's report & incident log
1:55 p.m.
Coroner called to the Chilly Buttes cemetery to investigate the discovery of a body.

SIXTY-2   EPILOGUE

Chilly Buttes wolves taken down
Ignacio Hawk, reporting

Contractors working under the authority of the Idaho Fish & Game Department tracked and exterminated all but one of the infamous Chilly Buttes wolf pack near the Settler's Cemetery yesterday. This according to Fish & Game spokesman Jonathon Bunch.

     Bunch said that this pack was selected because of its association with several scavenging incidents in Custer County. He explained further that there has been a strong push by the Governor's office to have the wolf population in Idaho thinned considerably. "It's what a majority of Idahoans want," he said.

     Aerial teams working from a helicopter and a fixed-wing aircraft coordinated with horse teams on the ground had been watching the pack for several days. On Thursday, the trackers noticed the pack digging in what appeared from the distance to be a fresh mound of dirt just outside the cemetery boundaries.

     This is the same pack of wolves that was suspected in either the killing or scavenging of Gerald Cahalan, a hunter from Pocatello, last October up the Elkhorn Creek. The cause of Cahalan's death was ruled a hunting accident but many suspect the wolves had a hand in his death.

On Friday morning, the teams dispersed and the air teams approached the pack from the north by way of the Willow Springs summit. Two shooters on horseback came from the opposite direction up the Big Lost River Valley and crossed Trail Creek Road near the cemetery.

Given the wide open ground in this area, shooters in both the helicopter and fixed-wing aircraft were able to kill 8 of the 10 wolf pack members before they reached cover along the riverbed. A large white wolf and what is thought to be one of her spring pups disappeared in the thick brush and cover.

A tracker on horseback flushed the younger wolf near Lincoln Redd's Bar R Ranch and shot the animal. The white wolf managed to elude trackers and is still on the loose.

A spokesman for Sheriff Tilghman says that his office is investigating the remains of a man discovered where the pack had been digging. The sheriff says that the evidence so far suggests that the man was the subject of a gangland style killing. Both knees and elbows had been shattered by gunshot and his nose had been cut off. He had not been molested by scavengers according to the Sheriff.

The man's identity has not been determined as of this writing. Further details will be made available as they come to light.

This latest episode continues a wild fall and early winter in Custer County. At least two mysterious deaths in the mountains, a shoot-out with the sheriff that ended with a local resident killed and the sheriff wounded. And now we have the latest violent death under investigation.

Stay tuned Custer County and have a Merry Christmas.

Linda Davenport walked into the sheriff's office. "Sheriff have you seen Hawk's latest?" She held up the new edition of the *Salmon River Sentinel-Reader* and waved it above her head.

Tilghman looked at his pretty dispatcher and just nodded.

"Oh, and the prosecuting attorney called before you got in this morning. He says he needs to talk to you about the Wicks case.

Says to tell you he doesn't think there is enough evidence to prosecute the crazy old coot, especially since he withdrew his confession. Carl says he needs a body."

"Great! Is there any more coffee?"

"Yeah, want some?"

"Bring one of those stale donuts with it, will you?"

"The kind with the jelly center?"

"Yeah, that'll work."

Linda turned to walk out.

"Oh, and Linda," the sheriff called out. "Take one to Wishful in cell 4, will you?"

"You're so funny Sheriff. A real comedian."

Custer County sheriff's report & incident log
8:45 p.m.
Custer County deputies were called to investigate an abandoned black Hummer vehicle near where the pavement ends on Trail Creek Road.

SIXTY-3   WHATEVER HAPPENED TO...?

Mike Cahalan

DNA analysis confirmed that the body removed from the shallow grave at the Chilly Buttes Settlers' Cemetery was that of Michael Christopher Cahalan. When Grayson's Funeral Home brought the personal effects recovered from the body to the sheriff's office, two credit cards wrapped in five one-hundred dollar bills were among the items recovered. The name on the cards was that of Gerald B. Cahalan. Mike Cahalan was cremated and his ashes stored in the sheriff's evidence room pending any claim from next of kin.

Sarah Cahalan

Sarah Cahalan's body was never found in the Big Lost Mountains. Sheriff Tilghman, as a precaution, filed a missing person's report with the State, FBI and Interpol.

A woman who claimed to be Sarah's sister, a Jolene Katz from Washington State, filed to recover Sarah's BMW. The resolution of that request is still pending.

Linda Davenport

The dispatcher ran for mayor of Challis in the next election and won. Since the mayor's job was not full time she remained with the sheriff's office.

Bosco Fx

The forensics dilettante found that he could not leave the high country of Custer County. He put his million dollar rolling laboratory in storage and rented a small house in Mackay from the owner of the Bear Bottom Inn. Bosco Fx began to dress in the garb of a cowboy and took to writing western poetry, which he performed to delighted crowds at the cowboy church on Saturday nights.

Jamie Hightower

Jamie was released from responsibility for the death of Rave Elder. The sheriff testified at the inquest into the shooting of Rave Elder that Jamie Hightower was acting in an official capacity for the sheriff's department and had shot Elder to protect the life of a downed officer.

Jamie pleaded guilty to a charge of reckless endangerment for trying to scare the deceased hunter Gerald Cahalan and was given one-year probation. The judge allowed him to return to Texas since he was promised work at the Cal Farley's Boys Ranch in the Panhandle. Jamie was allowed by the sheriff to keep the .270 custom rifle since no one had claimed the gun.

Jeremy Junco

The director of the Citizen Advocates for Wildlife took the news of the extermination of the Chilly Buttes wolf pack bitterly. He immediately sent out an emergency request for donations from the members of the CAW to counter the new threat to the wolves of Idaho. The reaction was strong and the organization had one of the best fund-raising events in their history.

Chief Deputy Charlie Two Leaf

The chief deputy took a short leave of absence from the sheriff's office to search for the last remaining member of the Chilly Buttes wolf pack. The white wolf who had incredibly escaped the tracker's bullets, Charlie explained, was a complimentary symbol to the black wolf and represented continuity for his people. He said he wanted to see if he could find the female and help her reestablish on the Nez Perce reservation near Winchester, Idaho. Charlie Two Leaf felt like it was his obligation to help the lone wolf and that she would be welcomed on the rez and well protected from those who wished to exterminate the lobos in the state.

Bertha Selman

Bertha Selman collected Mike Cahalan's belongings and brought them to the sheriff's office in Challis along with some peanut butter supreme cookies she had baked. Before she left, she requested that the sheriff and his chief deputy stop by for tea the next time they were in Clayton. She also posted a notice on the sheriff's bulletin board that the landlady had a vacant room for rent.

Sheriff Chester A. Tilghman

Chester A. Tilghman was reelected sheriff. The sheriff had several opponents in the election all who claimed that the county was becoming lawless and dangerous under his administration. Sheriff Tilghman refused to debate and stood on his record of over 30 years. He received 90% of the vote.

Howard Jasper Wicks

Howard Jasper Wicks, sometimes known as Wishful Wicks, was discovered dead on Christmas Day in cell #4 of the Custer County Jail. Wishful died of suffocation at the hands of Milford Means a cellmate. Means had been arrested Christmas Eve night for a disturbance at a local Challis west end bar. When asked by the sheriff why he killed Wishful, Means said he didn't remember; he was too drunk.

Charges for the alleged death of Sarah Cahalan were never brought against Wicks since he withdrew his confession and her body was never found.

Wicks was buried in a pauper's grave at the Chilly Buttes Settlers' Cemetery. Sheriff Chester A. Tilghman and Chief Deputy Charlie Two Leaf were the only ones attending. There was no known family to notify.

Victoria Wilds, Ph.D.

Professor Wilds took her well earned sabbatical and joined her friend Jennifer in the wilds of northern Idaho for an extended visit. Victoria was known to occasionally visit Sheriff Tilghman in Challis and the gossip was that she and Tilghman were a bit more than friends.

The rumors were confirmed when shortly after the Sheriff was reelected for his seventh term the couple announced that they had been wed a month earlier in a private ceremony in Boise. The headline in the local newspaper simply read: Well, Well, Well!, over the byline of Ignacio Hawk.

Hot Sauce

The sheriff's canine companion recovered from his brush with death and returned to the sheriff's side (more correctly to the crook of his arm). Sheriff Tilghman was not so happy with his crime fighting dog however when he got the bill from the vet. Among the charges was an item for emergency treatment for the vet who had suffered a dog bite from the pocket-sized pooch.

Afterword

By Chris Anderson,
Executive Director, Wolf Education & Research Center

The story you've just read no doubt touched one or more nerves with you as a reader, whether identifying with the indignant angst of a fifth generation rancher attempting to preserve, cultivate and protect opportunity from the land, an enthusiastic and idealistic naturalist of the vast wilderness that is the West, or the self-described savior and protector of our natural predators. RR Carroll, through his insightful and adept storytelling, does a masterful job of introducing many of the difficult and critical aspects of managing a land that wrestles with its own wild nature while allowing humans and animals to occupy her.

While the interpretation of this struggle is quite profound in its presentation, the subject is as old as time, possibly best portrayed by the love-hate Cain and Abel described relationship between the Cahalan brothers, in "The Big Lost." Furthermore, it is by accurate design that with each additional character revealed, we possibly identify with their perplexing struggle that we in the West have become accustomed to.

In the end, the resulting destruction that is often followed by gratuitous self-interest takes its toll on the story's cast as Carroll's characters embody our complex human struggle for place and purpose in the often wild frontiers of the West. And in the end, without human intervention that mediates a broader and more respectful tone, there will no doubt be further destruction in the real life struggle to resolve our brewing conflict.

While we humans continue unfolding that which is the mystery of our own place and purpose, we each face equally confounding suspense in the landscape of North American politics, land management practices and rights, and the proper balance between the interests of preserving the landscape that allows the earth to provide home and developing opportunity for future generations.

All too often, our attitudes about nature and the wilderness of the West are brought to the surface by the polarizing nature of our politics, elections, and special interest groups—each with a panhandler's stake to drive into the earth to mark our territory. As the leader of an advocacy group for the conservation of gray wolves, it's troubling to consider the immense expense of resources toward the promise of solutions that have, quite frankly, to date left all parties empty-handed and even more furious with each depredation that occurs, whether it be livestock or confidence in our leadership.

The Wolf Education & Research Center (WERC), since 1996, has worked regionally to internationally, bringing research, training biology students, and producing and sharing information about wolves that has far-reaching implications. Historically, WERC was placed strategically into the Idaho landscape by a group of wolf enthusiasts, among them a prominent film-maker whose work enjoyed more than decade of introducing the public to our curiosity and affinity for gray wolves through the subjects of his lens, the *Sawtooth Pack: Wolves of the Nez Perce*.

More recently, with the resulting mortality of the *Sawtooth Pack: Wolves of the Nez Perce*, in 2008, we rescued five additional wolves, called the *Owyhee Pack*, from the brink of destruction and brought them into the program with the purpose of helping people

"Get Face to Face with Wolves" as our program promotes. Together with the remaining Piyip, the last Sawtooth Pack member, the addition of the *Owyhee Pack* serve as ambassadors to their wild cousins by allowing individuals to experience a glimpse into the wilderness at our 300 acre wildlife sanctuary on Nez Perce Tribal land. This is done both literally and figuratively as we each develop our values, teach others, and commit ourselves to the wilderness and her predators—*our place and purpose.*

Located only a short drive southeast of Lewiston, Idaho on the edge of a town ironically named Winchester, the Wolf Education & Research Center greets thousands of individuals from civic clubs, universities, elementary schools, high schools, and other curious travelers who find their way to the scenic Hells Canyon Recreational Area in the panhandle of Idaho.

Many of the complex issues described in "The Big Lost" are the daily topics at WERC, dealing with the vital discussions such as trophic cascades, the importance for understanding the effects of removing top predators from food webs, as humans have done in many places through hunting and the natural and often unavoidable encroachment of urbanization.

Additionally difficult topics include the co-existence of humans, specifically ranchers and farmers, and the predators that typically enjoy the same landscape. If the land is ideal grazing ground for cattle and sheep, it is often also good grazing ground for a wolf's natural prey. This is where the most difficult mediation begins as groups such as WERC attempt to inform ranchers of non-lethal choices to live successfully in the predator's ancestral home.

The conversation is seldom won through the polarizing language of fear that we see portrayed in RR Carroll's story and unfortunately all too often in the media. It seems that one extreme side of the argument wants to show gut-wrenching pictures of dead wolves and their orphaned wolf pups while the opposing extreme shows an equally inflammatory picture of sheep or calf entrails strewn across a meadow—both side making claims of the inhumanity of the result.

Is it possible that both parties have truth in their presentation? Possibly, but often organizations on both sides see the tragedy not as an opportunity to enhance and strengthen our wilderness' balance but rather an opportunity to call each other's troops to arms and raise countless dollars in the process, while leaving the real victims—wolves and their neighboring citizens who are trying to co-exist, with no real solutions.

A healthy wilderness is a delicate scale that was originally imbalanced by the cumbersome settlement of humans throughout the world, not only North America. It's not a new tale. As I write this afterward, Sweden struggles to maintain any commitment whatsoever to their very finite number of wolves while Kazakhstan boasts more wolves per square mile than any country in the world. The countryside surrounding radiation riddled Chernobyl, Ukraine has seen a remarkable increase in wolves due to the total absence of man in competition with wolves for prey.

So, why is it in a country such as the United States, where resources of every imaginable kind abound, we cannot see a clear solution that serves the interests of each person and group who's stake is firmly planted in the rich soil of our wild lands? I am confident that preaching to our own choirs has not rewarded us with the sweetness of the fruit of change.

While the author's tale is presented as fiction, the details of the subject are spot on target as we deal with the various issues related to wolf recovery and conservation, among them the human aspects and our variety of positions and interests.

Somewhere in the middle, however, is where the solutions lie as we work to respect the heritage of our American wild lands, her native people, her adopted immigrants, and our generous land of opportunity.

Somewhere in the middle of this debate is where we build a future of informed and patient advocates. We must collaborate with those who work toward stewardship, toward that inner wilderness of our diverse choices, livelihoods and traditions with an equal respect for humanity and a clearer call to be better servants of our resources—among them the wolf.

With respect to our mutual stewardship,
Chris Anderson, Executive Director
Wolf Education & Research Center

Join the discussion and learn more about wolves and their vital importance in healthy ecosystems by visiting www.wolfcenter.org or by writing to WERC, PO Box 12604, Portland, Oregon 97212. You can write to Chris Anderson at chris.anderson@wolfcenter.org.

About Chris Anderson:
Chris Anderson is a Hood River, Oregon native who grew up enjoying the pristine wilderness of the Columbia Gorge and Mt. Hood National Forest scenic areas located in the Cascade Range. He currently resides in Portland, Oregon where he directs the Wolf Education & Research Center. He began working with wolf recovery issues in 2006 after visiting a Washington based organization and learned of the importance and plight of wolves in the region as an integral part of restoring balance to the West's wilderness.

Chris Anderson is a business and nonprofit management consultant and is founder and president of a Wyoming based science education company that works with educational institutions across the United States and Canada. His science company is directly involved in conservation of owls throughout the Western United States and more than 600 nesting sites have been created through their efforts. He is the former chairman and current vice-chairman of a 501(c)3 organization, Co-Serve International, and through that work consults and promotes leadership development in Afghanistan, Ukraine, Kazakhstan, the United States, and other developing countries, with an extensive background in the development and funding of humanitarian outreach projects in Oaxaca, Mexico.

Follow the work of WERC and related posts about wolf recovery and conservation on Facebook by visiting http://facebook.com/SawtoothPack and become involved in the discussion today. You may also connect with Chris on LinkedIn at http://www.linkedin.com/in/ccanderson